ILLEGALLY YOURS

LAWS OF ATTRACTION

KATE MEADER

Copyright © 2019 by Kate Meader

Cover artwork: © 2022 L.J. Anderson of Mayhem Cover Creations

All rights reserved.

ISBN 9781954107212

To Jimmie,
The adventure continues!

CHAPTER 1

Lucas

Remember that song by Queen with the banging bass riff? *Dindin-din-din-din, another one bites the dust . . .*

This is my life right now.

I'm at the Library, a tasty little spot in the basement of the Gilt Bar, giving one of the crew a righteous send-off. James Henderson is a friend, and the brother of Max, a partner in our family law firm, Wright, Lincoln, and Henderson. He's getting married in a couple of weeks, and to say it's been a whirlwind is an understatement. I suspect his fiancée's knocked up, but Jimbo's keeping mum.

Max has set up a whiskey tasting for the stag party. I'm more of an ale drinker, but I like to know all there is to know about everything, so I'm up for learning how to tell the difference between this glass of yellow shit and that glass of yellow shit.

"So, what time do the strippers get here, mate?" I ask with my cheekiest grin.

Max flashes his perfect American teeth. "Get a couple of drinks in you and the stage is yours, Wright."

Up on my feet, I shake my most excellent arse. "I'll fucking do it, too!"

This makes the rest of them laugh, but turning to sit, I find a woman staring at me like I'm an idiot. More important, this woman is wearing a bloody catsuit.

It clings to every curve—and she's got a lot of 'em—and covers up all the body parts I'd usually be assessing. This cover-up is sexier than if she were naked.

The only parts I can see are:

1. Feet in strappy sandals that show a tease of skin and purple painted toes. This bodes well because purple denotes royalty (think the late, great Prince) as well as wisdom, dignity, independence, creativity, mystery, and magic.
2. Arms that look toned and strong, one with a tattoo of some Asian symbol.
3. Her face. *Duh.* Did you think she was wearing a mask like Catwoman?

The suit is zipped up to her chin, but above her jawline is the best part: a face that launched a thousand ships.

Or hard-ons.

Okay, *my* hard-on.

It's more striking than pretty, this face. Regal, even. Big eyes with melted chocolate drops for irises. Cheekbones that almost rival mine. Warm, brown skin with golden undertones. A sparkling stud in her nose that tells me she likes to go against the grain. And her hair . . . there's tons of it, a mahogany wave ribboned with copper and red. I could go on, but she's quickly recovered from the sight of my booty shake and is now passing out sheets of paper.

"Hi, guys, I'm Trinity. Welcome to the Library and to your whiskey tasting."

Everyone returns her greeting and I hate them all for daring to talk to her. Her voice has a natural rasp, sexy as fuck. I try to catch her attention with one of my dazzling smiles, but she's already slinked off, gliding on ball bearings, to get the first round of drinks in.

I track her moves, jealous of every interaction she has with other members of the rotten human race. I consider myself an excellent judge of character and I'm especially conscious of the vibes we put out into the world. People respond well to Trinity's energy. A quick smile and pat on the arm for a customer in her path, a wave at someone who has just walked in, a familiar shoulder nudge to one of her (male) coworkers behind the bar.

"Other people first"—that's the vibe I'm getting from Trinity. What impression did I make on her, I wonder? According to *Chicago* magazine, I'm a "Chi-Town Hottie on the Rise"—it wasn't called that, but it may as well have been—aka, one of the city's best and brightest divorce attorneys. (And still single, ladies!) I tend to get pegged on sight as the cheeky upstart. The good-time Brit. I find it useful to let people make a call and then, *boom!* I crush those assumptions with a quote from Rilke or the like. No flies on me.

Back in our orbit, Trinity places a tray of glasses with a finger of whiskey in each on the table.

"The first thing you want to do is check the color," she says. "Turn your tasting chart over to the blank side and hold the whiskey against it. You could be looking at pale gold, straw, amber—"

"Piss," I interject, because apparently I have verbal diarrhea. Everyone glares at me, so I class it up with its scientific term, "Sorry, *your*-ine."

Trinity's lovely dark eyes narrow ever so slightly, and she announces, "That's not a standardized color."

"Sorry, we can't take him anywhere." So says James, the groom-to-be, though he's barely containing his laughter.

"How'd you get to be a whiskey expert, Trinity?" I ask her, needing to establish a connection.

"Years of training. Next, you'll want to assess its clarity and viscosity . . ."

Summarily dismissed, I follow the instructions. Of course, I have an opinion on everything. My so-called friends should tell me to shut up, but it's like a fire hydrant of inanity has been wrenched open and I'm incapable of closing it.

Here's how I fill out the sheet, accompanying commentary for free.

Appearance: Still going with urine, because I started off so well.

Nose: Engine oil with hints of vanilla and cabbage. Sure, why not?

Palate: Umami. I don't know if this is correct, but I like saying the word. Say it with me, kids. *Umami.*

I suspect this is all rubbish, because one of the flavor profiles is "Band-Aids." I mean, that can't be right.

"What the hell are we doing drinking booze that tastes like Band-Aids?" Not that this particular whiskey does—I think—but now that I try again, I'm getting a medicinal flavor I didn't notice before. "How is that supposed to be appealing? No one says wine tastes like sticking plasters—"

"Sticking plasters?" Max interjects with a raised eyebrow.

"Sticking plasters, Elastoplast . . ." I wave my glass, sloshing the remaining spoonful. "What we call Band-Aids in the old country, Maxie. Try to keep up. If someone said, *'Sip on this twenty-seven-year-old aged malt, it's got a lovely Band-Aid flavor,'* any normal bloke would be backing out the door *tout de suite*. And don't get me started on 'forest fucking floor.'"

My tirade against the tyranny of whiskey-tasting profiles has silenced the entire group. I peek up to find Trinity glaring at me in a way that makes my dick go *schwing*!

"Tell the truth, love, it's all a load of cobblers, innit?"

She weighs me for a moment and clearly finds me wanting in every way. "Actually, no, it's science. Scotch, you know, *from Scotland,* is made with malted barley, which is barley soaked in water and dried with peat fires. Peat has a chemical compound called cresols, which are a subcategory of phenols, or carbolic acid, which is found in products like Lysol and Sharpies and—"

"Band-Aids," I say, because I actually know this.

"Band-Aids," she affirms, clearly not pleased with how I needed to get the last word in there. I'm being an arsehole, but I can't help it. I'm a sucker for competence porn, and this, along with her self-assured beauty, makes me nervous. Rather ridiculous, because nothing makes me nervous.

"I'll get the next round in, gentlemen," she says, with emphasis on *gentlemen* to indicate I'm most definitely excluded. "Drink plenty of water."

With Trinity out of earshot, Max turns to me with palms up.

"If you're trying to impress her, you are fucking up royally."

"You think?" My gaze follows her to the bar. She's doing a fine impression of ignoring me, the little minx. "Thought I was winning her over."

"Tell her the color of your last dump," Grant mutters. "I'm sure she'd love it."

That cracks the crowd up, especially coming from the usually taciturn Grant Lincoln. He's my other partner in the firm, though he and Max are closer because they went to law school together. Grant's from Georgia, looks like a Bratva enforcer, and is of a slow and methodical bent, the perfect foil to my hyper personality.

I glance over at Trinity, who's still not paying me any heed, and consider my options. I've never met a woman I can't crack with my inordinate charm, razor-sharp wit, and all-around smarty-smarts.

Trinity, love, prepare to be conquered.

CHAPTER 2

Trinity

*R*ich, overgrown frat boys in slick, overpriced suits. Come the zombie apocalypse, these guys will be the first to get bitten.

"Come the zombie apocalypse, we'll have no one to charge exorbitant prices for fancy whiskey tastings." So sayeth Gideon, my coworker and closest pal. Apparently I had muttered that observation out loud.

"You don't think zombies can appreciate the finer things?"

Chuckling, he strokes his hipster beard. I'm not a fan, but I love the guy anyway.

"I think our awesome palates will be worth jack in the new world order. It'll kill or be killed, Trin. But you already look like Lara Croft in your"—he waves a hand over me in my cat-suited glory—"whatever this is. I'll just cower behind you seeking your badass protection."

This yields a laugh from me, which is in short supply these days. Thirty-four years old and I can't seem to get anything firing on all cylinders: my career, my love life, even my family relationships. I think of my sister, Emily, and feel a twinge of too-familiar guilt. She's going through a contentious divorce from her asswipe of a husband. I'm trying to be supportive, but the urge to scream *I told you so!* is the devil on my shoulder.

I measure one-ounce pours into lowball glasses for the second round with the bachelor party. Whiskey tastings are very fashionable with the overgrown frat boy set these days and I should be glad, because I'm a niche girl in a niche industry. A Black woman in a very white, very male field. The looks I get when I enter a tasting room usually range from *huh?* to disgust.

My sister doesn't understand my career choice. I may as well be "peeing standing up," she tells me. Sure, this job means that I'm more likely to buddy around with guys—definitely less drama—and I have to say I enjoy not having the drama that seems to follow my sister around.

However, I wouldn't say no to a little excitement . . .

I glance over at the bachelor party to find *him* looking at me: Hottie Brit. I immediately avert my gaze, but not before I catch a smug lift at the corner of his mouth. He thinks he's got me.

They're all annoyingly good-looking, even the guy who looks like a WWF wrestler. Grant, I think someone called him. The brothers Max and James Henderson I've met before when I used to bartend in the Gilt Bar upstairs. Max is a divorce lawyer, so I'm guessing some of the others are in the biz. When they walked in, I noticed the chatty Brit first because who wouldn't? The cheekbones are young Jonathan Rhys Meyers. The hair is late Harry Styles. The suit is . . . I don't know anything about suits, but this one is clearly expensive. Shiny, too, like shark hide. I imagine if I touched his arm, I'd come away with some slimy protective coating.

Then he opened his mouth, the first word out of it *piss*.

I didn't hear the accent until he amended to *urine,* pronounced *your*-ine. Kudos for making piss sound exotic.

He appears younger than the rest of them, whether it's attitude or the way they dote on him indulgently. Like he's the crazy loon in their care, the little brother that needs to be watched like a hawk because you never know what he'll do or say next. I've lived most of my life playing caregiver. I certainly don't need that dynamic with a man.

Pity, because I could come from listening to him talk . . .

The night proceeds per its billing. Whenever I stop off at the bachelor party's table, I'm treated to another Shakespearean soliloquy from Hottie Brit.

The latest: *"Leather and tar? Love when my drink tastes like the bottom of a biker messenger bag."*

Max mouths *I'm sorry* every time, but I don't mind—you quickly develop a thick skin working in bars—and I especially don't mind when Max drops a couple of C-notes on me just before he leaves with the group.

"We had a really nice time, Trinity," he says. "And sorry about Lucas."

I assume Lucas is the British guy. "Not a problem. Glad you had fun."

He squints, looking a little pained. "We're now headed to meet up with the bachelorettes for Abba night. The fun is only beginning."

My laugh is real instead of the fake one I manufacture for most customers. Max Henderson would make someone a nice husband, and being in the divorce business he'd probably know how to make her a nice ex-husband as well. Hottie Brit—Lucas—looks over his shoulder as the party troops out, but I'm already turning away.

Not falling for your cheekbone glimmer.

"Taking a break," I tell Gideon, who waves me away. It's

early July, and in evenings past, I would've headed out to the alley, not to smoke, but to inhale some fresh garbage-tinged air while checking my Insta and centering myself for the rest of my shift.

Not tonight, though. Not for weeks since it happened.

Standing safely inside near the back office, I shoot a message off to my nephew Chase: *Wassup?*

I get an eye roll emoji back because he loves my nineties throwback references. Five minutes of dueling emojis later, I return and my jaw drops at the sight of who's sitting at the bar.

Hottie Brit has returned. Or never went away.

Before he sees me, I take a moment to watch him unobserved. Long fingers are wrapped around a pint glass, which we don't see a lot of down here. The Library is a fancy cocktail kind of place. That too-long-on-top dark hair is mussed, as if he had to abuse it to temper his energy. A small scar bisecting his eyebrow makes him a little less pretty and a lot more interesting.

The air around him thrums even as he sits still, like a Broadway musical might break out any moment.

Gideon squints to tell me Hottie Brit is out of here the minute I say the word. I smile to let him know I've got this. Maybe HB didn't stay for me, though deep down I know that's not true. My pulse picks up at the thought. It's been awhile—a long, lonely while—since anyone this attractive has hit on me.

I'll let it buoy me and fuel a few British-accented fantasies later.

As soon as HB sees me he switches off his phone and places it facedown on the bar. I'm oddly touched.

"Hello, again. Lucas Wright at your service." He offers his hand, curiously formal.

I'm stunned enough into grasping that hand, its warmth

life affirming and not a little zingy. "Trinity Jones. Literally at your service."

He smiles. Charmingly crooked, it lights up his eyes, his cheekbones, and my very neglected lady parts. His irises are the blue of a curaçao cocktail, one with a sting in its tail.

He still hasn't released my hand. "I'm not really a whiskey drinker, hence my—"

"Resistance to the tasting?" I finish for him.

"People usually make fun of things they don't understand, right? Give me a nice pint any day." His self-deprecation throws me for a second, and while I try to measure how calculated it is, he leans in slightly. "Does this mean we can't be friends?"

My attitude toward him is far from friendly. Not exactly hostile, but something more discomfiting: a wriggle in my stomach and a lurch in my chest. The first I attribute to attraction, the second . . . I'm not sure yet.

I release his hand. "I've no doubt a guy like you has plenty of friends."

"You can never have enough friends, Trinity."

"Or friendly bartenders to unload your troubles on."

He flicks a glance to Gideon, who's watching us from a semisafe distance, ready to lunge into action at the first sign of trouble. "Now Treebeard over there doesn't look so friendly."

Treebeard? That's perfect. I can't wait to tell Gideon. "Just protective. We look out for one another here."

HB holds up his hands, palms facing me. "I've been warned!" Then he waves at Gideon, who hipster-scowls back. The exchange makes me smile, but I turn away to grab a bar towel before Lucas can see it. Can't make it too easy for him.

"So, Trinity, I have a proposition for you."

"Oh yeah?"

"Uh-huh. Now, I imagine you get this a lot, working here." He waves around, somewhat effusively. This guy has an entertainer gene. Probably can sing and dance as well.

"I've had a few . . . propositions."

"I bet. Slimy, handsy old geezers incapable of making eye contact and drooling all over the bar." He makes a point of looking at a spot two feet south of my face.

I point at my chest. "Uh, my tits are up here, asshole."

He grins. "Just taking the lechery to its logical conclusion. The lecher so drunk he can't even lech right."

"Don't think *lech* is a verb."

"Is when I do it."

This makes no sense, but I laugh, the sound unrestrained and genuine, and catch Gideon out of the corner of my eye. He disapproves. Whatever. I can laugh at funny, hottie, nonsensical Brits if I want to. It's not as if I'm going to let him banter his way into my bed. It's just nice to be the target of an attractive guy for once.

"So, Trinity, about this proposition."

"Hmm." I'm not quite ready for us to go there when I'm rather enjoying the chase.

"Do you do private tastings?"

Disappointment chills my gut. HB had been doing so well.

Maybe he needs inspiration. "I'm always up for spreading the love of hard liquors."

He nods. "That's brilliant. Because I know a woman who would really, really dig you."

My brain screeches to a halt, stutter-steps forward, and knocks against my skull. Ouch.

"A woman?"

"Right. Now, she's a bit stroppy, and it's sort of weird, as she's the ex-wife of one of my friends, but we're still friendly even though I hate picking sides, especially when mates are involved. Anyway, you're exactly her type and I told her I'd set something up and—"

He stops speaking because I've poured three quarters of a pint of ale over his head.

"Hey!" He stands dramatically, shaking his head like a dog coming out of water—also dramatically—which results in sizable beer droplets landing on a glaring guy two stools to his right.

"Pervert!" I manage to splutter.

"How am I a pervert?"

"Your proposition to a woman you've just met is a . . . threesome?" I think that's what he offered, but the minute it leaves my mouth the doubts set in.

Lucas leans over the bar and grabs a towel, a fluid move indicating that this is not the first time someone has unloaded a glass of alcohol over his head. "My proposition to a woman I've just met is a business one. A lawyer colleague is looking to set up an after-work event for women in the legal profession and I thought this might be a good suggestion."

I freeze, horrified by every word and my actions of twenty seconds ago. "But you said she was my type."

"Right. Badass professional who knows her stuff."

Rolling right over the compliment, I struggle to defend myself. "I thought—"

"That I was coming on to you? And using another woman as a tactic? To set up some sordid encounter?" Each question raises the stakes, shooting the situation to a pyramid of idiocy with me sitting as queen in a throne on the top.

Oh God oh God oh God. How could I have gotten the signals so wrong? But the banter and the smiles and the eyes. I could also ascribe it to my frame of mind these last couple of months since The Incident. I'm easily spooked and ripe for disappointment.

Gideon appears about thirty seconds too late and pinches HB's shoulder. "Okay, out."

Lucas is wiping the beer off his suit with the towel. "I'm going to clean up and wait for you to calm down, Ms. Jones." Slipping Gideon's grip and shooting me a much-deserved glare, he stalks off to the restroom.

Gideon looks confused. "What happened there?"

"You were kind of late defending my honor, dude."

"I was on the other side of the bar. As soon as I heard the word *pervert,* my Spidey sense went into overdrive."

"Figures." I shrug. "I might have misunderstood. I've been out of the game for a while."

After a few minutes, Lucas hasn't returned, so I head toward the restroom to make sure he's not crying, passed out, or bumping a line of coke. (We see it all here.) I run into him in the corridor outside the restrooms. The beer-slick hair and eau de IPA should really detract from his hotness. It does not.

I lead with, "Sorry?"

"Sounds a little too like a question."

Still with the drama. "Uh, you set me up. If I had a nickel for every time I heard *'Do you do private tastings?'* I wouldn't be working here."

There's that lift at the corner of his mouth. I swat him with the bar towel I'm carrying. "That's what you wanted me to think!"

"No. Okay, maybe. I was having a little fun. Should have realized a woman like you would use the weapons at your disposal."

"Somehow I don't think I could ever match you for weaponry." I narrow my eyes when really all I want to do is keep them wide and soak in his beauty. Life is so unfair sometimes. "You a lawyer like Max?"

"Not like Max. Better than Max."

It's not bragging. We muse on this for a moment until I break the silence.

"So you really wanted to throw some business my way?"

"I do, or rather I did before you sprang for the beer-drop option. Aubrey is a lawyer friend of mine who sometimes organizes after-work networking events for my ovary-sporting colleagues. They're always doing wine tastings, so I thought this might be a fun change for them."

It wouldn't hurt and might get some new blood for the Whiskey, Women, and Song events I'm trying to get off the ground.

"That's kind of you. If you still want to pass on my card . . ." I lower the zip of my catsuit, extract a card from my bra, and hand it to him.

"Smooth." His thumb rubs across the card, appearing to absorb the warmth of the skin it was recently next to. He places it in the breast pocket of his suit jacket and pats it once, twice. I shiver at the thought of this sensual connection between us.

"Here, let me give you mine." His hand brushes the waist-band of his pants, then a flick of his finger and thumb unhooks the fastener.

Unhooks. The. Fastener.

Wait, what? He's not . . . No, no, no. This can*not* be happening.

He inches his zipper down slowly, slowly.

Here? No, no, no, not *here*.

Finally, I squeal, "That's where you keep your business cards?"

He laughs, big and bold. "Nah, just a little payback."

My mouth drops open. He wouldn't have stopped unless . . . Would he have? I have no idea. The unpre-dictability of it—of him—sparks through me, lighting me up. While my life has seen its fair share of events from out of left field, as a rule I crave stability in my day-to-day. I have people relying on me to be their rock, so I can't afford to . . . indulge.

But damn and hell, I wouldn't mind indulging in Lucas Wright.

"Not going to make this easy for you, Trinity."

"You're not?" Visions of Lucas not making it easy—in fact, making it very hard—dance through my sex-starved brain.

"Did you really think I'd ask you out?" He waves around. "In a bar? Just like that?" The cliché appears to offend him.

I swallow, once again blindsided. He's not interested. At all.

I really am losing my touch.

I laugh it off. "Believe me, I've heard everything."

"I figured as much, which is why I'm not going to beg for a date. At least, not yet. You're not sure about me, Trinity. You think I'm too young or flighty or ridiculous. You think I'm as smooth as slime and a bit of a lad. Well, whatever you think, I have undoubtedly heard, a million times over. Want to know what I think?"

"I suspect you're going to tell me."

"*I think* . . . that it would be good for us to wait."

I barely restrain from screaming at him to just do me. I'm pretty confused at the pinging signals not hitting their targets.

He inclines his head, his gaze magnetized to mine. My heart is knocking around my chest like a pinball. Another pat on his breast pocket, like my card is a talisman, and my pulse spikes thinking of it next to his heart. Silly, really.

But his next move isn't silly. It's dangerous. One of those long fingers traces its tip along my jaw. His eyes widen, his nostrils flare.

"Wh-what are you doing?"

"Not sure yet."

Kiss me.

Do I say it? I have a habit of talking to myself, speaking my innermost thoughts aloud. His lips have not latched on to mine so I'm guessing I didn't. But something's happening here. He's kissing me with his eyes, seducing me with his intensity, with every sharp inhale of breath I see him almost struggling to take.

His hand anchors to my jaw and sneaks around to my nape. My blood runs hot, and I'm hyperaware of everything: his full lips. The eyebrow scar. The wicked cobalt blues. The supermodel cheekbones. A dash of russet in his eleven o'clock shadow.

The fact that we have yet to kiss. Gah!

Yet I am being ravaged. My breasts feel heavy, the spot between my thighs hot and slick. There's power in the anticipation, though I'm not sure who holds it.

"Trinity?"

"Yes?" I'm basking in the glow of gimme-the-good-stuff.

"Still think we should wait." The glow dims and flash-freezes. Before I can protest he adds, "Because once we start this, I'll be going all in."

"Once we start what?" I can hardly speak the words. I am furious.

"The ride of our lives, Trinity."

He gives me another smile that leaves me in a daze. I've no idea what's happening here but I feel itchy and very, very dissatisfied with my Lucas-free life.

"See you around, Whiskey Woman."

And then he's gone.

CHAPTER 3

Trinity

"*I* have wine!"

At the front door, I brandish the bottle of Pinot Noir in my sister's face and wait for her to crack a smile. Rays of lip-curving sunshine are few and far between these days for Emily, so I cheer a mental touchdown when she lights up.

She holds the door back to let me in. "I just put Ari to bed and I'm ready for wine and whining."

Oh, I'm so here for that. I'm also not opposed to the idea that her five-year-old is sleeping. Arianna is a demon disguised as a cherub-faced innocent, and I'm the only one who sees the evil lurking beneath.

"Where's my favorite nephew?"

"In his room. Brooding."

Uh-oh. Unlike his sister, Chase is usually a pretty good-natured kid. The separation has been tough on everyone.

I hand off the wine. "Open this, Ems. I'll pop up to say hi."

First I take a look inside Arianna's room. She's expelling

18

fluttery breaths, and as adorable (looking) as that sounds, I know better.

I knock on Chase's door. "Hey, put your pecker away. I'm coming in!"

A huff that's half laugh, half acknowledgment comes back. Popping my head around the door, I find him lying on the bed reading a comic book. My sensitive sommelier nose adjusts to the boy funk. Chase's room is probably typical for any fourteen-year-old kid who likes both the Marvel and DC universes (I know, weird) and has an artistic-sporty vibe. Hunky Spanish soccer players battle for wall space with half-naked lady rappers.

"Hey, Aunt Trin."

"Hey, Whiskey Chaser, what's up?"

"Just doing homework." There's an open laptop with what looks like a Word document on it. He should be enjoying his break, but he had a less-than-stellar last few months in the school year and has to make up for it this summer.

"Comic book report?"

That yields a grin. He really has the best smile that flashes at you so suddenly that when it's gone you wonder if you imagined it. His dad's, Brian's, smile. A light dusting of freckles over pale skin dots his cheeks. His copper-brown hair is standing on end as if his homework has been making him tear it out.

"Just taking a break before I get back to it. I have to analyze FDR's relationship with Winston Churchill."

"Ooh, I got this one. Fuddy-duddy white dudes talking a lot about, uh, cigars."

He makes a play of typing something on the laptop. "The extra piece I needed!"

"Shut it, ya cheeky boy." I take a seat on the bed. "Seen your dad lately?"

The air chills. "He came to soccer practice last week. Took me out for a chocolate malt after. Like I'm six."

"Hey, I'm thirty-four and you won't see me saying no to chocolate malts."

He shrugs. "It's just weird. I mean, he doesn't even . . ." The words peter out.

"He doesn't even what?"

"Nothing." His fingers trace the cover of the magazine. It's Wonder Woman, looking like she's ready to kick villainous ass.

"Anything else going on?"

Another shrug. We used to talk more, but he's at that awkward age where he doesn't want to be too friendly. His parents' situation isn't helping and I'm trying to be supportive, yet not interfere. Interference—or running it—is generally my jam.

"Want to catch a movie on Saturday? New Ant-Man's out." I hold my breath, worried he'll push me away.

"Most underrated superhero."

"He is quite small," I confirm, and that makes us both laugh.

"It'd have to be the afternoon. I have a soccer match on Saturday morning, not that I'll get much time on. Been playing like crap lately."

Chase used to be a whiz on the field, but I suspect he's going through a phase of bored resistance.

"Maybe I'll come see. Any hot single dads there?"

He rolls his eyes. "More like desperate married moms who have it bad for Coach."

"Then I'm definitely there." I pinch his cheek because I know he hates it and head back down to see my sister. She's in the living room with a serrated steak knife, a torn-open package of Dubliner cheese, and a box of Ritz.

"Classy," I say, and we both giggle.

Emily—or Ems as I like to call her when she's not pissing me off—is a blond, petite porcelain doll who, now that she's hit thirty-two and is going through hell with Brian, is starting to show her age. (For the record, I found my first gray hair at sixteen and it's been the greatest cover-up in hair science ever since.) We couldn't be more different: me with my big-boned sturdiness, brown skin, and rebellious hair, her looking like a cross between Baby Spice and Disney Princess.

That's right: different dads.

Mine died when Mom was six months pregnant, a boating accident at twenty-five. She married Evan, one of my dad's friends, right after I was born, and Emily was dropped off by the stork eighteen months later. Evan and my mom packed it in when I was eleven years old. He was a good stepdad, but his first love was always Emily. I get that. It hurt a little, but I've gotten over it.

Once it was just us three girls, we would have the odd "uncle" stop by to try us on for size, but nobody who stuck around. Mom was pretty encouraging of us to "be our own person," which was code for *I'm going out on a date and you need to babysit your sister, Trinity.* To say I feel protective over Emily is a massive understatement. There might be less than two years between us, but I practically raised her. All my efforts as a teen went to ensuring she was safe, that homework was checked, bullies were crushed, boys were vetted. Sure, Mom was there on the periphery, but I was running the Jones household with an iron fist.

Then my mom and stepdad died in a car accident during a rare interlude when they'd decided to give it another shot. I was nineteen, Emily was seventeen, and it left us raw and a little bit wrecked.

Emily hands off a glass of wine. "How's His Highness?"

"Grouchy. Having to do schoolwork when it's summer is the worst."

"Well, he has to catch up." She takes a slug of wine from a glass that is already half empty. "I know this last year has been hell on him, but it's been hell on us all."

"True." I take her by the glass-free hand and lead her to the sofa. "What's the latest?"

"He just switched lawyers because—oh, I don't know why. Now he has some shark who's telling him to push for sole custody!"

I jerk my head back. "What? But I thought we—*you* were going for shared custody. Brian works long hours and takes all those business trips. How the hell is he going to be there for them?"

"I don't know. My lawyer says it's just mind games. Tactics to keep us guessing so I'll be grateful when he hands me a pittance. Brian's worried I'll spend all his money on"—she gestures dramatically to the coffee table—"cheese!"

We both start laughing, because Brian is a notorious penny-pincher. He runs a restaurant investment group that owns twelve high-end establishments in the Chicagoland area. The man is doing very well, but God forbid he spend any of that on his family.

I look around at the perfect living room in their perfect Lincoln Park town house, which is sparkling clean, not because Emily likes to stay on top of it, but because they have a housekeeper who lives off site and comes in to make meals and generally tend to their every need. It's a different world.

"He wants us to move somewhere cheaper, like Uptown or Edgewater." She whispers the neighborhood names like they're shantytowns and saying them louder would conjure up hobo clowns. "My Pilates class is right around the corner from here. Where am I going to go in Edgewater?"

Jesus. "Well, *I* live there. We recently got running water and electricity. We even have a farmers' market!"

She smiles ruefully. "I'm sorry. I'm just so pissed at him. This is my children's home and he wants to sell it out from under us. As if they haven't been through enough upheaval."

I top off her wine, then take a sip of my own. We sit in silence, thinking on how life can get so fucked up that you don't even realize it's happening until you're waist deep in shit.

"My lawyer said I should get a job."

Emily has—or had—a nanny for Ari until she came home one day and found Brian giving the nineteen-year-old Danish au pair a gold star on her performance review. If you know what I mean. Even with the nanny, she never worked, so getting a job is a scary proposition for her. She met Brian when she was seventeen, was knocked up within three months, and married within six. She's smart and funny and kind, but she's not the most prepared to be out on her own.

I blame myself. I should have insisted she go to college. Brian wasn't as wealthy then as he is now, but they could have found a way. I would have helped despite the fact I despised—*despise*—Brian with the heat of a thousand suns.

But we can't change the past, only the future. Ems needs to restart her life.

"Getting a job isn't such a terrible idea, is it?"

"Of course not. It's just—what can I do?" She shoves her wineglass forward. "The bar where you work, maybe?"

"That's a night job. You need to be here in the evenings."

She blinks. "I do?"

"For the kids."

"Right." She deflates right in front of me.

I throw an arm around her. "Don't worry. We'll sort it out! Now tell me what your lawyer said about Foreskin going for sole custody."

She smiles grimly at my nickname for Brian. "That fathers' rights are all the rage. It used to be the mom was practically guaranteed to get sole custody, but the courts are completely woke up now."

"Woke up?"

"Yeah, woke up . . ." She squints. "Woken? It's something Chase said in between grunts and shoving cereal into his mouth this morning."

"Woke. You mean woke."

"That's what I said!"

I chuckle because we're so, so different. I've always loved it, but lately I wish she was more like me. More self-aware. For so long, she's lived in this Lincoln Park yummy-mummy bubble, everything in her life taken care of.

Brian's leaving has made her just a little bit woke.

"Maybe I should get another lawyer. The one I have always sounds so bored with me when we talk. Like my problems don't mean anything to her. I don't think she's doing all she could. I have to keep this house!"

"You need a shark." I think of that murder of divorce lawyers in the bar two nights ago. I haven't heard from Hottie Brit's friend yet about setting up the networking event for female lawyers. Neither have I heard from HB himself.

"Once we start this I'll be going all in."

The kiss that never happened is imprinted like a stencil on my brain. He was right about what I thought of him: too young, too flighty, too smooth. And the fact that he knew enough to peg my thoughts on the topic makes him much more interesting. A bit of a conundrum, that.

"I know a divorce lawyer, a customer at the bar. Max Henderson."

"Where have I heard that name?" Emily cocks her head. "Oh, he helped Magda with her divorce a couple of years ago.

She said he's gorgeous and very, very good. I called his office when all this started and he wasn't taking on clients."

"That was six months ago. Maybe I could run it by him when I see him again."

"Maybe sooner." She turns on the doe eyes and I roll my not-doe eyes in return before caving like a cheap suitcase. She knows I'll do anything for her.

"I'll give him a call tomorrow."

CHAPTER 4

Lucas

I love where I work. The 333 West Wacker building overlooks the Chicago River, its green-mirrored shine reflecting the beauty of the Riverwalk onto its face. The offices of Wright, Lincoln, and Henderson are on the twenty-fifth floor, and we're expanding this year, taking on two more associates.

The business of human misery is good.

It's not all union dissolution, but it's the majority of our work. If I were still living in the UK, there wouldn't be this much action, but Americans are notoriously litigious. No one wants to discuss anything. Lawyer up is invariably the first option. I should be glad, but sometimes I just want to tell my sad and angry clients to have a cup of tea and call me in the morning.

I walk into our office building, salute Mac, the security guy, and find an open lift. It's just after eight and amazingly not busy. As the doors close someone calls out.

"Wait, please wait!"

I keep the doors open because I'm nothing if not a gentleman, but my good manners are about to be tested, because in walks temptation herself, Trinity Jones.

"Oh, hi!" She blinks and looks out into the building foyer as if maybe she should get into a different car.

The doors close on her escape route and I ask the immortal question: "Which floor?"

"Twenty five."

We both look at the numbers panel where twenty-five is already selected.

Now my firm doesn't have the entire floor—yet. We share it with a boutique brokerage firm and a venture capitalist outfit where the guys order in cases of Grey Goose like they've got stock in it. I could ask Trinity if she's repping GG, but I'm guessing she's here to see me. Besides, I'd much rather drink her in. She's wearing a cream dress with little red flowers on it, its neckline what my mum would call peasant style. It shows her collarbone in all its kissable glory. Her hair is a hullabaloo, a minitantrum on her head.

"Humidity, one. Trinity, zero." Chuckling at her own joke, she thumbs at her head, and I laugh along with her. Then I touch my breast pocket where I placed her business card this morning. Her golden-brown eyes dart there. She swallows, then licks her lips.

Am I wearing the same jacket as two nights ago? No, I am not. I have merely switched the card to each new jacket I don. And if you're wondering if this is normal, rational behavior, I can safely assure you that no, it is not.

The card had sat next to her skin, the warmth of her tits keeping it toasty, and the mere thought of that was enough to keep me half hard for the last two days. I was supposed to give it to my friend Aubrey, but instead I shot her an email with the details so I could keep the card—Trinity Jones: Whiskey Woman.

How brilliant is that? I like this woman, enough that I didn't call her.

This might appear counterproductive, but I meant what I said. She's seen Lucas the clown, and God knows that joker's okay for a laugh, but Ms. Jones needs more than a good-time Charlie. She needs a guy who's worthy of her.

I'm delaying things while I work out how to conjure up *that* guy.

The lift makes a smooth and fast ascent. When the door opens onto my floor, I let her go ahead of me. She looks right toward the other offices, then turns left toward mine, and I walk behind her as she pushes through the glass door.

My heart booms triple time. I'm wondering when she's just going to fess up to her reason for being here.

No sign of Casey, our receptionist, so I have to do the dirty work myself. "Who are you here to see?" I ask Trinity's hair.

"Max."

Max? Before I can enquire further, a pretty Black woman in her forties appears. Sadie is our office manager, though it's more like office mother. She spends her days telling us off. Enjoys the hell out of it, too.

"Ms. Jones?"

"Yes, hi, I'm Trinity. I have an appointment with Max." She sounds nervous.

Sadie smiles to put her at ease. "He just called to say he's running late, but I can set you up in the conference room with—"

"Tea. We'll have tea in my office," I say before Sadie can finish.

Two sets of eyes turn on me. Sadie squints, which is code for *explain yourself.*

"Ms. Jones and I have already met," I reply, putting both authority and Britishness into my speech, though I feel a bit silly talking like this to Sadie. She's never going to let me live it down. "I'm happy to entertain her until Max gets here."

To Trinity, I gesture to a door: "My office is through there."

She's not buying it. Instead she looks to Sadie for confirmation that this is okay. I also look to Sadie with "the look," one that begs her to help me out.

The woman who holds my future sex life in her hands dangles me on the hook for an extralong second before finally relenting. "I'll bring the tea through in a moment."

As soon as Trinity's in my office and out of earshot, Sadie grabs me by the lapels and growls, "What are you up to?"

"So suspicious."

"She seems—"

"Out of my league?"

Sadie smiles, a don't-bullshit-me tilt to her head. Because I'm a couple of years younger than Max and Grant, she lavishes me with more of her eagle-eyed scrutiny. She's also a notorious gossip, which is fine because I'm a notorious gossip myself.

"That girl will chew you up, baby."

"I can only hope!" I drop a kiss on her head, step back, and smooth my lapels. "How do I look, Mom?"

"Away with you. And I'll be interrupting in about seven minutes with tea. No shenanigans."

"Seven minutes? Challenge accepted!"

I should tell her that she needn't worry. Not because I'm one of those man-ho players with a different woman warming my bed every night. Sure, I do okay, but that's not the issue here. The problem is that most women can't handle my energy. I'm pretty high on life a good chunk of the time, which is great for short term, but scares the crap out of most potential mates. As much as it pains me to admit it, I'm like my mother in this respect—but where she channeled it into crazy shite, like dragging us all over the UK to hippie music festivals or to Spain to pick grapes, I've funneled my energy into being the best at bloody everything. And while I can make a play for Trinity and have a little fun, I'm fairly certain she'll tire of me quickly and won't be sticking around past breakfast.

Leaving Sadie chuckling, I walk into my office and shut the door.

Trinity is patrolling the walls, checking my diplomas. "How old are you?"

"Twenty eight."

"Damn. So you were . . . twenty when you got your law degree from Oxford?"

I smile. "Yes, but the system is different there. You read law at the undergraduate level. Then I did a postgrad here and passed the bar exam."

"Read law?"

"That's what we say to describe getting a degree."

"We?"

"The British, love."

She snorts. "But you must have started college at, what, sixteen? So you're some sort of smarty-pants prodigy over-achiever?"

"Is there any other kind?"

She shakes her head, half annoyed, half amused, and walks over to the window. The view is spectacular, yet she makes no comment, clearly determined to remain unim-pressed. Her circuit takes her to the jigsaw puzzle I have set up on a drafting table on the west side of the office.

"Narnia," she mutters, a reference to the puzzle's subject matter.

"The kids like it."

Her brow creases slightly at the mention of kids, perhaps. I like to keep the little buggers entertained while I chat with

Mommy or Daddy about how much they hate their significant other. And sometimes working the puzzle helps me unravel a few knots of my own.

I gesture to the sofa on the other side of the room. "Have a seat."

Ignoring that, she sits in the less comfortable chair opposite my desk and crosses her legs. The dress rides up a touch, showcasing a flash of smooth, shapely thigh. I take a seat on my desk, ensuring she has a good view of Hot Guy in Suit.

We're both givers.

She peers up at me through her dark lashes. "I suppose you're wondering why I'm here."

"You don't have to tell me."

"Lawyer-client confidentiality?"

"Well, no. Technically whatever you discuss with Max is the same as discussing with the firm. But I won't pry if you'd prefer."

Clearly torn, she examines her nails. Uncrosses her legs. Recrosses them. This sexy sequence sends blood shooting to my groin.

Finally, she barks, "It's not for me. It's for my sister. She's in the middle of a divorce and he's being a dick."

Ah, the circle of life. "Divorces tend to bring out the worst in people."

"Yes!" Visibly upset, she shoots up, hands fisted on hips, eyes to the floor. "I hate to see her like this and what it's doing to the kids. . . ." She shakes her head, unable to finish her thought.

Standing, I move in and place my hands on her arms. Her skin is hot to the touch, feverish, even, and makes my fingertips sizzle. Hating that her gaze is dipped and not meeting mine, I touch a finger to her chin and raise her focus to me. Those golden-brown eyes flame, set aglow by our proximity.

"Trinity, love, it's okay. You've come to the right place.

We've got a lot of experience dealing with this. Now, how come she's not here today?"

"I thought I'd help her out by doing a little research. She's my baby sister and I usually vet things for her. Old habits, I suppose. Also, she's got a—a class."

"A class?"

"Pilates." She steps away from me and takes her seat again. "I know you think that's weird, but her life has been totally upended this last year, so I'm trying to help her maintain some sense of normality. Balance. I don't want to have her switch lawyers until *I'm* sure it's a good idea."

Sounds like Ms. Jones has a few control issues. I file that away.

"So, she already has legal counsel?"

"Yes, but I don't think they're doing enough. Apparently Brian's lawyer is a shark, so I think we need a bigger shark." She looks me up and down, and I see her appreciation for my form reflected in her eyes. Some people think that sitting while the other party stands gives the upright party too much power. Not Trinity. She recognizes that her current position affords her the best view. I look pretty fine from the gutter.

"Would you call Max a shark?"

"He's excellent at his job."

An awkward pause overtakes us. I can tell she's a little embarrassed that she's not asking me outright to represent her sister. That's okay. I presented a certain image on our first meeting and it's stuck with her. Besides, Max would probably be better for this because his client list is mostly female. I lean more toward men—in my practice of the law, that is.

I have good reasons.

The door opens—no knocking, mind—and in comes Sadie with a tray. She takes a gander at our positions, gives a small yet knowing *huh,* and sets the tray down on the desk.

"Any sign of Max?" I ask.

"Why? Do you care?" Practically sung back at me, of course.

"Thanks, Sadie, that'll be all."

She smiles at Trinity. "I don't think you need any help, but I'm right outside if this one gets fresh."

"Thanks, Sadie!" I repeat over Trinity's husky chuckle.

Once we're alone again, I take a moment to pour tea, doctor it up per her request, and hand it off with a double-chocolate Milano perched jauntily on the saucer. I sip my own, closing my eyes in pleasure. You can take the boy out of Britland, but you can't take Britland out of the boy.

We've each downed a cookie in comfortable silence—except for a breathy, slightly orgasmic noise from Trinity—when I restart the interrogation. "Tell me more about your sister."

Her face lights up, the worry of a moment ago faded for now. "She's eighteen months younger than me and we've always been close. Our mom was a bit—neglectful, I suppose. She was usually on the lookout for a new man and all her energy went to that, which left me to be the grown-up. I made a lot of the decisions where Emily is concerned and I suppose I can't help continuing to watch over her." There's that brow crimp again as her mind wanders to the past and a time when something went wrong. A decision she regrets where her sister is concerned. "My mom died in a car accident when Emily was seventeen and I became her guardian. She's been sort of sheltered, which is probably my fault . . ."

She's still speaking, but I've stopped listening. A chill has descended over my skin.

"Trinity," I interrupt.

She blinks at the sharpness of my tone. "Yes?"

"What's Emily's full name?"

"Emily Anne Carson."

The chill becomes a freeze, but I need to ask. "And her husband?"

"Brian. Brian Carson. Why?"

Fuck. "Trinity, we can't talk about this anymore."

"About what?"

"The divorce proceedings between Emily and Brian Carson."

Confusion blights her expression. "What's going on?"

"Our firm is already representing Brian Carson in this matter. Brian's my client."

CHAPTER 5

Trinity

I'm waiting for the punch line, but Lucas either has really poor comedic timing or is completely serious. *Shit, fuck,* and a million other swear words climb up my throat.

"That can't be right. Brian Carson? Partner in the IGC Restaurant Group? Prematurely balding, bit of a paunch, father-of-two Brian Carson?"

"One and the same."

The teacup in my saucer has started to shake. Lucas relieves me of it and places it back on the tray, then hands me a second Milano cookie.

"Sugar's good for shock."

I don't need to be told twice. I inhale that cookie, using the chewing motion to give me time to wrangle my emotions.

"But Max could still represent my sister, right?"

"Not in this. No one else at this firm can represent Emily Carson. That would be a conflict of interest."

He hands me another cookie, and while I shove it into my mouth, I break down what he's told me. When I called to make an appointment with Max, I didn't give details, just that I wanted to talk about *my* divorce. It sounded better than saying I'm here because my sister is a special snowflake who needs her every move to be curated and vetted.

Of all the law firms in all the world . . .

I stand, because if I remain seated, I will finish that entire fucking plate of Milanos.

Lucas straightens and smooths some cookie crumbs from his thighs. The way his suit pants stretched taut around his thighs while he sat on the desk was a praise Jesus moment, for sure. The man is one incredibly fit specimen.

And Brian's legal counsel.

"Unfortunately, it also means that you and I can't be in any sort of relationship while I'm representing your brother-in-law."

My heart plummets like a rock to the Chicago River twenty-five floors below us. "You think I care about that?"

"Don't you?"

"Of course not! That's not why I'm here. I came to see Max, remember?"

"I remember." He says it quietly, like he's referring to another memory, say, two nights ago when he told me I was about to embark on the ride of my life, with Hottie Brit as the driver.

"You were the one who started this," I say, not even sure what I mean by *this.*

"So you're mad I didn't call."

"I-I am not—mad! You think I've been waiting around for you to pick up the phone? Or I'm here to put my ass back on your radar? Or I care that this conflict-of-interest business kills *this* before it's even started?"

So this litany makes it sound like I care. Considerably.

Also, apparently I have my own definition of what *this* is and it involves lusty, sweaty nights tangling up sheets with the man before me.

"It's not completely impossible, just tricky. I'd need to get my client's written permission."

"You mean if I wanted to—to—"

"Kiss me?"

My breathing locks up and I can feel color rising to my face. So much is inferred from that query and kissing is the least of it. "Brian would have to give his blessing?"

"In a manner of speaking."

"Well, good thing I don't want to kiss you." Damn, I want to kiss him. Bad.

The mention—twice—of the word *kiss* lingers like temptation in the air. It's all I can think about. It's everything I want.

But then I remember that this guy just torpedoed me with terrible news, not about the doomed-before-we-begin thing, but about how Max and his firm are off the table. Even worse, they're representing Brian. The man before me is working for the enemy.

The man before me *is* the enemy.

"How long have you been his lawyer?"

"I can't answer that."

I growl. "How long?"

His eyes darken to a midnight blue. I want him to look at me like that forever. "A few weeks. He wasn't happy with his previous counsel and he decided a switch was in order."

Emily said Brian had hired a shark. It appears I'm looking at him.

"And you're pushing him to go for sole custody?"

"Trinity, I can't discuss this with you. All dealings with my client are confidential."

I open my mouth, in no doubt that I look like an oxygen-deprived trout. Confidential? I know that!

"He's—he's not a good person. He's the kind of guy who steals lunches from the communal employee fridge, who aims for puddles in crosswalks. He's one giant foreskin!"

His raised eyebrow makes me feel foolish. Sharks don't care about their clients' evil quotients or uncanny likenesses to dick jackets.

"Okay, whatever. I guess we're done here." I turn, practically stumbling toward the door. I have to get away. I need air and water and more Milano cookies.

A big hand emerges from behind me to touch the door, and I jerk in surprise. I know it belongs to Lucas, but I still jumped because apparently after The Incident, the slightest thing is enough to reduce me to a cowering bundle of nerves.

"Trinity. Wait."

I can't look at him. Why do I feel so betrayed? I barely know him, and except for that almost-kiss, there's nothing between us. But the sheer impossibility of it makes me realize I might have wanted something after all. A curveball in the otherwise predictable trajectory of my life.

Damn Brian and Em—no, not Emily. This isn't her fault, yet a little voice nags me. *It's never her fault. She's done it again. Taken away something you want. Something that should be yours.*

"I have to leave. You can't help me so it's best I go." I say this to the door.

"Look at me, Trinity."

My name sounds like a prayer on his lips. This is a terrible idea, but not doing it would assign it more significance than it deserves, so I turn my head. "Yes?"

It's as awful as I expected. Worse. Deep, cobalt blue pools of compassion stare back at me and I want to drown in their depths. You know you're in a bad way when you start thinking in clichés.

"I'm as disappointed as you are," he says gravely.

"Well, I heard such good things about Max, but I can always find another lawyer."

"That's not what I'm talking about."

I shrug. "It was nothing. *And* you smelled like a brewery."

"Surely perfume to a woman in your profession. Admit it, I brought the goods. The slight brush of my hand to your jaw, the focused lean-in, the promise of more."

He's doing it again, that charming self-awareness. My lungs have locked up. Useless, useless. "The hallmarks of a player."

"Not a line, Trinity."

I don't believe him. Neither do I care, because even a surface attraction from a surface guy is better than nothing. "Stop this. You just said it can't happen."

"Yes, I did. But the thing about divorce proceedings, Trinity"—he inclines his head so our foreheads are almost touching, his breath a ghost of a whisper against my lips—"is that they eventually come to an end."

But I want it now, I almost whine. I want the mouth and the clever hands and the sly, knowing laughs. I want the flutter in my chest and the heat between my thighs. I want the woo. And I want it in the not-too-distant future.

I am one greedy wench.

"We'll see if I'm still available," I say with appropriate hauteur.

"Brilliant. I won't be dating anyone else either while we wait."

This guy cannot be for real. "I'm not hanging around waiting for my sister to sign her divorce papers just so I can get laid!"

He nods. "No, you're not."

"Exactly. I'm not."

"Getting laid doesn't really describe it, Trinity."

It will be so much more. That's what he means. That's what I'm willing to wait for, apparently.

He opens the door, a smirk on his lips I'd like to slap into the middle of next week. "Enjoy that slow burn," he says.

"Enjoy your blue balls," I shoot back.

I smile thinly at a surprised Sadie and head off to start my day.

CHAPTER 6

Lucas

*A*ny asshole can father a child. Any idiot can provide the genetic material to create an embryo. I've advocated on behalf of plenty of guys who should have wrapped it before they tapped it because, in all honesty, they are not qualified to play daddy.

But I usually place myself in a client's shoes. If I had a mini-me running around out there, nothing would keep me from being a major part of my kid's life. Now some of the men I represent are douches. They've cheated on their wives, hidden assets in offshore accounts, have shady dealings in their past and present, and while they might be out-and-out assholes, it's important to remember this: Being an asshole and being a good dad are not mutually exclusive.

I truly believe that most fathers want the best for their children. Stable, loving environments are best for kids, just as nurturing relationships with parents and guardians are also preferable. If both parents want to be involved and are making a decent effort, then the gender of the parent should not be discounted. However, we still live in a world where motherhood is viewed as mandatory and fatherhood as voluntary. My take is that a mother's bond is not any more special than a father's.

So while some dads are assholes, they're still dads, and I'm here to fight for them.

I know, I know. I sound like one of those late-night commercials for a shady ambulance chaser. *We're family here at X, Y, and Z, Esquire. Let me fight for yours.* Cue awkward photo of attorneys plus whichever staff were forced to stare directly into a camera that day.

I tell you all this because Trinity's news that Brian is a dick, or more accurately—and hilariously—one giant foreskin, isn't exactly a bombshell.

The guy cheated on his wife with Freja, his nineteen-year-old Danish au pair.

At our first meeting, he slipped me a twenty (yup) and asked about the best ways to ensure his wife doesn't get a penny from him.

He also turned up at my office one day wearing a Coldplay T-shirt.

So, yeah, asshole.

But he still has rights, and I plan to help him be the best dad he can be. *We can rebuild him. We have the technology.*

Today I've called Brian to discuss the house. His wife—Trinity's sister, and man does that chap my dick—doesn't want to sell.

"Of course she doesn't, Brian. No one wants the upheaval of a home move, but your finances won't really support that mortgage and whatever you need for your new household. Unless you have some stash you're not telling me about."

"I told you everything. But she says it's tough on the kids."

"This whole situation is tough on them, but you have to provide." More than financially but I'm not here to judge. At least, not yet. "However, there's no reason why she can't contribute to the household finances as well. And part of that contribution is downsizing to something more reasonable."

I can practically hear his smiling sneer over the phone. "I knew you were the right guy for me. We're gonna crush her."

Clients who feel they might have a weak leg to stand on often give off this vibe of blowhard bluster. I'm not here to crush anyone. My job is to ensure that everyone gets what's fair and the kids come out of it unscathed. The little blighters invariably get the short end of the stick, and I'm determined that they shouldn't suffer any more than necessary.

My gaze wanders to the jigsaw puzzle in my office, thoughts of the past—of Lizzie—ever present.

"I'll put a call into your wife's lawyer and get the ball rolling. But I have to ask: How much of a hard-ass do you want to be on this?" The paperwork includes details on Emily Carson's work history, as in nada. It's going to be tough for a woman with no marketable skills to make headway finding a job. "Her lawyer will argue that she stayed out of the workforce to raise your children."

"Raise them? The nannies raised them. Hell, her sister spent more time with them than Emily did. Especially Chase."

I perk up at the mention of Trinity. "Really?"

"Yeah, she's always been there. Butting in. Giving unsolicited advice, making my son soft. My kids!"

So not a whole lot of love there. And I don't especially appreciate Brian's "making my son soft" comment. As far as I can tell, Chase is a great kid.

Brian continues. "Does she expect me to support her for the rest of her life?"

"No. Just until she remarries."

"Well, no one's going to take on a chick with two kids."

You'd better hope someone will, Brian, because your denial-of-alimony claim is not a slam dunk.

"Let me see what I can do." I click off, thinking of Trinity.

I should leave her alone, yet I'm drawn to her. To her tough shell hiding that soft center where her sister is concerned. I admire the hell out of a woman who steps up like that. Who puts family first, probably because I've tried and failed as a son and a brother.

We're always drawn to our opposites, magnet to metal. I need to play this carefully, because there's a really good chance that my attraction to Trinity Jones could make me screw up.

CHAPTER 7

Lucas

Some asshole snaps his fingers in front of my face to get my attention. Okay, not just any asshole.

Grant Lincoln, partner-asshole.

"Where the fuck are you, Wright? You've been walking around like a zombie all evening."

It's Sunday, and we're settling in for quiz night at the Frog & Footman. I flew in from London this afternoon and I didn't really feel like going out, yet here I am. My transatlantic trips usually leave me in a funk, and I'm not the only one in a mood. While Max is with us in body, he may as well be on another planet mentally, because he's having problems with his girl, Charlie. The man's not fit company for anyone.

When Grant's the cheerful one of our trio, you know we have fucking problems.

"Is this about Trinity?" Max asks.

Grant squints, par for the course when he's gearing up for an interrogation. He has a slow, methodical, southern style that belies the sharpest legal mind in the city. "Trinity? Why is that familiar?"

"She's the whiskey sommelier from James's bachelor party." The mention of this makes Max scowl because it forces his brain to Charlie, who has his balls in a vise.

"Wait. Sadie said something," Grant says, his brain churning through the details of my pain and plucking out the salient ones. "About wanting representation, but we already represent her brother-in-law?"

Max explains the situation fully. Perks up with the retelling, too. He especially enjoys the part where she was heard telling me to enjoy my blue balls.

Grant's shaking his head. "Only you, Lucas."

"Nothing happened."

"You don't sound too sure."

I stab fingers through my hair. "Nothing happened, but now all I can think about is the nothing that happened."

"It'll pass."

I narrow eyes at him. "Like it did for you?"

Immediately I regret my glibness, because it's clear that it didn't for Grant. He's been divorced for a year from Aubrey Gates—the woman I sent Trinity's contact information to for the whiskey tastings—and we all know he's not moved on. Law school sweethearts and Chicago's golden couple, they were separated by something catastrophic, something neither of them will share with Max or me. Me I can understand—I'm the (relatively) new kid on the block, and while Grant and I have known each other for seven years, there are still areas he won't open up to me about. But Max? He's known them since uni and they're clamlike on the topic of their relationship's demise.

"I have a date tomorrow night," Grant says.

Max and I unslump. "With who?" Said in unison, which

makes us both smile. This is what we need to get us out of our funk. Some vicarious bonking.

"Woman I met at Gina's bachelorette party." That's James's bride-to-be. "Kelly or Callie or something."

"You don't know her name?" Max asks, incredulous.

"She put her number in my phone and told me her name. And it was really noisy with fucking Abba playing and she was very, very drunk. Anyway, I called her and she just said hello when she answered."

"Like you do," I interject.

A Grant glower ensues. "No name. Not a clue. So we're going out to dinner and I have to figure it out. Secretly."

"You going to rifle through her purse when she's at the loo?"

"That seems . . ." It takes a moment for him to pronounce. "Invasive."

"Maybe. Maybe not." I grin, because it's kind of funny and I'm happy to see him making the effort. "Glad to see you getting your wang back in the game, Lincoln."

He looks uncomfortable. "It's just dinner."

"With a mystery woman!"

"I just—fuck, I have to move on. I've been in this holding pattern for over a year and I'm tired of it. When you told Max he had to be ripped out of his rut, it made me think. I wasn't going to even call her—whoever she is—but I figured you were right. We need to have our lives shaken up."

Three days ago, Max found out that I *might* have been fucking with his life. The Twitter version: I convinced his ex to dump a puppy on him in Lincoln Park while he was flirting with another woman with the aim of making Max mix up his routine, and maybe apply this freewheeling 'tude to the rest of his life. One of my finest pieces of work, I have to say. The evil plan hasn't quite come to fruition just yet— the fair lady has not been won—but it'll happen. And I'm proud to hear my wisdom might have had an impact on Grant, who's not really the advice-taking type.

"Ladies and gentlemen!" Quizmaster Steve's voice rings out over our heads, telling us the festivities are about to begin. "Make sure your entry fee is in the pot and your drinks are on your table. Phones off. The first round of questions will be the classic 'dead or Canadian.'"

Love it when they ease us in gently.

I stand and stretch, trying to shake off my jet lag. "Okay, I'll get the drinks in . . ." Max looks at me expectantly, so I add: "And how about I pay our entry fee, too, Mr. Fucking Trust Fund, even though I paid it the last three times?"

"I donated that trust fund to charity, asshole. Besides I don't carry cash. Like your queen."

"Very convenient."

I head up to the quizmaster and fork over the entry fee. It's only twenty bucks, but I like taking the piss out of Max because even sans trust fund he's still very, very rich.

"Team name?"

"Beyond a Reasonable Stout."

"Lawyers?"

"How'd you guess?"

Quizmaster Steve looks unimpressed as he writes it on the chalkboard. *Fuck off, it's cute.*

I turn to head to the bar to get the next round in and bump into the person behind me.

"Oh, sorry," I say to a rumpus of wild, beautiful hair shot through with red and gold. My gaze dips to full, kissable lips, then raises to the chocolate-drop magnets staring back at me.

"Trinity!"

"Oh, you."

"Here for the quiz?"

"Yeah, with my crew." She thumbs over her shoulder to a

table where I spot her coworker, the arsemonger barman I wanted to punch before he wanted to punch me, and a guy in specs and a Doctor Who shirt. He must be their geek. Every team has one.

"You guys any good?" I probe.

She folds her arms, immediately cagey. It hikes up her lovely breasts, amplifying some stellar cleavage peeking out of a black tank top, so the joke's on her. "We hold our own. How about you?"

"Maxie's good for movies, Grant covers American sports, while I'm our authority on science, history, pop culture, international sports, and politics."

"Is that all?"

I raise my hands in acceptance. "Yeah, you're right, I'm holding the bloody team together. They're fucking useless."

She wants to laugh, but she doesn't like me—or what I'm doing to her sister. I lean in close. "Can't we put aside who we are to each other and marinate in a bubble of mutual attraction for a while?"

She takes a deep breath, her eyes lit by the fires of indignation. "I can't ignore reality. You're trying to destroy someone I love."

"I'm trying to keep the playing field level. Everyone deserves legal representation."

"That's easy for you to say. You get paid and don't have to witness the mess. I'm left behind to pick it up. You can't seriously think I could forget about that."

I seriously thought we could.

I seriously thought she wouldn't take what I'm doing so personally.

I put one of my investigators on the case so I know more about where Trinity's coming from. Her mom and stepdad died when she was nineteen, leaving Trinity as her seventeen-year-old sister's guardian. Emily married Brian a year later, but Trinity is obviously incredibly protective of her. There's more here, a collection of jagged puzzle pieces I can't yet visualize as a single image.

"Two minutes, ladies and gentlemen!"

"I need to pay my entry fee," she mutters, looking away. Sighing, I step aside, order another round in, and when I turn back, she's at her table talking to Treebeard. He shoots a dagger of a look in my direction. I smile back, because after getting wins for my clients, fucking with twats like this joker is my next favorite thing.

I glance at the team name board as I walk by, seeking out Trinity's, and laugh hard, drawing a few weird looks.

Just the Tip, they're called. Lucas likey.

All right, all right, time to see how far I can get with the quiz—and the fair Ms. Jones.

CHAPTER 8

Trinity

Oh Lord in heaven, you have got to be kidding me . . .

Despite my chipper attitude on leaving Lucas's office, for the last three days I've felt like a balloon that's been slowly deflating. I was determined that our last encounter would be the end of any and all communication between us. Lucas Wright is Trinity Enemy No. 1 (okay, No. 2 after Brian), and there's a snowball's chance in Scottsdale that he'll ever get inside my panties.

This should be easy. It was merely an almost-kiss. And while he's good-looking, he's not exactly Idris Elba or Chris Hemsworth levels. (That I defaulted to guys with accents there is merely a coincidence. Quit judging me!)

I've no doubt I'll survive not getting it on with Lucas Wright. I don't have to see him. But the "don't have to see him" stratagem only works if I truly don't have to see him.

Working in a bar means that I usually choose not to spend all my spare time in other people's bars, but I haven't been out with the boys for a while. We used to attend the

Frog & Footman's quiz on a regular basis before my spare time was hijacked with first, comforting Emily, and second, The Incident a couple of months back that shook me to my core.

I want to get back to the person I know I am: the good friend, the bon vivant, the woman who might actually have a chance at sex with a guy. Not that quiz night is a magnet for talent, but at least I'm putting myself out there with two of my besties as my wingmen.

Gideon glowers as I take my seat. "Is that—"

"Yes," I say before he can finish.

"Universe must be telling you something."

"That it hates me."

Pete raises an eyebrow, then a pint to his lips. "What's the problem?"

"Thought you liked Hottie Brit." Gideon again, slightly accusing.

"Hottie Brit?" Pete cranes his head and immediately hones in on Lucas despite the fact there are approximately one zillion adult males here. "Guy with the cheekbones that could cut a tomato can?"

"The very one," I say with a glare at Gideon. I had shared the HB nickname with him in confidence. Of course I should realize that anything I say to Gid will be immediately passed on to his boyfriend. If I had a man I could trust, I'd probably tell him deep, dark secret stuff, too—like how I confided in Lucas the other day in his office. About my mom's neglect and how responsible I feel for Emily.

Annoyed with where my thoughts have strayed, I rush on to explain to Pete. "He was in the Library last week with a bachelor party and then—"

"Round one!" the quizmaster's voice booms to all four corners of the bar. "Dead, Canadian, both, or neither. An easy one to get you started. Alec Guinness!"

I jot down *dead* on our answer card. "He's Brian's lawyer."

"Who?" Pete asks. "Alec Guinness?"

"Hottie Brit," Gideon says, as if Pete's query was serious.

"Question two: funnyman John Candy!"

I make the annotation for *dead*. Pete takes the quiz sheet from me, crosses it out, and writes *both*.

"He's kind of hot."

"John Candy?" I ask, knowing we're not talking about him. *Sorry, John Candy, wherever you are.*

"So now she can't—" Gideon locks his two index fingers together to make a chain link.

"She can't what?" I say.

"Bang him."

Both Pete and I stare at Gideon.

"Honey, I know you're gay, but that's not how the hets do it," Pete says. "It should be—" He jabs a finger into his rounded finger and thumb on his other hand.

"You know what I mean," Gideon says, annoyed. "She thought he was a perv, poured a beer on his head, flirted her ass off. Some quality meet-cute stuff there. Now she's ready to get busy except they've got a *Pride and Prejudice* crossed with legal ethics thing going on."

The legal ethics thing I understand. The rest . . . "What?"

"Dwayne 'The Rock' Johnson! Dead, Canadian, both, or neither?"

I squint at Pete, who makes the call. "One of our neighbors to the north. Citizenship through his grandfather."

Impressive. "Where are you getting the P and P thing from?" I ask Gideon.

"Well, Darcy is pretty much responsible for destroying Elizabeth's sister's happiness. That's your main gripe—his impact on Emily's future. And he's British."

Gid might be onto something here. I'm not sure why I care anyway—it's just a guy. There are tons of guys and plenty who can service my sex-deprived body. It doesn't have to be *that* guy, and it won't be because he's the enemy. *Capisce?*

As luck would have it, Lucas is currently wearing an outfit designed to ensure he won't be getting any himself—as in sex. Green and blue plaid pants, or as he'd probably say—tartan trousers—that even fashion-challenged golfers would spurn, paired with red, bordering on pink tennis shoes. His well-defined chest muscles are undergoing a containment situation in a gray tee with the slogan: Show Me Your Torts. Really? Who's the audience for that?

He catches me checking him out and wiggles his eyebrows. Tingles shiver-shock across my body, making my skin tight and my belly loose. Apparently, *I'm* the audience for that.

Hunkering down, I devote the next few minutes to the rest of the questions.

"So endeth round one. Hold up your cards for collection!"

I can't help taking a quick glance in Lucas's direction. He's smiling back at me, smugly gorgeous. I scowl and look away.

Pete gives a slow clap. "Nicely done."

"Oh, shut it."

The powers that be count up the scores in the first round and make announcements.

"Who the hell is Without a Reasonable Stout?" Pete asks, immediately miffed that we're in third behind Blood, Sweat, and Beers and this interloper.

Again I glance over. Again I find a response, though this time it isn't a smirk, it's an all-knowing grin.

"Fucking lawyers," I mutter. Lucas Wright and his posse are going down.

After two more rounds—finish the lyrics (my specialty) and sports (Gideon's), we're in joint second behind Lucas's team. I can't believe those legal bastards are doing so well. Look at how one of them is dressed!

A ten-minute break halfway through facilitates visits to the smallest rooms and liquid replenishment. I run into Lucas outside the women's restroom because of course I do. He's leaning against the opposite wall, texting. I think he might be waiting for me and there's that flutter again behind my rib cage.

He raises his gaze. "Having fun yet, Ms. Jones?"

"I assume you guys are cheating."

He clutches his chest, wounded. "Care to make it interesting?"

My pulse skyrockets as the air's molecules start to whir around me. "What did you have in mind? We win, you tank my brother-in-law's case?"

"We win, you have to go on a date with me."

"You just said you can't. That we can't." And there I go sounding disappointed again.

"I said we would have to get permission from my client."

I scoff, imagining how Brian would love to lord that over me. No, thanks.

"Not interested in sleeping with the enemy."

"I can assure you there wouldn't be much sleeping."

He still hasn't moved from the opposite wall, but I sense the weight of him as if he was hovering over me. In his stifling presence, I feel drugged, a limp noodle of lethargic lust.

"As soon as you give me the green light, we can resolve all this unresolved sexual tension," he murmurs. Still not moving. Still projecting that tractor beam of raw magnetism.

"Don't worry. I can take care of it all by myself."

And *that* sounded like an admission that the UST exists.

"Are we talking toys here? Or are you thinking you can use some sort of placeholder to ease some of that pressure?"

He shakes his head like I'm a fool who doesn't understand what's happening. Like I don't understand the science of it.

"Don't worry yourself so much with what I'm thinking."

"Well, *I've* been thinking what our first kiss would be like."

Every part of me clenches in lust. It's just science, I insist. Chemistry.

"I'm thinking I'll back you up against a wall." Like the wall that's currently, barely, holding me up. "And I might grip your wrists and put them behind your back because I suspect you're kind of handsy."

I snort my disagreement. He can't possibly know I'd love to fill my hands with that most excellent ass . . .

He continues. Relentlessly. Cruelly, even. "Yeah, you'll want to grab my arse or run your fingers through my hair, but I'll need to put my foot down that first time. I'll need to impose my will, make sure you know I intend to kiss you thoroughly and professionally."

A pause makes the air around me sigh.

"My mouth will hover near yours, and our noses might kiss first, because noses usually like first dibs. But it won't happen until . . ."

Another pause. It's excruciating. I refuse to participate verbally. Meanwhile, my pussy is lining up to volunteer as tribute.

"You close your eyes, Trinity. And when you do, my lips will brush yours so fucking gently that you'll gasp. Your lips will part and your tongue—Jesus, that sweet, sweet tongue— will dart out to wet your lips and mine. An invitation. And then I'll know I can go all in. Move my lips over yours. Love that sweet mouth until you're moaning. Until it's mine."

He stops talking and the silence is worse. The silence is unbearable.

"Not happening," I croak, willing myself to walk away,

one heavy, lust-poisoned foot at a time. Behind me I hear—oh, God—*singing*. Instantly recognizable, it's that Billy Paul classic from the seventies. Remember it?

"'*Me-ee aa-and Mrs., Mrs. Jones, Mrs. Jones, Mrs. Jones, Mrs. Jones!*'"

"Stop that!" I hiss over my shoulder.

He does not. "*We got a thing . . . goin' on . . .*'"

I pick up the pace as I walk back into the bar. He doesn't follow, but the words of the song do, the part about knowing it's wrong but too strong to let go.

"Whatcha smiling about?" Pete asks when I sit down with a new round of beers. (I don't spend money on top-shelf whiskey in other people's establishments.)

I wipe that smile clear off, realizing that it stayed on my face all through that drinks order.

"Nothing." What is Lucas Wright's game? He knows zilch can happen—him for his ethics reasons, me for my own. I can't possibly be with a man whose aim is to inflict catastrophic damage on my sister. Yet he's doing his utmost to charm me and forge a connection between us.

I renew my commitment to the quiz. After three more rounds, we've caught up to the lawyers and are now running neck and neck. I had an especially good round on history (Sir Edmund Hillary, first man to climb Everest, was from New Zealand, *not* the UK—take that, colonial imperialists!).

I don't bother to be sneaky about my glance toward the lawyers as we head into the final round. I'm happy for them to know that they are about to be crushed in the hellfire of pub quizzery.

Max greets me with a cheerful wave. The other guy—Grant?—gives a subtle nod of respect. As for Lucas, he does a two-finger prong to first his eyes, then mine, and finishes with a thumbs-down gesture. All with a cheeky—and yes, sexy—grin.

How can I stay mad at this guy?

"Ladies and gentlemen, the final round!"

"Star Wars, Star Trek, or the Marvel Universe," Pete chants.

"The Chronicles of Narnia!"

"Fuck!"

So inevitably your average pub quiz hosted in your average British pub will offer a question or two on classic children's literature. And while our team is of an age where we should have read The Chronicles of Narnia, or at a minimum, The Lion, the Witch, and the Wardrobe, none of us have ever quite gotten around to doing the deed. Those books are thick! And there are seven of them! I've seen the first couple of movies, because awesome aunt here, but the questions are usually a touch too esoteric to be covered by those.

I recall that jigsaw in Lucas's office and another look his way tells me all I need to know: We're screwed. He's wearing that smile I despise that also happens to do things to me. Wicked, wanton things.

The quizmaster continues. "In the Lion, the Witch, and the Wardrobe, which of the Pevensie children is the first to step through to Narnia?"

Lucas and Co. get busy scribbling, while Trinity and Co. get busy grumbling.

We lose. Badly.

Flush with the pot for the evening, Lucas hops up on a wobbly bar table, does a dance that highlights his trim hips and amazing ass—even in those ridiculous plaid pants—and launches into a tuneless "We Are the Champions." Subtle he is not.

Max wanders over, Grant trailing him. Lucas is too busy signing beer mats no one asked for.

"How about we buy you a drink?" Max asks. "Show you we're not all sore winners."

"Sure you should be consorting with the enemy?"

He smiles kindly. "I think we can be adults about this."

Problem is I want to do very adult things to Lucas Wright. Absent that, I'll plunder him in other ways. "I'll have a glass of Glenmorangie eighteen year."

Max's smile stretches wide. "Why do I get the impression you're about to relieve us of our winnings in one round?"

"The hazards of drinking with whiskey experts."

Five minutes later, Max is in a deep debate with Pete over the damage someone called Steven Moffat has or has not done to Doctor Who. Grant and Gideon are talking about baseball. I'm on the periphery of both these conversations, wanting to contribute but having too little expertise, when I'm nudged by an elbow.

"Bad luck there, Ms. Jones," Lucas says. Whispers, really, which makes it all seem so much naughtier.

"I wouldn't say that. You won fair and square with your oddly encyclopedic knowledge about a children's book. Not weird. Not weird at all."

Something flashes across his face, a shadow that disappears as quickly as it came. "Can I help it if I'm a master of all trades?"

"Hmm, not the phrase."

"It is when we're talking about me. I'm very good. At most everything."

"Modest, too."

He tilts his head. "You have problems with self-confidence?"

"Just braggarts."

"Don't you consider yourself an expert in whiskey? Don't you advertise yourself as such? What's the point in pretending you're only somewhat knowledgeable at something when you're the best there is?"

I seek to unpack that. "People are put off by overconfidence," I say carefully.

"Should I substitute *men* for *people* in that sentence?"

A foreign heat warms my chest while Lucas's blue-on-blue eyes cut through me. My friends don't condescend about my ambitions, but my family—my sister—has never really understood why I chose my profession (*So manly! Unless it's a strategy to find a man? Is it?*).

I respond with, "A whiskey sommelier isn't a traditional job for a woman."

"The Chronicles of Narnia's not the traditional reading material for a divorce lawyer," he shoots back.

"So why do you love it?"

"Why do you love whiskey?"

I think of my granddad and the time when I felt safe and secure. "Nostalgia. Longing. Soothes the senses and feeds the soul. It also feels good to . . . understand an entire world of taste. Of sensation. It's a world I can dive into and control." I shake my head. "I'm not making much sense."

But I am to Lucas. I can tell what I've said has struck a chord somewhere deep inside him. A private place I'd like to visit. I curl my hand into a fist to stop from touching him.

"You, too?" I whisper, the intimacy of the moment shocking me. "With Narnia?"

Now his smile is tinged with sadness. "Me, too."

My heart contracts. Behind the clown in the ridiculous plaid pants is a man in pain. Worse, I want to know him.

Lusting after him was safer. Despising him after discovering his mission was logical. But this? Peeling back a layer in Lucas's good-time-lad façade gives me chills.

"I should go," I say, which conveniently coincides with Gid and Pete offering me a ride home.

Lucas nods, pulls away. Something shudders between us, and I tell myself it's for the best. "Yes, you should. See you around, Trinity."

Not if I can help it. I'm starting to realize that Lucas Wright is a hundred times more dangerous than I previously thought.

CHAPTER 9

Trinity

I'm careful by nature. A woman living alone, walking alone, in the world alone, has to be. Pepper spray is my constant companion because clutching keys in readiness for a good old-fashioned eye gouging isn't always going to cut it.

I have a residential street parking permit, but sometimes my late hours mean the rock 'n' roll spaces outside my door are taken and I have to park a block or two away. I'm constantly aware of my surroundings and I have that little canister of pain in my hand as soon as I exit the car. Not a big deal.

Until the night it was.

The weather was a little cool for May, but understandably so at one thirty in the morning. My street is tree lined and invariably quiet, but I ended up parking two blocks away from my condo building. No one was around. All I could hear was my breathing and the soft tread of my running shoes.

The alleys in my neighborhood are wide and well lit. I don't turn down them for any reason but I'm aware of them, like gaping maws as I pass. A block and a half from where I live, he grabbed me by the hair.

Surprised, I dropped my pepper spray, the sound a heart-crushing clatter as it hit the ground, the sound of my salvation slipping away. My scalp burned but adrenaline rose to soothe it—I swung out with my closed fist and connected.

He let go.

That's when I should have run. I know. But I was in shock and angry, and I wanted to confront this piece of shit who thought he could frighten me in my backyard. This gangly white guy with dark, greasy hair and burning, bloodshot eyes. He stood there, his palm covering his bloody nose—yes, I'd done that!

They'll have DNA if they need it. If they need to identify my attacker. My killer.

He lunged but I stepped back, then farther until I was in the well-lit street. My heel brushed the pepper spray canister but no way was I bending down. I was a block from my door but I knew I'd never make it. He was still coming toward me and I was still backing up when I heard it.

A car. It turned down my block and we both looked up as its headlights caught me and my cornered-animal fear. I blinked and my attacker ran back into the alley like the rat bastard he was.

I don't drive at night anymore. I have a postshift drink with my coworkers and use that as an excuse to always take a taxi. To always ask the driver to wait until I'm inside.

Neither did I tell my friends, because I didn't want it getting back to Emily. She has enough going on, and while I know she'd sympathize, a teeny part of me is terrified she'll blame me or the neighborhood or the fact I serve alcohol for a living. I'm supposed to be looking after her and she won't let Chase stay with me if she thinks the neighborhood is unsafe. Besides, it could have happened anywhere.

It could have, but it didn't.

It happened a block from my home.

It happened to me.

And I was forever changed.

ALMOST A WEEK after the pub quiz, I'm on my way to Lincoln Park for a little fresh air and sports ball. You might think that the offer of a fun day out in a beautiful park in our fine city would be golden. Alas, none of my friends are interested in accompanying me to watch scruffy fourteen-year-olds play soccer.

Gideon claimed he had to make a Home Depot run for lumber. Lumber? I call *liar*. The man hasn't built so much as a house of cards, never mind anything requiring wood. (Insert dick joke here.) Pete asked if there would be any booze involved.

It's 10 A.M. in a public park with teens, Pete.

He hung up on me.

Even Emily, Chase's own mother, couldn't be bothered. She wanted to have a girly mother-daughter mani-pedi day with Ari, the thought of which made me shudder.

So here I am representing the Jones clan and praying to God Brian won't be here.

The parking gods are shining on me as I score a spot on Stockton, just a couple of blocks from the action. Immediately I spy Chase in conversation with a tall kid over near the sidelines.

"Hey!" I barge in, ready to show my embarrassing love.

"Hey, Aunt Trin," Chase mumbles.

"Aren't you going to introduce me to your friend?"

Eye roll. "This is Carlos. He's on the team."

"Hi, Carlos. I'm Trinity, the cool aunt. No doubt you've heard all about me."

Carlos flicks a glance of *is this for real* at Chase. My nephew merely shrugs, then mutters that they have to get started.

"Okay, break a leg!"

"That's theater," Chase says with immense patience. "You don't say that to athletes. You *never* say that to athletes."

"All right. Break one of your opponents' legs. Crush them!"

Another eye roll from my nephew, but I tease a grin from Carlos. It's probably pity for Chase, who has to painfully endure me, but I don't care. Connections are being made.

Looking around, I spot parental types several feet off with collapsible chairs and most important, coolers. These look like my kind of people so I sidle over.

A woman peers up at me through unfortunate fire-engine-red bangs, halfway through tapping Franzia box wine into a Solo cup. She scoots an expressive eyebrow. "You here to judge?"

"Nope. Just felt like a weirdo standing over there by myself."

Mollified, she thrusts out a hand. "Glinda Parsons. My mom had a *Wizard of Oz* fetish, so yeah, I've heard all the jokes."

"Trinity Jones. My mom had a *Matrix* fetish, but fortunately pop culture has left that one on the slag heap of history. No more jokes that anyone under forty will get."

"Aw. So sad." A big, toothy grin. "I brought an extra chair unless you want to stand through this horror."

I grab the collapsible lying behind her, uncollapse it, and settle my ass into the minihammock.

"Wine?" she asks, shaking the Solo. A casual slosh of Robitussin red leaps the cup's lip and lands on the grass.

"No, thanks." I move on quickly lest she be offended. "So which one is yours?"

"The redhead. Never marry one unless he looks like Prince Harry, know what I mean?"

I chuckle and watch as the kids are corralled into a huddle by a man in shorts with dark, messy hair, oak-trunk thighs, and one of those broad triangular backs framed by big shoulders and trim hips. Nice tight ass, too.

My skin tingles. I recognize that form. It's haunted my fantasies and kept me awake at night . . . *What the actual fu* —*tbol?*

Lucas Wright *here*? This is the main attraction Chase was telling me about, who has all the moms in a tizzy?

"Is that their coach?" My voice sounds breathless.

"Oh yeah." Glinda's agreement has a lascivious tinge to it. "You think I'm here 'cause I enjoy youth soccer? No chance. We're all here"—she waves at the phalanx of support on the sideline, all of whom I notice now are women middrool— "for *that*."

That is pointing at areas on the field, instructing players to take up positions, I suppose. He probably won't even see me. I sink lower into my chair, but there's only so far I can go.

He turns. A pair of shocking blue eyes trap mine. That wicked, kissable mouth curves.

My face burns hot. I want to be anywhere but here.

"How long is this game?"

"They don't play as long as the pros. Only an hour."

"Glinda, I think I'll have that drink now."

"Do you know him? Lucas?"

I'd hoped that maybe the grin he dropped on me might

have gone unnoticed, but Glinda is on it like a soccer mom on the Franzia box.

"Vaguely. He's—" What, exactly? My thwarted lover? An eye-fucker par excellence? The man I can't stop fantasizing about? "He's my brother-in-law's divorce attorney."

Glinda's mouth screws up while she connects the dots and draws a fairly fucked-up picture.

"He smiled at you."

"He smiled at everyone." Which is true. He arced a pantie-melting grin over the entire group. There were a few sighs and at least one NSFW moan.

Glinda is unmoved by my hedging. "Well, we call ourselves Lucas's Birds, just a bit of fun. But you got the good stuff. The light-up-his-eyes that lights-up-your-vaj stuff."

I doubt she could see Lucas's heated blue gaze from here, but I know what she means. I felt his eyes on me all the way down to parts of me severely neglected of late. We both know nothing can happen here, so maybe that's why it all feels so naughty. Harmless, even.

The game starts, so I try to be a good aunt and do what I came to do: support my nephew.

Thing is, Chase used to be a demon on the field, but since his parents' separation, he's been having more off days than on. Today he's playing a midfield position, and within the first minute has made a poor pass that the other team inter-cepted. They score.

Carlos, on the other hand, is single-handedly keeping the team in the hunt with solid passing and flashes of speed down the line that never quite result in goals because he doesn't have the support. After a few moments of being a good little aunt, I can't help myself. I have to look at Lucas.

The team bench is on the other side of the field, but Lucas obviously thinks benches are for losers because he stalks the line the entire time. Having seen how parents can become ugly when their kid is playing sports, I expect more of the same, yet even in this, Lucas bucks my worldview. The man throws his entire being behind the kids. It's full bodied, done with affection, and vaguely unsporting, but only to the other team.

"Come on, mate, don't be such a jammy dodger!"

"Get in there, my son! Show that tosser how it's done."

"Right in the knob, you plonker!"

Half the time I've no idea what he's talking about, but it sounds like the encouragement every child should hear. Maybe every woman. Imagining Lucas calling me a plonker in bed should be the perfect damper on my fired-up lady parts, but I suspect the man saying anything in that accent will have me orgasming in seconds.

I can safely assure you that not one woman is paying attention to the action on the field. I hear snatches of encouragement on this side as well. Lucas's Birds are in great form.

"Those thighs are giving me life . . ."

"Lift your shirt . . . yes, yes, yes . . . Oh, God in heaven, the brow wipe . . ."

"He can get me right in the knob anytime . . ."

That last one doesn't even make sense! (Unless knob means . . . oh, I don't know.)

The first half is over in thirty minutes, the score 3-0 against, and the kids are taking a break with water and fruit gels near the goal. Lucas swaggers over, salutes the moms, and stops in front of me. Those Thighs of Thunder are hairy and look incredibly touchable.

"Ms. Jones, how are you today?"

It's cheekily formal. Doing my bestest impression of a moody eight-year-old, I peer up and mutter, "Fine, thanks. Didn't expect to see you here."

"You sure?"

This puts my back up. "Very sure."

He turns to Glinda. "Mrs. Parsons."

"Now, Lucas, I've told you a million times. It's Glinda."

Out pops the Lucas smile. Sunglasses make an appearance across the board and that thud you hear is the sound of someone keeling over. "Gavin's playing well today. You must be pleased."

"What?" Glinda is focusing all her attention on Lucas's crotch, definitely pleased about something. "Oh right. Yes. Thrilled. You're doing such a marvelous job."

"Thanks, Mrs. Parsons. Ms. Jones, could I have a word? It's about Chase." Without waiting for my answer, he moves away from the group.

I feel as though I've been dropped into *The Hunger Games,* not because the boys are playing lights-out, competitive football. No, I'm Katniss surrounded by a wolf pack of laser-eyed women who have spotted the threat in their midst.

I shoot a quelling glance at Glinda's eyebrow and push out of the chair. Lucas waits for me, hands on hips, his gaze tracking my approach.

"Yes?"

"How are you, Trinity?"

"You already asked that."

He frowns. "I did?"

"Yes, like sixty seconds ago." I wave behind me to the chair I just vacated.

"Hmm. Right." He sounds like he disagrees. "What did you say?"

"That I'm fine."

"Are you?"

"Yes!" I'm irritated that we're going in circles. I'm especially irritated that he's smiling at me, which is making me the center of attention—and Lucas's focus—much more than

I'm comfortable with. I've always been a sidelines kind of girl. "Are you *trying* to piss me off?"

"No. A little. I like seeing you fired up."

"Water bottle over the head if you don't watch out."

Another ovary-destroying grin. "So you're close to Chase?"

"Yes. Very."

His grin fades. "I don't think he likes footie all that much, which is a shame because he's talented. I get the impression he's here to please his dad, which I understand, but it might not be the best option for him."

I'm not sure what he's asking. While I mull it over, I pump him for intel.

"Is this how you met Brian? He heard you were a divorce lawyer and hired you?"

"Correct. We got talking."

I've done my research on Mr. Wright. If you're a father who feels maligned by the system, Lucas is your guy. He's built a reputation as a staunch defender of paternal rights and access. Has even written articles in law journals about it.

"I'm surprised Brian isn't here," I say, probing.

Lucas doesn't take the bait. "I wonder if you could talk to Chase about what he really wants to be doing. He wouldn't be bad if he applied himself, but he's missed a few practices and I'm not sure his heart is in it."

A whistle sounds and Lucas turns. "Okay, back to work! I'll see you after."

"What?"

"Pizza party, Ms. Jones. I'm going to need help wrangling the little buggers, especially if they lose as badly as I suspect they will. It would be really bad form to abandon me in my time of need."

And then he trots off that perfect ass and those Thighs of Thunder, leaving me in serious need of more Franzia.

CHAPTER 10

Lucas

We head over to Chicago Pizza and Oven Grinder Company right after the game (we lost 6–1). The guys are feeling dejected, but that'll soon change when I stuff their sad little faces with pizza and Coke.

Not all the kids can make it—just five of them, as most have other activities on their jam-packed agendas. American kids' lives are scheduled up the wazoo, I've noticed. No worries, though, I'm fine with the numbers, and I'm especially fine with my co-chaperone who has agreed to drop off half the kids after.

The pizza place is historic because it *might* have been used as a lookout point for the St. Valentine's Day massacre across the street in 1929. Built into the basement of a town house in tony Lincoln Park, it's small and doesn't take reservations. But I know the owner, Reggie, and he's set aside a six-seater booth at the back.

"Kind of a tight squeeze, Reggie." Not that I object to tightly squeezing anywhere with Trinity. At which point

Reggie, who is clearly a man after my own heart, directs Trinity and me to a separate table in the corner. Brilliant.

Trinity looks like this is less than brilliant. "But—" Flustered, she waves a hand over the kids, who are busy crowding into the booth. Carlos and Chase on one side, Sam, Jonah, and Shawn on the other. "We have to sit with the children. To watch them."

"Who's chaperoning who now, Trinity?"

"Pretty sure it's whom," she says, taking the seat I hold for her.

"Sure thing, Ms. Grammarian. And don't worry. I'll watch the little shits with the hawk eyes I'm not allowed to use on you. Because. Ethics."

She doesn't want to smile, but she's helpless in the face of my charm. By the time this divorce is settled, we'll be so ready. The hottest slow burn in history.

Trinity's looking around, so I take this opportunity to study her. She's wearing ripped jeans and a white T-shirt that contrasts beautifully with her skin. Her bra is lacy, a fact of which I'm acutely aware because it creates an embossed pattern where her gorgeous tits press against the erotically thin fabric.

"Okay, guys," I call out to the team. "Let's get our orders in for pizza pot pies because they take awhile to bake."

"Pizza pot pies?" Trinity asks with fitting amazement. "That sounds awesome."

"You have no idea, Ms. Jones."

Chase shoots me a look, then catches his aunt's eye. Something is communicated between them, then Trinity frowns at me as if to say I need to knock it off. A little harmless flirting won't breach any code of ethics here. Of this I've been convincing myself since day one.

Once our orders are in, Trinity goes straight for the

bread, immediately followed by the jugular. "So why divorce law?"

"Are you one of those people who think lawyers are scum and divorce lawyers are the scum on the scum?"

"No. But I saw those diplomas in your office. You graduated early from a very prestigious university in England. You moved away from where you were raised and made your life in another country. You've dedicated your career to fathers' rights. I think you're the kind of guy who could do anything he puts his mind to, yet you've chosen to do this. Divorce. Custody battles. A specialty that deals in a very unique branch of hurt. I'm guessing some guys do it for the money, but you could probably make more in personal injury law or something corporate. You have reasons that mean something significant to you."

Well, then. I've never had anyone cut to the heart of it like that. To the heart of me. Her insight deserves an honest response.

"My parents divorced when I was eight. Dad was a mild-mannered accountant by day and, well, a mild-mannered accountant by night. Boring as fuck, the kind of bloke who liked his hard-boiled eggs done for exactly three minutes and his underpants dry-cleaned with medium starch. I loved him to bits. He was smart, my dad. And when my mum divorced him, it destroyed him. Destroyed us, because we should have stayed with him."

How he and my mother ever survived eight and a half years of marriage I'll never know. She was a wild child who thought she could settle down once my dad knocked her up after a one-night stand. He adored her, you see. Stepping up was never not an option for him.

"So you fight for dads who you think get the shaft from the system?"

"You could say that. I mean, my parents really should

never have married. Millie, my mum, was—*is*—a free spirit with hippy-dippy views on parenting. She was a big fan of treating children like adults and letting them make their own decisions. Want Kit Kats for dinner? Go ahead. Want to wander barefoot and camp out in the garden for a week? Knock yourself out. Which is great when you're a little kid, but not so much when you're older and want stability. Or clean clothes. Or report cards signed."

No, Millie wasn't a great believer in structures like compulsory education or organized religion. Everything was controlled by the patriarchy. And damn, she knew how to work a judge during a custody hearing—probably where I get my own gift of persuasion in a courtroom.

My sister and I should have lived with my stable, boring dad, but instead sole custody was awarded to my mother because she turned on the waterworks. We saw him once a month for a year, but then he got transferred to Edinburgh for a job. May as well have been on another planet.

"Sounds like you practically raised yourself." Trinity's words pull me out of the bitterness swamp that threatens to engulf me whenever I think of my dad and the real, life-altering consequences of custody being awarded to the wrong parent.

"In a manner of speaking."

I recall our meeting in my office, when I found out who she was and who she couldn't be to me. "You said your own mum was on the neglectful end of the spectrum."

"Yes, but it made me self-sufficient." There's more challenge in there. *I don't need anyone, especially a man,* she's telling me.

I emerged from my childhood similarly independent, yet still shackled to the reckless decisions my mother had made. I also recognize that it takes a village. To raise kids. To make a life. To become a full-fledged person. Trinity might think she needs no one, but I have what it takes to change her definition of need. Self-sufficiency is unnecessary when Lucas Wright is at your beck and call.

"What are you smirking at?" she asks.

"Just thinking of all the things I plan to do to you once the obstacles are out of the way. All the dirty things."

She shakes her head. "You think you can emerge from this without any blood on your hands?"

She means the divorce and what will happen to her sister. She'll use my job to justify the thickness of her walls as long as it suits her.

"I think you need to stop worrying about your sister and start thinking about yourself."

"And conveniently once I start thinking of myself, it has knock-on benefits for you."

"And my dick."

She gasps and flicks a glance toward the boys, who are too busy to pay heed to us horny adults. "Not in this lifetime."

But I can hear it in her voice. Trinity Jones is coming around.

CHAPTER 11

Lucas

My mum's a thief. Yeah, I said it.

She justifies it with her bullshit theories on capitalism and socialism, and how the world belongs to the downtrodden. The meek shall inherit the earth and all that.

When my twin sister, Lizzie, and I were kids, Mum made us steal for her. Well, *made* is too strong. Encouraged, more like. She'd send us into the local shops with instructions to grab what we could using the five-fingered discount. Anything we could lay our grubby little hands on: food, booze, sweets, clothes. You name it, we lifted it.

By the age of eleven, Lizzie looked fifteen and was beautiful with it. My youthful bones were exactly that—youthful. I was scrawny and underfed and had the look of a tinker. Matted hair, dirty fingernails, muck baked into my skin by the sun we frequently slept under. When Mum took us on the road, we spent most of our time crashing in German forests and on Spanish beaches, living off welfare and baked beans cooked over campfires.

It's our adventure, she'd say. And at first, we loved it. But Mum realized she'd lose alimony payments and social security benefits and risk the wrath of the authorities—the man, she'd call them like a seventies jive talker—if she kept us out of school, so by the time September rolled around, we'd be back in merry old England.

I loved school, which might sound weird. But after the unstructured existence my mum foisted on us for months, I loved the stability, and I especially loved to read. I wasn't genius level, but I did have a whiff of prodigy about me—I was definitely too smart for my year, so I leaped ahead. And even though I was small for my age and then worse, *really* small compared to the older kids in my class, I was able to get by on personality.

Funny and hyperactive, I managed to make friends with all the high school cliques: the sporty ones, the nerds, the popular kids, the outcasts. Existing at some level above it all, I was lucky to have my supposedly hot sister (I didn't see it myself, but my friends were really into her) smoothing my entry into the right circles.

You might be wondering what any of this has to do with my mum's thieving ways. Hold up, I'm circling back to it. You see, Millie didn't limit our extracurricular activities to our travels abroad. No, she had no scruples about doing it in her own backyard. We lived in Hammersmith, a working class neighborhood outside London, and "shopped" on King Street, the main thoroughfare (cool fact: not named for the king of England, but for Bishop John King, who gave land to the poor in the seventeenth century).

Boots, the pharmacy chain, was one of our favorite haunts to lift from. Lizzie liked it because of the beauty products, while I was a fan of picking up condoms, which I could sell to kids, and deodorant, especially as some fucker at school had said I smelled. So what if he was right. I decided to do something about it.

And one day I was caught, my first time getting pinched. Of course, Lizzie, aka the Artful Dodger, scarpered, leaving me, aka Oliver Twist, high and dry. I was arrested and brought to the police station—only eleven years old. But I was lucky. My guardian angel appeared in the form of Quentin Scarborough.

Mr. Scarborough was my teacher and he'd been watching me in school (not in a creepy way!). We called him Queer Quentin, not because he was gay but because his name was posh.

Yeah, the razor-sharp wit of the young.

The fuzz couldn't get ahold of my mum, so they called the school to find my dad's number. Mr. Scarborough showed up at the police station instead. Mum was nowhere to be found (surprise, surprise), but Mr. S was on hand to fix things.

I really liked him, but I was too cool to show it.

"What are we going to do with you, son?"

"I ain't your son, guv." (I was a tough little shit.)

He chuckled.

I sneered.

A week later, I took an exam. Weird punishment for shoplifting, but Mr. S had a plan. His favorite quote was from Robert Browning: I judge people by what they might be, not are, nor will be.

I passed that exam, scored a scholarship to King's College, a fancy boarding school with notable alums like Orlando Bloom of *Lord of the Rings* fame as well as a handful of Eastern European aristos, and the rest is history. Up to Oxford to read law at sixteen, graduated at twenty, postgrad in the States at twenty-one before most American kids have even entered law school. How's that for getting ahead? And all because of my sticky fingers.

Mum never forgave me.

Of course she didn't come right out and say that, but I honestly think she would have preferred if I'd been locked up. I'd become part of the establishment she hated, a toff, a bloody wanker. She still takes the money I send her, though. She sees it as a redistribution of the wealth.

I see it as a payoff so I don't have to spend a single moment with her. A payoff for my guilt, too, because that path Mr. S put me on veered away from Lizzie. *Two roads diverged* . . . I got sent to fucking Hogwarts and a new, shiny life, while she was left in the clutches of the Dursleys.

Even when I go back to London to visit Lizzie, I make sure I avoid my dear old mum. Worst son ever, but then I learned from the best.

CHAPTER 12

Lucas

"Hey, good practice, mate."

Chase is sitting on a park bench, gym bag at his feet, eyes on his phone screen. Barely looking at me, he replies with, "Liar."

Cheeky bugger. Taking a seat beside him, I glance at my phone: 9:12 P.M. All the other kids have been picked up.

"You wound me, mate."

"Uh, you're a lawyer so I doubt you have any feelings to wound. Also, I was terrible in practice and we both know it."

Sharp like his aunt. "Wouldn't go that far. Though I don't think you dig it all that much. I mean, you used to, but now? What gives?"

"I'm just trying it out for a while."

I nod, knowing this has something to do with his dad and whatever's going on at home. My heart keens for him. "So, where's your ride?"

"I'm staying the weekend with my aunt but I guess she's running late."

I remain quiet and so does Chase. Not awkward, it just is, but then we start chatting about movies and music. After a few minutes the long shadows of the evening have descended over the park, and Chase has not-so-surreptitiously texted his aunt a couple of times with no response.

"Where's your mom?"

"She went to visit my grandparents in Rockford with Ari. And Dad's on a business trip to New York."

"Where does your aunt live?"

"In Edgewater."

A couple of miles north of where we are. "I'll drop you off."

He's a kid, used to having people chauffeur him around, so he merely shrugs his agreement.

"You like her?" Chase asks, once we're in my car.

"Who?"

"My aunt."

I hide my smile. "What makes you think that?"

His side-eye makes clear why he thinks that. "She dates weirdos."

"Oh yeah?" I try not to sound too interested. Fail miserably.

"One guy was a performance artist. He'd cover himself in peanut butter and read really bad poetry onstage. She sent me a video."

This is my competition? I remain silent.

"I don't think she dates anymore. Not for months anyway." He looks out the window. "I stayed over once and she was crying in the kitchen one morning."

My heart lurches. "Everyone gets the blues on occasion."

"Not Trinity. Nothing gets her down. But she said she just wasn't feeling well. Now she works a lot and doesn't go out much, except to hang with us when Mom goes out for her martini nights with friends."

Trinity babysits while her sister paints the town? Filed away.

A few minutes later, we arrive on a leafy street in Edgewater, in front of a nice brownstone walk-up. Chase is already muttering his thanks, one foot out of the car.

"Hey, wait up, mate, I'll walk you in."

He rolls his eyes but I don't take offense. I'd be the same way. When I was his age, I was definitely wandering the streets alone. But I'd never want it for my own kids.

Chase presses the intercom buzzer. Nothing. After about twenty seconds, he presses it again.

"You sure she's in?"

"Yeah. I mean, she didn't answer my text but she should be expecting me." Impatiently, he hits the button again. Finally, we hear a muffled "Yeah?"

"Trin, it's Chase. I'm supposed to be staying over tonight. For the weekend?"

"Chase?" She sounds drunk or confused. "Oh, fuck." Then louder: "Sorry. Come on up."

"See? Fine," Chase says, though his eyebrows are practically joined as one with the crease of his brow.

"Think I'll say hi to Aunt Trin."

"Your good deed is not going to get you in her pants, dude."

Smart-arsed little shite! He goes up ahead to the third floor, which is as high as it goes. The door is slightly ajar then is pulled open to reveal Trinity in all her mad-haired glory. Her eyes are watery, her nose is red-raw, and she's holding a tissue in her hand.

"Chase, I'm sorry. I've got a cold and the meds knocked me out. I meant to set an alarm to pick you up." She spots me lurking behind him. "Oh, hi. Thanks for bringing him over."

Chase is hovering at the doorway with his gym bag. "I need to take a shower after practice. Thanks for the ride,

Coach." He thrusts out his hand, very grown-up. I give it a firm shake.

"Anytime."

In he goes, which leaves me with his hot aunt. And yes, even ravaged by the effects of illness, she's still gorgeous.

"Well, uh, thanks," Trinity says again.

"You look terrible, Aunt Trin," I say, sliding by her and shutting the door behind me. "Have you eaten?"

"I was going to order pizza—what are you doing?"

I'm pushing her back toward the sofa. "You need to rest and let me take care of dinner."

"But—I can make a phone call to a pizza place." She coughs in my face. I take it like a man.

"Or you could let me cook up something quick so you could get back to bed and won't have to wait an hour for delivery. How about scrambled eggs on toast?"

"You shouldn't be here."

"Why?"

She tilts her head. "Because of your professional ethics."

"Nothing in the rules about being a friend. I can do that and not cross any lines, especially when . . ." I wave a hand over her.

"Are you saying you don't want to jump me when my nose is running and I might cough all over your dick?" She looks mortified, color flushing her gilded skin. "I didn't mean that."

"Such a sweet talker."

"Forget I said it. In fact, forget everything you've seen here."

I shove her—not too gently—onto the sofa and lean in close enough to acquire a good share of germs.

"Not likely to forget that there'll be blow jobs on the menu the first time. Way to sell it, Jones."

She closes her eyes, likely trying to will away her embarrassment at being caught even thinking about my cock. Perhaps even will me away entirely. "I was just trying to be funny in the face of bizarre circumstances. You're the enemy, remember?"

I wonder if she really thinks that or if she's trying to convince herself because she's afraid of how amazing it could be between us.

"Enemies make the best lovers, Trinity."

At which she sneezes, without warning, right in my face.

I suppose I asked for that.

"Sorry," she mumbles, but there's a twinkle in those golden-brown eyes that wasn't there before. She's not sorry at all.

Smiling, I head into the bathroom to wash my face before making dinner.

CHAPTER 13

Trinity

$\mathcal{M}$y head feels like it's enclosed in bubble wrap.

Luckily I had a few staples in—eggs, onions, mushrooms, tomatoes—so that tricksy bastard was able to throw together a light meal for the three of us in less than ten minutes. Curled up in misery on the sofa, I could hear him in the kitchen with Chase, who was on toast duty, discussing the best way to scramble eggs. (The key is a touch of milk and an electric mixer to get air in for maximum fluffiness, apparently.)

I'm a terrible aunt for forgetting to pick up Chase. I suppose that's why I let Lucas gently manhandle me and take over. Guilt. Whatever Lucas is making is probably healthier than pizza and I'm in no state to provide for my nephew.

About 10 percent of my taste buds are in working order, however, enough to know that what I just shoved down my throat was very tasty. What's sitting across from me in my breakfast nook is very tasty as well. Lucas wears a Nike tee

85

and shorts that reveal those Thighs of Thunder. They should be spindly, the stems of a pelican, the legs of a man who spends all his time at a desk, but they're not, and this seems rather cruel.

"Take care of the plates, mate," Lucas tells Chase, "while I take care of your aunt."

Chase grins at me. I scowl back.

"What's that for?" my favorite nephew asks.

"Just do the dishes."

Another smile, this time shared with Hottie Brit.

No, I'm no longer calling him that. He's an interloper, a bossy know-it-all who's out to destroy my sister in the name of giving Brian the best possible defense. But every time I see him, another knee-melting exchange inevitably pushes my objections further to the back of mind.

He stands and starts stretching. Hands in the air, which pulls his shirt up to showcase the V. You know the one I mean, the lickable one crafted by the gods.

Next, he puts a sneakered foot up on the bench in my breakfast nook and does a couple of lunges. Then he switches to the other leg.

"What are you doing?"

"Limbering up."

"For what?"

He frowns. "Carrying you to bed, love."

"I do *not* need to be carried." Yet my traitorous stomach wriggles at the thought. Other parts of me like it, too.

However, my head's in charge, even if it's saturated in cold meds. I search for indignation. "Also, I'm not sure I appreciate the implication that you need to limber up and might throw your back out from lifting me. I can walk just fine."

Up I get. Too fast, alas, and I sway a touch, making a grab for the table.

"Just let him help, Trin," says Chase in a tone that tells me I'm being difficult.

I'm too tired to argue. "You'll get sick," I mutter into Lucas's neck, which is warm and has a concave spot where it joins his shoulder that's perfectly designed to fit my nose.

"Don't worry about me, love."

But I do worry. I've always worried. About Ems and Chase and Ari and even my mom, who never worried about me.

It's no fun always being the grown-up.

He sits me on my bed, and I try to imagine it through his eyes. Framed whiskey posters and images of the motherland, Scotland, fill the walls along with my sommelier diploma, which feels positively lame when compared to Lucas's big brain qualifications. I kick a thong under the bed.

"What do you sleep in?" he asks. "Something lacy and sexy?"

I point to an oversized, washed-out University of Illinois tee slouched over a chair. He hands it off, then turns before I have to ask him and walks out of the room. Quickly I undress and put on the tee, then slip under the safety of the covers. I need this space between us because apparently my germs aren't enough to create a barrier.

On his return, he brings a couple of Tylenol, a glass of water, and a box of tissues. He sits on the side of the bed.

"Want these now?"

"I'll wait. See if I have problems sleeping first."

He pulls the covers up to my chin. "What's the protocol here?"

You sneak under the covers and show me what I'm missing. "With what?"

"Chase. Tomorrow's a school day, so I'm guessing you don't want him up all night watching TV."

"He's usually pretty good at self-policing."

He bites down on his lip. It's hot. Why is it hot? Probably because *I'm* hot, feverish with this damn cold.

Then he kisses my forehead. I almost swoon, not because of the sweetness, but because of—oh, hell, it's really sweet. I so want to hate him for making Ems's life miserable. I need to hold on to that.

"I'll be out here if you need anything."

Before I can question that more thoroughly, he's gone and I'm falling into a deep slumber.

I WAKE with a stuffed head and a desperate need to pee. It takes me longer than it should to sit up, swing my legs out of bed, and shuffle to a stand.

I'm a mess.

Mornings with a killer cold are usually worse, so I'm hoping I'll feel better before I need to head into work tonight. When you live on tips, nights off are disastrous to the bottom line. At the same time, I know Gideon won't want me behind the bar, infecting the clientele.

A voice filters in from the living room and a moment of panic overtakes me. I grip the door frame and hunt for a weapon. The lamp? My Kindle?

But Chase's laugh loosens my battle-ready muscles. Right. Who else would it be?

Walking out to the living room, I already know who's with him, yet I wasn't expecting to be greeted with the sight of a pair of perfectly taut, clenched buns attached to a body contorted into downward-facing dog. Using one arm!

"So what we talked about last night?" Lucas asks, addressing Chase. Neither of them have seen me.

"About playing soccer?"

I hold my breath, waiting for more.

"Do it only if you like it, mate. Not for anyone else, okay?"

"I like being part of a team," Chase says. "Even if I'm no good right this minute, being part of something makes up for it."

My heart clenches. This sports ball business is helping my nephew deal with the trauma of his parents' separation. I'm also in awe of Lucas for stepping up and talking to Chase like this.

And he's still suspended above the ground with that single arm holding him perfectly still!

"Keep that pose, mate."

Chase is also trying it but he doesn't have Lucas's stamina. His knees drop to the floor, unable to maintain the position.

"Yoga's fuckin' hard, man," my nephew says.

"Uh, language."

Chase twists and grins at me. "Hey, you're up."

"Yeah, and you're doing yoga."

"Just giving it a shot," Chase says. "Lucas says it frees the mind."

Lucas is still balancing on one hand, which really should not be possible. With a little bunny hop, he jumps up and faces me. He's wearing the same shorts as yesterday but no shirt.

It is glorious and I am miraculously cured.

Just kidding, but hell, this is better than a cup of morning joe. I spy tattoos. A full, colorful sleeve of a serpent on his left shoulder, a band of astrological symbols on his right bicep. What looks like a witch's hat and the name Lizzie ringing it over his left pec. I hate this woman already.

Lost in a lust fog, I barely notice that it's—*he's*—speaking.

"What's that?"

"How'd you sleep?"

He moves in and holds my upper arms. He's done that before, a subtle display of caring coupled with dominance. Intellectually, I don't approve, but as his heat pulses right through me, I figure that intellect means diddly when I'm breathing Lucas Wright's air.

"Did you stay the night?"

"On the sofa. I thought you'd probably want to sleep in and I could get this one off to school." With a conspiratorial eye roll, he thumbs behind him to Chase, who's busy on his phone.

"You don't have to—"

"Help?"

I'm not used to this. I've always been a lone wolf where this kind of thing is concerned. I like making the calls and maintaining control. It comes from raising Em. When you're sick you just get on with it.

"You shouldn't be here," I say, not wishing to list the reasons in front of Chase.

My sensitive nephew picks up on the vibe and stands. "I'll get ready for school."

"Put your cereal bowl in the dishwasher, mate," Lucas says, never taking his eyes off me.

Chase rolls his eyes but does as he's told. Lucas leads me to the sofa, sits me down (more gentle shoving that I'm strangely starting to enjoy), and grabs an afghan. Silently, he makes a meal out of wrapping me up, arranging cushions, and generally ensuring my comfort.

Standing back, he assesses his work. With a disapproving head shake he moves a pillow so it's supporting my side more firmly, tucks the blanket underneath my body more securely, then takes a seat beside me.

He's still shirtless. I might be as sick as a dog, but even I can appreciate the way his arms flex as he positions me for his pleasure, the way the ropy cords of muscle strain slightly against his skin. He also happens to smell incredible. Didn't he come from soccer practice last night?

I lean in and sniff, wondering why it's familiar. "Did you take a shower and use my body wash?"

"Yeah, after you conked out last night I took the liberty of not stinking up your sofa with my sweaty body. You're welcome."

Taking liberties is right. I can't believe he just stuck around without invitation. Last night, he was here, in my home, mere feet away from my room. I'm about to take him to task when he utters this gem:

"And then Chase and I went over his maths homework." Plural like they say in the UK.

"You did?"

"Yep. Bloody algebraic equations—that brought it all back." He chuckles like algebra is his happiest memory. I move away a couple of inches because I'm beginning to deduce that Lucas Wright might not be all there.

"So." He rubs his hands together. "What about breakfast?"

"No appetite."

"Okay, how about a cup of coffee? That's probably all I can manage anyway before I take His Lordship to school."

"You don't have to do that. The coffee, the ride." I make to get up, but I'm—what's the word?—swaddled. The fucker has *swaddled* me on the sofa.

I feel helpless but strangely helped. I usually wouldn't like this level of bossiness, but since he arrived last night, he's exuded a forceful calm, which is strange because he's usually so high energy and on all the time. For one day I can accept his comfort. I'm ill, suffering lowered immunity, and someone else is taking care of business.

"I wouldn't say no to coffee," I whisper.

He grins huge. "That's my girl!"

He bounds off to the kitchen like a friendly Irish setter. There's a cooking show on the TV, currently on mute, that *Great British Baking Show* that Gideon and Pete are always raving about. They claim it's relaxing.

I don't really know how to relax, especially not lately. I don't think watching amateurs bake bread will do it for me.

Chase comes back in, hair brushed, backpack at the ready. He takes a seat beside me. "You okay, Aunt Trin?"

"I've been better. Sorry I've ruined your weekend. I don't want you to catch anything, so it might be best if I called your mom and sent you to Rockford to see your dad's parents."

"Can't. I have a game tomorrow."

"You might not be playing if you get sick."

"I'll just stay away from you." He moves to the other end of the sofa.

"That's not how germs work, young man. I've probably infected every surface."

"I'll risk it."

Lucas returns with a cup of coffee and pops it on the side table on a coaster. "You ready, mate?" he asks Chase.

Chase stands. "Today's a half day so I'll be back at one. Maybe I should bring the spare key?"

Lucas folds his arms. "Better buzz. I'll be here looking after your aunt and I'll need it to get back in."

Now wait a second . . . but Chase is already heading for the door.

"You don't have to come back," I call out to Lucas, with a nice, juicy lung hack to sweeten the offer. "Don't you have a job?"

"I have some work I can pick up at my place along with my laptop. I need to get a change of clothes anyway."

"I don't need you to take care of me."

He hunkers down beside me and lowers his voice. "Chase

has to stay the entire weekend, but it sounds like he'll need rides to places. He already told me he wanted to head over to play video games at Carlos's house tonight. I'm going to hang around so you can focus on getting better. Now, I'll admit that covering up your legs with that blanket nearly bloody killed me, Trinity, but that's my burden and I'll carry it like a man."

How is that relevant? "But—"

"Listen, love, I'll come back with . . ." He raises an eyebrow. I want to lick the scar bisecting it.

"What?"

"You tell me. I'll come back with . . ." He flourishes a hand, encouraging me to fill in the blank.

Oh, if I must. "Ham, egg, and cheese from Dunkin'."

"Ham, egg, and cheese from Dunkin'. Got it. Anything else?"

I think on it a moment before inspiration strikes. "Tampons."

"Which absorbency?"

Oh, he's good. "Regular." I don't even need them, but I refuse to back down. "And Cadbury Crème Eggs. Two, please."

"It's July."

"When I was a kid, that's what my mom would get us when we were sick." Yeah, I went there. Played the dead mom card. Just how far is he willing to take this Good Samaritan act?

He smirks. "I'll see what I can do."

As he stands, I'm treated to the intoxicating sight of Lucas's exceptionally well-toned, perfectly muscled body filling my eyeballs.

"See you in a few." He heads to the door.

"Aren't you forgetting something?"

"What?"

"Your shirt."

He gazes down fondly at his pecs as he's just realizing now that he's half naked. "It needs a wash. I don't think anyone will mind me walking around shirtless, do you?" And with a cheeky wink, he's gone.

CHAPTER 14

Lucas

*D*o you have any idea how hard it is to find Cadbury Crème Eggs in July?

Trinity Jones does, which is why she set me on this quest.

But she doesn't know that if I want something badly enough I will make it happen. I once BASE jumped off a mountain in New Zealand to impress a girl (she banged the bloody instructor instead, but it was a good plan all the same).

An hour after dropping off Chase, I slip into her apartment quietly, just in case she's sleeping. Placing my computer bag on the ground softly, I move into the living room to assess the lay of the land. She's there where I left her, though she's adjusted her head so it's on a throw pillow and it's easier for her to catch a few Zs. Most people look calmer when asleep. Not Trinity. The crimp between her eyes deepens with each inhale, her dreams apparently filled with worry.

I set the bag from Dunkin' on the coffee table.

Without opening her eyes, she sniffs the air like a hunter for prey. When her eyelids flutter open, there's no missing the appreciative once-over she gives me.

"Covering up won't cure me."

I could have stayed shirtless but had to make myself semi-decent before I picked up her sandwich. No shirt, no service, etcetera. Stinkin' rules. Now I'm wearing yellow and green striped board shorts—they're slimming—and a black T-shirt with the slogan Keep Calm and Call Your Lawyer.

"Society demands it. Too many car crashes as I walked down the street."

She smiles, despite her best efforts not to. It's fun finding cracks in her façade, though it's easier today given her weakened immune system.

"Ready to eat?"

"God, yes." She sits up and I hand off the sandwich, then grab her empty mug.

"Another round?"

"Maybe water? I might try to nap more after this."

She still sounds terrible and doesn't look so great, but it's a good sign that she wants to eat. I bring back water and a couple of DayQuil I bought at the store.

"No, thanks," she says. "Don't like putting chemicals into my body."

"Should I tell you about the egg sandwich now or later?"

She scoffs. "Not bad chemicals."

"Whiskey?"

"Natural chemicals."

I take a seat at the end of the sofa, lifting her feet to slide in and settling them on my lap. I position them so they're not resting on my dick and we can all pretend I'm not dying to jump her despite her illness.

I am a fucking saint.

She sits up slightly to eat her sandwich and drink her

water, and we remain in easy silence watching Mary Berry and Paul Hollywood biting into what looks like a cheesecake.

"Thanks for bringing me breakfast and for . . ." She waves to fill in the rest. "No luck with the other?"

"Tampons in the bathroom." I extract my phone from my pocket. Lay it down on the coffee table. Then I unpocket my find and place it beside the phone.

She stares at the Cadbury Crème Egg like it's a bomb. "Only the one?"

"Don't get greedy. I'll keep the other one in reserve."

"But how?"

"A gentleman doesn't reveal his methods." I can tell I've thrown her and I'm glad to do it. She needs to recognize that this path has one destination. *Me and Trinity sittin' in a tree. F-U-C . . .* You get the idea.

"You want to eat it now or take a nap?"

"Nap first, treat later." I nod, then remove myself from the sofa.

"Wait. Are you . . . leaving?"

"No. Just going to be in the kitchen working. I'll pick up Chase in a couple of hours and then get out of your hair."

She's clearly fighting her pleasure at learning I'll be sticking around. "And Chase? He was okay when you dropped him off?"

"Yeah. We had a little chat."

"About?"

"Whether he should be playing footie. I see kids do that sometimes, trying to please their parents. It can be exhausting for them."

She looks relieved that I brought it up. "I've been trying not to interfere, but I know he's having a rough time connecting with his father. He does seem less miserable lately, though . . . I'm sorry if I came off as ungrateful. I'm just used to fending for myself and you're—"

"The last person you want help from."

That cute worry dent I want to kiss appears between her eyebrows. "Yes. I know you're doing a job representing Brian, but I can't separate that from who you are."

I wonder about her antipathy to Brian. It seems a bit over-the-top. "What did he do to you?"

"To me?" Her voice raises slightly. "He's being a dick to my sister."

"That's their business, right? Why is it so personal to you?"

"My sister's happiness is very personal. Is that so strange?"

I suppose not. I'm pretty damn protective of my own sister. But it niggles at me all the same.

"Take that nap. I'll be in the kitchen, so give me a shout if you need anything."

I KNOW AS SOON as Max opens the email he'll be calling me, so I'm already walking to the bathroom, creeping past a sleeping Trinity on the couch, when the phone rings.

"Yep?"

"Why am I messengering depositions to a strange address in Edgewater?"

I roll my eyes as I shut the bathroom door behind me. "As you already know who lives here, why don't you just get it all out, Maxie?"

"What in the *actual fuck* are you doing? Do I need to cite the American Bar Association's model rule on conflict of interest?"

"No, but I feel a boring speech coming on, so have at it."

He intones like it's Shakespeare. "Rule 1.7 states, and I'll skip to the pertinent part: 'A lawyer shall not represent a client if the representation involves a concurrent conflict of interest. A concurrent conflict of interest exists if: there is a significant risk that the representation of one or more clients will be materially limited by the lawyer's responsibilities to another client, a former client or a third person, *or by a personal interest of the lawyer.'*"

"I know the rule. I've been following the ru—"

He cuts in. "Yet somehow you're working today in the apartment of one Trinity Jones, sister of the respondent in a case where you are representing the petitioner. Tell me why this doesn't fall under personal interest."

"Because I haven't had sex with her," I whisper.

"But you want to."

"Of course I want to! Dammit, I'm a walking ball of blue over here. This is complicated. I coach her nephew on my football team—"

"You mean soccer."

"Max, if you interrupt me one more time, I'm going to hang up. Then I'm going to come into the office and shove ten Milano cookies and seventeen puzzle pieces down your throat."

He sighs dramatically.

I start in with my explanation, the one I've crafted to justify every decision I've made since the day I first set eyes on Trinity. "Chase, the son of my client, needed a ride to his aunt's house while both parents are out of town. The aunt is sick so I'm sticking around to run errands and pick up the kid—all done *in service to my client,* who is currently unable to fulfill his on-site parental duties. Now, tell me how this is in *my* personal interest when everything I'm doing benefits my client."

"Don't try to argue your way out of this with twisted logic, Wright. You wouldn't be the first guy to invent some jumped-up excuse for why he should be screwing a woman who's off-limits."

"There is no relationship here. There won't be as long as I'm representing Brian Carson." The case is nowhere near finished so I'm pretty sure Trinity and I are going to miss our window. This makes me incredibly sad, not to mention sexually frustrated. For several weeks now I've been forced to beat the bishop twice a day. I've had offers, but all other women repulse me because they're not Trinity.

Thing is, I like her. (Okay, more than like. Shut up.) I think she needs a friend. I can be that friend and not be derelict in my duty.

I'm sure of it.

"So do I need to come and pick up the depos myself or are you going to send them along like I asked?"

"Expect them within the hour. And Lucas?"

"Yeah?"

"If you're so sure this isn't a conflict then you should probably run it by your client."

I know he's right. I hate it but I know it.

CHAPTER 15

Trinity

*A*ll morning, Lucas works in the breakfast nook in my kitchen. From my position on the sofa, I can see his long legs stretched out under the table. I can let my grasping gaze linger over his fingers as they tip-tap on his keyboard, all while imagining those fingers tracing sensual circles on my body and slipping into warm, tight, wet spots. My cold misery should make thoughts of sex with this guy—with any guy—unlikely, but I think Lucas Wright would tempt a dying crone for one last shot at ecstasy.

He also talks to himself, just like I do. Every now and then, I hear him muttering, "Fat chance, mate," or, "Not on my watch, you muppet." Then he'll peek his head out of the nook, checking to see if he's woken me.

I keep my eyes closed. I like him here. The comfort of it. The safety of having a good man in the house. I don't like to think on that too hard, so I just accept it as part of my illness and push it to my brain's attic.

Chase's classes get out at noon on Fridays. Lucas leaves to pick him up and I'm ashamed to say that the minute the door closes, I rush into the bathroom to wash my face and put on lip gloss. Oh, God, my hair! A dab of coconut oil and a good comb-through saves the day, leaving me looking about 20 percent less awful. Winning!

On their return, Lucas approaches me with a thermometer.

"What's that for?" I'm already recoiling.

"Chase seems to think you'll want to head into work tonight. I'm here to check your temperature so we can make a call on that."

"We?" He takes advantage of my open mouth to slide the thermometer in.

"Close your mouth, love. You smell like summer, by the way."

After ten seconds, he removes it and stares hard. As I feel feverish, I suspect the answer is one I don't want to hear.

"One-oh-one. No work for you."

"I have to go in—"

"And infect everyone you pour drinks for? Nope. It's okay. Gideon's fine with you not working tonight."

I slide a look to Chase, who is reading a comic in the armchair opposite. "Did you give him my work number?"

My nephew looks mildly offended at my accusation. "Uh, no. I gave him Gideon's number when we didn't get an answer at the bar. Not open."

I sit up straight. "You can't just decide I'm not going into work." But my case falls apart in a splutter of coughing.

Chase shrugs. "Can and did."

What the hell is going on here? This is some sort of conspiracy of . . . caregiving.

"I need to call Gideon." I grab my phone, noting that there

are already a couple of text messages from him I must have missed while I was in the bathroom.

Don't come in.

Followed by: *I mean it.*

God*dammit.* A complete conspiracy!

"You owe me fifty bucks," Chase says.

Lucas pulls out the money and hands it over to my scheming nephew. "He said you'd be difficult. I said you'd be immensely grateful and now I'm out fifty dollars, Ms. Jones."

"I'm sure you can afford it, Mr. Billable Hours."

We spend the rest of the day binge watching the baking show. I'm not ashamed to say I quickly develop a crush on Paul Hollywood, he of the master baking knowledge and just enough dickishness to compensate for the suspect goatee. Or maybe it's the accent. I could get used to that British accent . . .

Lucas and Chase make chicken and pineapple quesadillas for dinner, and afterward we watch some German time travel thing, but I can't focus on the subtitles, so I fall asleep.

The headlights blind me. Welcome. So welcome. I wave but the car won't slow. I have to jump back to avoid being mowed down. My almost-savior speeds to the next intersection, and onward. Away.

"Nooo!"

I turn. He's still there. He takes a step.

My eyes snap open. Lucas. He's cupping my face and staring at me with such intent I almost sink into him. Attempting to get my bearings, I pull back.

"Wh-what are you doing?"

"You were having a nightmare."

I'm back in my bed but the cover is on the floor. It's just me with my T-shirt riding up and my black silk panties barely covering the assets. How—? When—? Vague memories of being carried here strain through the sieve that's my brain.

"I-I'm cold."

In a few seconds, the comforter is back where it belongs and the barrier is between us again, just as it should be. But hoo boy, it's getting harder.

"What time is it? Where's Chase?"

"It's just after eleven and he's in bed. Needs to get up early for the game tomorrow."

The game. I'm so out of it that I completely forgot.

"I was just about to leave when I heard you getting stroppy."

"Getting stroppy?"

He smiles. "Yeah, thrashing about. Being generally difficult, but you're excused because you were sleeping and you're ill. Want to tell me what's going on?"

"Just a weird dream." I search for a suitable lie. "I was forced to wear plaid and stripes to a wedding. Super disturbing."

He remains silent, his disbelief a third person in the room.

"You should head out," I mutter. "I've taken up enough of your time."

"Well, I'm really here for Chase."

"That's nice of you."

He shrugs. "I'm a nice guy."

I'm starting to agree. "Maybe you could stay awhile. Until I fall asleep anyway."

His breath hitches at my pseudo invitation. "On the sofa?"

"I don't want you to get sick."

"I won't get sick."

He waits. And waits. I suspect he could wait me out forever.

My fingers are possessed by a spirit. I watch in horror as

they creep toward the edge of the comforter and peel it back a dangerous inch.

Foxy fast, he stands and rips off his shirt, as if he's afraid I'll change my mind. And he's not far wrong, only I'm thinking my mind will be changed to pro-Lucas, a state of existence where this man takes me places I've only imagined existing.

"You have tattoos." They look old for someone so young, a few of them stretched out. Some look like astrological signs —a bull, a fish, a crab. And now I'm hungry.

"Mostly from when I was a kid. Traveling with crusty hippies and New Agers."

I pull back the comforter without thinking, the last barrier to him joining me. A silent but clear invitation. This is crazy, but I need his heat. I crave his energy.

He pulls down his jeans and kicks off his shoes and socks. Then he's in the bed.

With me.

"Just until I'm asleep," I say to give him an out. Myself, too.

"Right."

"Is the front door locked?"

"Locked it when I came home with Chase."

Home. "Could you check?"

Avidly, I watch how the black cotton of his boxer briefs perfectly cups his ass cheeks, how the muscles bunch as he leaves to pander to my insecurity. I might be ill, but I'm most certainly not dead. He's back in ninety seconds. "All safe."

None of us are safe.

He slips under the comforter. I let out the breath I've been holding.

"I'm not sure what we're doing here."

"I'm just taking care of everyone," he says, his voice rough. "Clients, sons of clients, enemies of clients."

It's more than that. So much more, but if I question it, I'll chicken out. I need to let the mantle of suspicion slip. I'm not looking for anything more than friendship (lie, lie), and while Lucas is the worst candidate because of his representation of Brian, he might be the best because of his representation of me. These last twenty-four hours, he's been here for me. Technically, for Chase, though we both know my nephew is the handy-dandy construct that's facilitating what's happening between us (sorry, Chase).

My fingers brush across the tattoo on his pec I noticed earlier, which I now realize is a Hogwarts sorting hat. How did I miss that? "Who's Lizzie?"

His shoulders stiffen. "My twin sister. She lives in London."

"You must be close?"

"Yeah, we are. Mind readers. The whole twin telepathy bit. I visit a couple of times a month to see her."

You know when someone dispenses information in quick bursts, like they want to parse it out on a need-to-know basis? That's what Lucas is doing. He doesn't want to talk about Lizzie because she's a source of pain. He's not ready to give up that hurt, and maybe I'm not ready to take it on in a meaningful way.

He smiles but the implication is clear. *We won't be talking about it. We each have roles and mine is to entertain.*

I know all about roles. We lock ourselves into them because the prospect of breaking our chains terrifies us. Comfort lies in the familiar, security in the cage.

"You still cold?" he asks.

I nod.

"Turn over."

I do, let him envelop me in a human spoon, take all the heat and kindness he wants to give me. There's a bit of drama surrounding my hair (*so much of it*, Lucas whines) and a threat to separate us with pillows if I don't stop squirming against his groin—he's hard, I don't take it personally—but then we settle in like this is what we've always done.

"How'd you get into the whiskey business?" His breath is warm against my neck, and not facing him makes it feel both more and less intimate.

"My granddad, my mom's father. He was a big whiskey drinker and I remember sitting on his knee while he sipped and smoked a cigar. Mahogany. Leather. Cologne. All these things knit together in my mind, creating these memories, crafting a world. It was a time in my life when I felt . . . safe, I suppose. Whole and not judged. The first time I tried whiskey—a Glenmorangie—it was like coming home. You know that feeling when something fills your nostrils and makes your heart burst?"

"I do."

"What does it for you?"

A beat passes, then another, a stretch that makes me question whether he heard me.

"Books," he finally says. "Library books." He chuckles against my neck. "*Stolen* library books."

"Um, the point of the library is that you don't have to steal them, dummy."

"I know, but when I was a kid, we traveled a lot and I wanted to have something to carry with me. Something to read when my mum was off doing her thing."

"What was her thing?"

"Men. Weed. The night sky above our heads. She didn't want to be tied down."

I can feel his tension surrounding me, taut as a rubber band. I relax, hoping it can help him soften against me. Let him feel some reciprocity for the care he's given me today.

"Sounds tough."

"I survived." There's bitterness there, painting the words

with something that sounds like a combination of grief and anger.

"Tell me about all the traveling when you were a kid."

"Not as glamorous as it sounds. I prefer being settled in one place. Stability is preferable to adventure, I find."

I might have agreed with that once, but here with Lucas I'm not so sure. Each new moment with him is an adventure, and I can see myself getting hooked on Lucas-fueled adrenaline. "I've always wanted to travel. Planned a distillery tour to Scotland once to see where my babies come from."

"What stopped you?"

Emily got pregnant with Ari and she needed me to be around. "Life got in the way."

"Yeah, that happens."

Maybe because I feel secure for the first time in forever, or maybe because he's convenient—yes, let's go with the last one—I'm overcome with the urge to share more.

"Some guy jumped me on the street a few months ago," I say. "A block from here."

Pause. "Took care of him with Trinity ninja moves, I assume."

"Of course." I chuckle through the pain, but it devolves into a sob.

His hold tightens, yet somehow it makes me breathe easier.

"No—nothing happened. Not really. A car came along and he ran off, but . . ."

"But what, love?"

"It spooked me, is all. City living, right?"

"Sure, but now you don't feel safe and you're mad because you used to feel safe."

Trust the shark lawyer to cut to the heart of it. It's not just that—I used to feel a lot of things. Adventurous, desirable, my own person. Now I feel like a shadow in service to this version of me I've created to get through it all. The best sister, the great aunt, the good friend. A bit player in the story of my life.

"Did you report it to the police?"

"Yes. They weren't all that helpful, almost as if they blamed me for being outside in the dark."

I didn't tell the guys. They'd be sympathetic of course, but I wasn't in the mood for the speech from Pete about how I needed to be more careful. Ever since he's known me when we met in freshman year at college, I've given off an air of invincibility. I've always had to be the strong one, even when I didn't feel like it.

"What did your sister think?"

"Didn't tell her." Immediately I launch into a defense of Emily. "She's got so much going on, worrying about where she'll be living in a few months." I know it's a dig at him, but it's my way of deflecting. I can own it—in my head. "It's also left me questioning my instincts."

"With me."

"Among other things. You're here and I like that you're here, but normally, I wouldn't." I turn over. He needs to hear this face-to-face. "Normally I'd find you abhorrent." I speak these words to his perfect cheekbones and his supermodel lips and his strong brow and twinkling cobalt eyes. "But my current situation has left—"

"You weak and at my mercy?"

"Yes. I don't want to be taken advantage of."

He nods, thinking it through. "I'm the one in danger, Trinity. What's happening here between us is potentially detrimental to both my balls and my career. I'm not afraid to be honest and tell you that I want you. You can sneeze in my face, set impossible quests, play the grouch, and use your sister as an excuse—I'll still come back because I already know this is worth it. And as soon as you know it, we can make it happen."

His words stir my blood. "You're crazy."

"Maybe. Or maybe I'm completely sane."

This bubble we've created will burst soon. He'll go back to being on Brian's side and I'll go back to . . . wherever I've gone these last few months. For now, I'll hold on to the heat.

I'll hold on to Lucas.

Lucas

"Lucas!"

During the Saturday game, Brian sneaks up on me on the sideline of the footie pitch in Lincoln Park and claps me on the back. I don't like when the mums or dads stand beside me. I'm trying to focus on what my kids need, and the parents—especially the female parents—are usually focused on me. "How's my boy doing?"

"Pretty good." Actually, better than good. I'm not sure if it's down to our chat, my yoga tips, or he's got something else going on. Maybe telling him that it really doesn't matter freed up his mind.

Max's warning pops into my head for a very annoying visit. "So, Brian, we need to talk about something that's come up."

"With my case?"

"Yeah, with your case. It's about Trinity."

He stares at me. "What about her? Has she been bad-mouthing me?"

That he immediately went there irks me. That he's right irks me more.

"Nothing that affects your situation."

"Wait, how do you even know Trinity?"

"I met her at the bar where she works before I understood her connection to you. I was interested, but as soon as I realized who she was, I backed off." Sort of.

"You're interested in Trinity?"

"Is that so strange?"

His eyes have turned into dark, shiny, shifty buttons. "No. Well she's older than you by what? Five or six years? Not exactly in the full bloom of youth, you know."

Brian has strange ideas about what qualifies as the full bloom of youth. Oh yeah, he's dumping his thirty-two-year-old wife for a nineteen-year-old nanny.

On the pitch, Denny Macklin is showing off with the ball instead of moving it into goal-scoring position. "Macker! Stop pissing about and get forward." I mean, really.

I turn back to Brian. "Anyway, it's no longer a consideration, because as soon as she found out I was representing you, she threw up her walls."

He coughs out a laugh. "Sounds like Trinity. She's not exactly the warm fuzzy type."

This puts my back up, but I can't defend her because it would sound like I have far too much skin in the game.

He's still talking. "And Emily can barely make a decision without checking in with her sister first. It was always that way. Trinity's just as responsible for the demise of my marriage."

"She pushed you into having an affair?"

Brian scowls, and I'm happy to have earned it. "That's merely a symptom. Any divorce lawyer worth his salt should know *that*. We had a lot of problems, plenty of them to do with Trinity interfering, telling Emily how bad of a husband

I was. The affair . . . that only happened because Emily decided she wasn't happy and started withholding. That was all her sister's doing."

Sure, my wife doesn't understand me. Does he really think I haven't heard a million variations of that hoary line?

"So." Brian sniffs. "You want to bang her?"

Sometimes I represent scum. I've always been proud of my ability to treat all my clients the same regardless of how charmless they are. As Max is constantly telling me, everyone deserves a fair shake.

But Brian—or should I say, Trinity—has made this personal for me.

It's been almost a week since I saw her. Once Chase was back home with his mom, my excuse to hang at Chez Jones no longer passed the smell test. But damn, I'd enjoyed playing house. I know I took advantage, but she let me in. I liked being on the inside where I could insinuate myself under her skin.

Holding her close in bed was like living in a dreamscape. She'd felt so soft and warm and I'd felt so hot and hard. (I know, feverish, on both sides.) And when she told me about her assault—about that fucker who made her feel unsafe—I wanted to hold her tight and never let go. But I knew if I stayed with her any longer I'd break every ethics rule in the book, so I eventually dragged my sorry arse to the sofa and shot for a couple of hours of shut-eye before my boys' game last Saturday.

Brian's query about my desire to bang Trinity is a wood-pecker taunt in my head. What a prince.

"True, I wanted to date her, but I can't because that would be a conflict of interest." I will be saying those three fucking words on my deathbed. "Nothing has happened, although I should probably tell you that I gave Chase a ride to her place when he was staying there last weekend and I stuck around because she was sick and needed help."

"Help? What kind of help?"

"Making dinner, dropping your son off at summer school, that kind of thing."

His response is a little too long coming and emerges begrudgingly. "You did that for Chase?"

"Full service over here, Brian."

"But nothing happened with Trinity?"

Something hot and jagged burns in my chest. Does my client have a thing for his sister-in-law? That's all I bloody need.

"Nothing *can* happen. I'd have to either remove myself as your counsel or ask you to declare in writing that it's okay."

"Fuck, no. You'd need my permission?" His colorless eyes fill with imagined power. I understand now Trinity's initial horror when I mentioned running any potential relationship by my client. The notion that Brian Carson, of all people, might have some say in who I can be with disgusts me.

I'm not about to hand this guy my balls on a silver platter. I'm not going to ask Brian Carson permission, which means I'm not going to do anything about Trinity.

This makes me both angry and sad.

"You've nothing to worry about, Brian. Nothing will happen with Trinity, so we're all good." I clap him on the back hard enough that he coughs.

The dominance might have shifted back to me, yet why do I feel completely and utterly powerless?

I RUB MY EYES, anxious to remove from them the remnants of my transatlantic flight. Larkvale is quiet. Always is on a Sunday.

I get a few nods of recognition. My chatty charm can wait until later. This quiet shadow world an hour outside London is waking up and no one's quite ready for what I have to offer, not even me. I slip inside the cheerful room and take a seat in my familiar spot by the bed.

Lizzie's hand seems thinner than two weeks ago, a bony claw covered in waxed paper. I give it a gentle squeeze, waiting for a response.

Always waiting.

For fifteen years my beautiful sister has lain prone in this bed, her every need attended to by angels wearing scrubs. I've not been the best brother. I send money. I visit when I can. Twice a month on a Saturday night, I trudge to O'Hare and take an overnight flight to London. I spend a few hours with her. Talk to her doctor and nurses. Make the staff at Larkvale laugh uproariously. The day ends with us all feeling better about ourselves.

Does Lizzie feel better? She knows I'm here. Her eyes follow me around like one of those haunted house paintings. Once they were bright and mischievous. Now they're dark saucers, behind which her mind shifts in and out.

She's in what the doctors describe as a minimally conscious state. She doesn't speak, at least not verbally. But I know she hears and I know she answers me in her head.

Hi, bruv. 'Bout time you showed yer ugly mug.

She should be dead, according to the nurses. I overheard them once chatting about how it's a miracle she's lasted so long. Is there ever a more overused word than *miracle?* Forever thrown around like it's the only option, like it's this gossamer thread that tethers her to reality. Her body might be lacking, but her mind is still fighting to keep her in this world.

"Hey, Lizzie, it's me." Who else would it be? Certainly not her mother.

Reel it in, mate. She's not here. She's never here.

Before the indignant anger I usually keep for the courtroom can surface, Jenny, my favorite nurse, pops in with the flowers I brought in a vase.

"These are lovely! Much better than the petrol station ones some of the other residents get."

"Yeah, I nicked them from some geezer's garden on the way down from the city."

She chortles, knowing I'm fibbing. The flowers cost me a bloody fortune, just one bloom in my ever-present bouquet of guilt.

"How's she been?"

Jenny leans over and smooths a strand of dark hair on Lizzie's forehead. "She had a bit of a cold last week—" At my look of concern, she speaks up to put me at ease. "Not bad enough to call you."

"I can be on a plane immediately. Don't think the fact I'm in another country would ever keep me away."

"I know. We all know. But it wasn't necessary. She's fine now."

Relatively.

I'm okay, LuLu. Just a case of the sniffles.

Three months ago, she developed a nasty chest infection that lingered. It was touch and go for a while, and there was a lot of checking in and mentions of paperwork. As her legal guardian, did I want to put a do-not-resuscitate order on record? I don't want her to suffer if it comes to that, yet I'll do my damnedest to hold on to her, even from across the pond.

And why do I lay my hat in Chicago when I could be here, closer to my sister, available at all hours when she has a cold?

A few years ago, the crushing weight of it all pushed me to a decision. Selfish, perhaps, but we're all selfish creatures at heart. The change of scenery was necessary and I figured the bigger salary from the higher billable hours would assuage my guilt. Moving Lizzie into a private nursing facility with better care than the National Health Service would work for her. Reducing my visits to twice a month would work for me.

I slip Jenny and company a few quid every month to ensure Lizzie has someone doing the tasks I can't, the little things outside of the basics of cleaning, feeding, and medicating her. Reading to her, mostly. And though she can't play jigsaw puzzles anymore, Jenny plays for her.

In unspoken agreement, we both stand before the puzzle set up on the desk near the sunlit window. Another Narnia—Lizzie loves the Chronicles—this one is about a third of the way done.

I grab a piece. "Yes!"

Jenny plays annoyed. "Ooh, you spotted it before me, you bugger!"

I slot it in, completing Aslan's mane.

"Don't know how she could have missed that one, Lizzie. It's pretty obvious, right?"

Tee hee.

I love Lizzie's laugh. It plays in my head when I'm down. Unbidden, I think of another woman's giggle—a naughty, sexy one, all the more satisfying for the work it takes to earn it. What would Trinity think of Lizzie, and vice versa? I suspect they'd get along. Both brave, no-nonsense, take-no-guff women.

I wanted so badly to stay with her, come up to her place after the footie game and make dinner. Look after her. She needs looking after, does Trinity.

But I have a standing date with Lizzie.

Chatting with Brian yesterday placed my problem in stark relief. Trinity is a complication I can't allow, not if I want to maintain my ethics, my job, and possibly, my sanity.

Seeing Lizzie today confirms it. I don't have the bandwidth to give a woman like Trinity what she needs.

"Well, I'll leave you two to it," Jenny says. "We got to chapter 18 of *Prince Caspian.*"

"I caught up on the plane." When I'm not here, I read the chapters I know the nurses cover so I'll be ready to pick up when I visit. I pluck the book from the shelf, even though I have it on my e-reader. There's something about holding the weighty tome that makes it feel like I'm doing something. Doing more.

One more chapter, bruv.

I take a seat and answer the request Lizzie made in my head.

"One more chapter, Lizzie."

CHAPTER 17

Trinity

*P*rotip: Don't wear leather pants on a hot summer day.

Bonus protip: Don't wear them to a whiskey-tasting function in a fancy suite of law offices. Not terribly professional, plus they're tight enough to give my uterus a massage—and not in a good way. It's mid-July and I'm sweating like a hog. Most attractive.

But I'll focus on the positive. Introducing people to the wonders of whiskey is one of my favorite things in the world. I wasn't always a whiskey drinker, even though it was part and parcel of the memories of my youth. I'd sit on my granddad's knee in his old leather chair that "talked" when he filled it. *Gertrude's glad I'm home,* he'd say, and I'd laugh because calling a chair Gertrude was cray-cray. Pops drank Scottish single malts—Glenmorangie was his tipple of choice—and he would let me sniff the glass.

I hated it. The fumes, the sourness, even the color put me off. But those hours with Pops were the best. I didn't know my dad's family—they didn't approve of his relationship with my mom. Pops knew the score. *You have strength you can't even imagine, Trinity. Resources that will carry you through in a world that will judge you for things you can't control.* Whiskey meant comfort and safety, and those memories lay dormant in my DNA, waiting until the day I was ready to call upon them when I met a guy from Louisville.

Beau MacRae was a Kentuckian master distiller, specializing in whiskey and bourbon. I was working in a bar during college when he came in and proceeded to give me an education. A late bloomer in a lot of things—sex, being one of them—I learned plenty from Beau. He was older (yeah, my daddy issues were probably showing), and after a month, he was on his way and I was left with a newfound love for whiskey and a recognition that I might not be so bad in bed after all.

That didn't mean whiskey was going to be my life, but the more tastings I attended and the more I learned about the culture, I realized that I might have found my calling. While wine tastings are a no-brainer with women, whiskey is a more recent phenomenon.

For today's tasting, I've brought a selection of my favorites to a law office in the same office building as Lucas's. Not that I'm thinking of him.

I'm pushing a dolly with a case of my wares toward the elevator when a voice calls out loudly behind me.

"Hey, Whiskey Woman!"

Now I know that's on my business card, but it doesn't mean I like hearing it fired at me across a crowded lobby in a downtown Chicago skyscraper. Turning, I see Lucas heading my way with a big doofus grin on his face. My heart flips, but I don't let my pleasure show on my face.

"Trinity!"

"Could you keep it down?" Heat is rising in my cheeks as people check us out.

"Why?" He looks around, then throws his arms in a wave around the lobby before adding in a high volume, *"Do you hate the attention?"*

I can't help my chuckle, because while I do hate the attention I don't hate Lucas.

"How we feeling today? All better?" He takes ahold of the dolly and starts a push to the elevator. One of them opens, expelling its suited contents, and Lucas rolls the dolly in ahead of a couple of people waiting. "Excuse me, need the room here. Better take the next one, mate. She has a wicked bad case of the flu. Projectile vomiting and the like." Over his shoulder he yells at me. "Come on, Trin! Time's a-wasting."

I make it inside just before the doors close. Lucas presses the button for the thirtieth floor, home of Kendall LLP.

"You don't have to do this."

He smiles, a beautiful curve that does things to me. "I know. But I'm going your way."

He's going my way. I like how he says that.

After a moment of electric silence, I ask, "So. Everything good? No cold?"

"I'm impervious, Jones. Though maybe not to that smile of yours."

I haven't seen him in over a week. The weekend I was ill, he dropped Chase off after his soccer game that Saturday and didn't come up to say hello. Or goodbye. Initially, I'd felt slighted because he'd spent the night in my bed. Listening. Holding me like I mattered. Then I decided to buck the fuck up because I don't need a guy. I don't need *this* guy.

"Listen," he says. "I'm sorry I didn't stop in after Chase's game on Saturday, but I had something to do I couldn't get out of."

Exit my head immediately, sir.

"No big deal. I didn't even expect you. Barely noticed you weren't there. In fact, I haven't wasted a single second on you since."

Too much?

His devastating grin tells me it's much too much.

"Oh, shut up."

"Didn't say a word." He continues to grin like he's won a prize. Like he's won me.

It's getting increasingly hard to dislike him. But it's all a game, isn't it? None of his charm changes the fundamentals of what we are to each other. He won't do anything, as it would be an ethical violation, which is fine because I won't do anything as long he represents Brian.

And if he decided to just ignore all that, what would it mean for Emily's case? Would Lucas have to give up Brian as a client? Would that be better or worse for Emily?

It might be better.

It might be tons better.

I blink back to reality when the elevator reaches the thirtieth floor. I can already tell that these offices are more moneyed than Lucas's. Original abstract art slams my eyeballs—the paint is chunky and tangible—along with weird bronze sculptures of people boning. The receptionist fixes me with a glassy stare before lighting up at the sight of Lucas.

"Oh, hi, Mr. Wright!"

"Shelly, I've told you, it's Lucas!" he booms. "And I *love* the hair. New do?"

Blushing madly, she preens a touch. "Just yesterday. I can't believe you noticed. My boyfriend didn't even compliment me."

Lucas's head shake embodies the pain of slighted women the world over, and he adds "Men!" for good measure. Shelly titters in self-commiseration.

"Sweetheart, we're here for the whiskey tasting. This is Trinity Jones—she's the sommelier."

It's not my first time encountering disbelief when someone hears what I do for a living. "Oh. Right. Ms. Gates said to go to the library. That's where they're hosting it."

"Excellent! I know the way." Lucas grins. "And when I come back I want that boyfriend's name. I might have to call him and give him what for!"

More giggling from Shelly, and we're on our way.

Lucas greets everyone effusively, I assume because they work in the same building? I know less than zero about lawyerly collegiality, but it seems strange that all the people we pass high-five him (the men) or double-cheek kiss him (the women). Apparently, I'm in the presence of minor royalty or a boy band star.

We walk into a room with plush leather chairs and leather-bound volumes, a library just as Shelly said. It's empty until I hear behind me, "Wright, I should've known you were here. The pheromone levels of the office are through the roof."

Lucas sets the dolly down and turns to a voice I recognize, having spoken with it on the phone. Like the place, it's grand with hints of Boston.

"Aubrey, meet Trinity, your sommelier for the evening." Lucas says. "I don't like whiskey, but she seems to really know her shit."

Silver-gray eyes snap fiercely to mine. A blue-black curtain of hair falls past her strong jaw, floating like a cloud over the shoulders of a navy power suit. Aubrey is, in a word, stunning. Her beauty is sharp and angled, and I imagine her ripping defendants to shreds with her gorgeous white teeth and stamping on their exposed intestines with her stilettos.

She holds out her hand. "Lucas's recommendation would

normally be worthless given his boundless enthusiasm about the most ridiculous things, but I trust him on this."

Unsure why, I decide to take her at her word. Maybe I just want her to like me. I shake her hand, enjoying her firm grip.

"So I thought maybe we could set up over here." She gestures to a sideboard. "Will that work?"

"Perfect!" I take the dolly from Lucas—or try to. He makes a meal of wheeling it over and lifting the cases onto the sideboard.

"I've got this, thanks."

"No problem." He leans in, smelling like a dream, making me dizzy with lust. "Back to your fuck-off, I-don't-need-a-thing self, I see."

I open my mouth, both annoyed and surprised at his prescience.

"It's okay," he says into the gap. "Pretty fucking hot, but then you know that."

"You're impossible."

"Am I? Or am I impossibly sexy?"

A few women in suits and heels start to trickle in, so I try to morph into my professional self. Hard to do with Lucas smelling and looking like a god and my leather pants cutting off all circulation to my ass. "I need to set up."

"Okay, I'll be over here watching you be a whiskey ninja."

Aubrey's slight cough interrupts us. "You're sticking around, Wright? Since when are you a member of the Chicago Bar Association Alliance for Women?"

Lucas smiles at Aubrey. "Now, Ms. Gates, you know I'm not. But the alliance's rules clearly state that anyone can attend one meeting per calendar year without paying dues."

"Anyone with tits."

"Really, Aubrey? I'm pretty sure that's nowhere stated in the bylaws. Do you need me to whip them out?"

Aubrey expels a sigh and turns to me. "Get out now while you can, Trinity. Do you want to be arguing with *that* all day and night?"

I laugh, thinking that maybe I do. Shocked at where my thoughts have veered, I shift to business-friendly as a couple of women approach the sideboard.

"Wow," one of them says. "I've never met a whiskey sommelier before. Can't wait to hear all about it."

This is directed at the penis in our midst. *Sigh.*

Lucas is as quick as a tick. "Ladies! Let me introduce you to the star of the evening, Trinity Jones. She's a certified whiskey sommelier who also runs Chicago's chapter of Whiskey, Women, and Song. No one is better qualified to educate you on the finer distinctions between bourbon, scotch, malt, and whiskey—both with and without an *e*. This woman knows her bloody stuff, I can tell you."

The women stare at me, Aubrey stares at Lucas, and I stare at my feet. I'm embarrassed . . .

Why am I embarrassed? Because Lucas is loud and he has focused on me in a way I'm not used to. Is that so terrible? With this guy, I feel like for once, I'm the center of my own universe instead of a distant satellite.

The thing is, I *do* know my bloody stuff. I am good at this and I shouldn't have to apologize for being the one person in the room who knows more about whiskey than everyone else put together.

"Hey, guys! Let me get set up and then I'll be more than happy to talk whiskey—with and without an *e.*"

I catch Lucas's eye and feel a thrill that's foreign and confusing. He's proud of me. I can't remember someone giving me that, or at least, not the way Lucas bathes me in it.

That feeling is more dangerous than anything else in his arsenal.

CHAPTER 18

Lucas

I'm standing at the back of the library at Kendall, a glass of untouched scotch in my hand. This is me being supportive. Trinity gave her tasting spiel—totally rocked it, by the way—and now she's flitting between groups, asking for opinions, weighing in with her own. As we all know, I'm a competence porn addict and I can't take my eyes off her.

Sure, that's my reason.

It might also have something to do with the way those leathers of hers fit her arse like a rubber. I mean, no one should look that good in leather trousers, but Trinity pulls it off because she's a goddess. Throughout the evening, I've caught her looking at me—or maybe she's caught me looking at her. Every time our gazes connect, supernovas collapse, galaxies self-destruct, and planets emerge from the antimatter.

I want her. Badly.

"So. Wright." Aubrey stands beside me, also with a glass of

scotch, but she sips from it slowly. She comes from some blue-blooded family in Boston, so I gather she knows how to drink this stuff right.

"Aubrey," I say gravely, but I can't resist a little eyebrow wag to lighten the mood.

"What's with you and Whiskey Woman?"

"It's complicated."

"It always is."

We're quiet for a moment, but I've never been good with silences so I break it. "I think I need to uncomplicate it. Just do it."

"I assume you've had a good reason not to Nike the fuck out of the situation already."

I do. The conflict-of-interest issue is a legitimate problem. I value my clients, my job, and my ethics. But I don't want to miss my window with Trinity.

"She's the sister-in-law of a client." I fill her in quickly because I'm always up for a legal opinion, particularly of the female variety.

"Don't do anything you'll regret."

I turn to her. "Like you and Grant?"

The color drains from her face. It's as if I've struck her. "What did he say?"

"Not a word." This frustrates me because I don't like playing guessing games. "Look, I know you and I don't know each other all that well, but if you ever want a friendly ear . . ." She's good friends with Max, but with Max and Grant being partners in the same firm, Aubrey probably feels she was cut out of the loop post-divorce. "Grant's a friend, but he's pretty closed off about you."

"I screwed up, Lucas."

I'm so startled by her admission that I make a weird sound in my throat. Her smile is wry.

"Sorry, I offered and—"

"You didn't expect me to take you up on it?"

"Well, people don't really think of me that way."

"You might play the clown, but I know there's more. She does, too." She nods at Trinity, who's looking my way, her eyes alight with appreciation.

Does she know it? Do I even want her to?

I think I do. I think I want her to know everything.

Oh, I like her, bruv.

"What happened with Grant?"

"I . . ." Aubrey shudders out a weary sigh. "I thought I knew myself, but it turns out I didn't know me at all."

"I don't understand what that means." I can't help her if she talks in riddles.

She pats my arm. "Forget what I said about not doing anything you'll regret. Go for it. Swing for the fences. Seize the fair maiden. And, Lucas?"

"What?"

"Let her see you. All of you."

I'm not sure she's ready for that—or that I'm ready for it —but I can take a step in the right direction.

I know now what I have to do.

CHAPTER 19

Trinity

I smile at the last couple of women who are signing up for the Whiskey, Women, and Song mailing list.

"So, only women at these things?" one of them asks.

"Think of it as a safe space, a place for women to meet and not feel the pressure to be *on* all the time."

"I like the idea," her friend says as she writes down her email address. "As long as it's not filled with lawyers."

Her friend cackles and they walk out the door laughing.

Wow, this has been a really positive experience. Good people, even with the "mistaken identity" snafu at the beginning, a brand of shade I've been living all my life. I'm smiling as I turn, eager to share my good vibes with someone.

He's gone.

One minute he was talking to Aubrey, the next, the air is a void I feel like a punch. What the hell is wrong with me?

It's just a hot guy. There are lots of hot guys. And this one is the wrong, hot guy. Too gorgeous and too much trouble and—

"Hi."

Thank the gods, he came back.

"Thought you skedaddled out of here."

"No, you didn't." He lifts the case of half-empty bottles onto the dolly and secures it with the bungee cord I use. "Ready?" He's already dragging my wares into the corridor.

I follow, noting how quiet it is in the office. We pass a couple of open doors with people at desks, heads down, poring over depositions or whatever lawyers pore over at seven in the evening. But other than them, no one is around to watch our departure.

Lucas calls for the elevator.

The air crackles with possibility. I'm suddenly very nervous.

The doors open and we step inside. Lucas situates the dolly and then he backs me up against the wall before the doors have closed. His eyes burn into me, branding me with sensual purpose.

"We good?"

I nod.

"Say it."

"We're goo—" His mouth descends on mine. We're goo. *I'm* goo. A hot, melting puddle of neurons and blood vessels and other things that make up my weak, weak body.

I'm not good at being kissed. I don't enjoy being on the passive end of a smooch, so I do what any modern woman who hasn't gotten any in a while would do:

I eat Lucas's face off.

I can't help it. One touch of his mouth to mine and it's a flame to kindling. My lips take on a life of their own: greedy, grasping, gimme-all-the-sugar. He moans at the contact of our tongues and that moan sets off vibrations throughout my body. Every cell is on fire.

We're both fighting for supremacy here, neither of us willing to surrender. It's war. It's brutally beautiful. How wonderful to feel so well matched with a kiss.

I'm ready to see how well we fit in all the other areas. His chest to mine, our hips rocking together, that moment when he sinks inside me, deep and true. I need it so badly I can already feel it. I want to feel *everything* with this man after so long sublimating my needs to others.

Seems we're on the same page. We both go for the respective ass grab, and this simultaneously mutual move shifts something. Separating, we laugh into the kiss.

It's a lovely moment that I'll never forget. But it breaks the spell and twists it into something else, something deeper as we stare at each other for a long, ultra-charged moment.

"Wow," he murmurs.

"Yeah. Wow."

The elevator doors open. Aubrey is on the other side, her cat's mouth curving into a grin. Neither of us has pressed the button to escape this floor.

Lucas hits twenty-five and smiles at Aubrey. "Take the next one, princess."

He's back to kissing me before the doors close.

I know there are a million reasons not to do this. I can only think of the one reason why we must: I need Lucas Wright more than I've ever needed anything.

I need something for me. Someone who sees me, if only for a sparkling star-filled moment. I expect I'll fall back into sanity, but hopefully, not too soon.

The elevator doors open again, this time on the floor of his offices. Lucas stops kissing me long enough to pull my case of liquor out into the hallway and toward the glass door of his suite. His other hand is on my ass and he's trying to wave at a scan pad on the wall.

The thing won't beep green. Not enough hands, stupid tech . . . I don't know!

I try to keep my end up by burying my nose in his neck and licking his skin. He tastes better than the best bourbon.

"Love, just a sec." Growling, he waves his security card again and the door clicks. Once inside he leaves the dolly by the door. "Should be safe there. But you're not."

I giggle like a lovestruck fool.

"You think that's funny?"

I giggle again. He pulls me flush against his body.

"Love hearing your laugh, gorgeous girl."

"Gorgeous *woman*," I insist. "I'm mature. And too old for you." God, I sound drunk, yet I've barely touched a drop.

"You need a younger bloke to keep up with you."

Maybe. Or maybe I need someone with boundless energy and sparkling eyes who looks at me like I matter.

"You talk too much."

"So I've been told. I'm going to be chatty, love. Can't help it."

I love his honesty. It's so strange to think that, considering what he does for a living, but there's no artifice about him. And if there is, I don't want to know.

"Where are we go—?" But he's already hoisting me up around his hips as he walks, still kissing me. We're heading to his office, where I'm gently placed on the sofa.

"You're sure?" he asks, and I'm surprised to hear hesitancy from someone who's usually so cocky.

"Never been surer."

That smile again. I could exist on its heat. Live on its luminosity.

I unbutton my pants, hoping against hope that my muffin top doesn't suddenly go splat with the release.

I'm not fat, but I've definitely got a little extra padding on the hips. And the waist. And the thighs. Now that the pants are no longer doing their job, I need to get this done and dusted. Most guys don't really like to linger on the buildup, which is fine given where we are. I'm sure Lucas doesn't want a long, slow screw in his place of work. Something fast and furious should get us both there.

To distract him, I curl a hand around his neck and pull him in for a kiss. His dreamy, answering moan tells me I probably got away with it. My suspicions are confirmed when Lucas pulls on my zipper and yanks down on the waistband of my pants. Boy's in a hurry.

Then the unimaginable happens: My pants get stuck on my cupcake-padded hips.

He pulls away from my mouth, searching out the problem. The problem, however, does not want to be immediately resolved.

"Maybe if—"

"Just a bit this way—"

"How about—"

"Uh, let me stand." I do, trying to pull my pants down at the same time for maximum efficiency. Part of the issue is that they are not only tight, but far too warm for a summer day. We manage to get them past my hips . . .

. . . where they become sweat-bonded to my thighs. Mother. Fucker!

Lucas is on his knees between mine, his shoulders shaking with laughter.

"I don't know what's so funny. If these stay on, you're not getting any, Lucas!"

Back on his haunches, he's now laughing his head off.

"All right, forget it!" I make a move, but I'm thigh-cuffed by my stupid pants. What was I thinking?

"Oh no, you don't." He pulls me back with a tender shove,

placing me knees first on the sofa so I'm ass-out. A teeny-tiny thong is all that separates me from undiluted pleasure.

Oh, and my cock-blocking leather pants!

"Lucas, I—"

"Hush, love. I've got this."

Unable to see exactly what's happening, the next thing I feel is the strap of my thong sawing against my pulsing pussy.

Oh. My. Lucas.

His breath feels hot and urgent against my ass cheeks, then lower in between my legs. Something wet—his tongue, it has to be his tongue, *please let it be his tongue*—paints a line of desire along my inner thigh. Then the other.

Then in between.

"Luuuu—*caaaas.*"

I try to force my thighs wider to give him better access, but my pants have me in a bind. This scenario is a microcosm of our overall situation, both of us locked into unchangeable positions. I can't move. I can't get off this way. I can't—

One of those long, lovely fingers traces a path between my folds and makes sizzling contact with my clit. I jerk at the touch.

"Oh! Yes, yes. Do that again."

He does it again, applying more friction this time. Harder, faster. My hips flex to meet his strokes, trying to ignite a fire.

Things are definitely starting to smoke. My thighs shake and the orgasm slams through me like a summer storm. One second I'm as frustrated as hell, the next I'm sprinting up a peak like I'm being chased. The view up there is spectacular.

That's when I hear it. A ripping sound, followed closely by Lucas swearing. But my thighs are free with my pants now shoved to my knees. He flips me to face him.

"Sorry—I had to—"

"'S okay."

Now it's a race to see who can get naked quicker. He wants to help me and I desperately want to help him. We're both so damn helpful that we're divested of clothing in seconds flat, except for my thong.

Naked Lucas is about as wow as it can get. I've seen the epic chest and the load-bearing thighs, but the whole package sends a flood gushing between my legs. He kneels on one knee to the right of me, his cock jutting forward like a joystick I want to put into fifth gear. Just give that knob a twist. Savoring me, he cups and palms my breast. No more urgency, only a languor that thrills me.

But I know his patience has to be hard for him, so I'm prepared to sacrifice my love of the leisurely approach this one time.

"You don't have to go slow. I know you must be ready." We've both been ready for weeks.

With a long finger, he pushes my thong aside, lingering where I'm pulsing and wet.

"Think I need to get right in this pussy."

This pussy—*my pussy*—flutters in anticipation.

"Oh yeah?"

He smiles. The wickedest, sexiest smile I've ever seen, punctuated with a dirty lick of his lips I can already feel between my thighs again. "Oh yeah. I want to rub my face right in there, right where you're soaking wet for me. I want to drink you down, Trinity Jones."

I've never been so turned on in my life and I just had a top-notch orgasm at the hands of this man. I don't know if I'm going to be able to survive his tongue on me again or actual P in the V.

"You want that, love?"

"Yes."

"Tell me what you want."

"You. Your face. In my—" He takes my thong and rips it apart before scooping my butt cheeks up in a lift, like he's about to gulp from a goblet.

The moment his tongue touches my flesh, I jolt upward, an involuntary flex of my most sensitive tissues. This only spurs him on. He's undeterred. Unrepentant. He's a man on a mission and that mission is to lick me dry. This will likely be impossible because the sheer pleasure is making me gush. The more he licks, the wetter I get.

His moans vibrate against me, amplifying the sensation of every suck, sip, and lick with his tongue. Invading, conquering, owning. I grasp his hair, pull on it hard. He raises his head and the sight of him, smothered in me, takes me to another level.

"Do you mind?" he pants. "Genius at work here."

"Get to it," I demand with a lusty giggle, amazed that this is actually *fun*.

He gets to it. On it. In it.

There's nothing better than a guy who enjoys you, and Lucas enjoys me. It's more liberating than I could have possibly imagined. When I come again, it's as if invisible bonds have dissolved.

As if anything is possible.

CHAPTER 20

Lucas

*T**high shudders.*

My goal when eating a woman out is to get them. Trinity's not only shuddering, she's writhing as she comes. I'm so bloody turned on that I feel like I'm the one who had a whopping great orgasm. Almost.

Watching her let go is a dream come true. She's a mass of curves, a symphony of song. I love how open she is, how her gorgeous skin glows with the exertion, and I haven't even put her through her paces yet. For now, she's sprawled on my office sofa, her thighs wide, her body inviting me to get snug and deep.

She sits up and grips that part of me dying to slide into her.

"You've been so patient, Lucas." Long, deep strokes of her hand send me on the path to mindlessness.

"Christ, Trinity. I'm going to blow if you keep that up."

"Hmm. Blow." And then she swipes her tongue over the head of my dick like it's a lollipop.

Shit shit shit. This isn't happening.

Well, it is, but not like this. Not with what I imagine will be a top-of-the-line gob job. I lean down to grab my trousers, but she's still holding on to that very motivated part of me.

"Love, I need a condom."

She still holds on. Laughs while I try to maneuver my wallet out of my pocket. Laughs as I tear open the condom package and smooth the condom on.

That's when I do what makes the most sense to show her this is no laughing matter.

I grab both her ankles and yank her forward on the sofa. With trembling hands, I coast up her legs, her thighs, until I'm palming that sweet ass. The one I intend to own.

Falling to my knees, I ease her forward so I'm lined up to the beautiful target perfectly.

"You ready for me, love?" I tease my cock head along her lips, separating, tormenting. Mapping my way like a Victorian-era explorer.

She whimpers. I ease in slowly like I have all the time in the world, though every inch outside her tight confines kills me. The ride in brings me back to life, her grip on my dick a current sparking waves of electricity through my body.

"Jesus," I manage.

"Oh god oh god oh god."

I stay seated inside her for a moment, knowing I can't last but wanting to give it the old college try. I need her to remember this. Remember me.

"You trying to kill me?" she whispers, her dark chocolate eyes melting to a burnished gold as her gaze meets mine.

I lean in to kiss her, taking her lips softly, then with more urgency as I pull back and thrust hard. Her lips part, my tongue tangles with hers. One of her hands curls around my neck, the other grabs a handful of my arse.

"That's it, baby," she urges. "Don't stop. So good."

It is. We are. Together, we're making something incredible, every stroke bringing me deeper and closer. Bringing me to the heart of her.

"You're so beautiful." I plunge back in, taunting her to tighten her grip. "Never felt so good."

Her eyes darken even more, a deep caramel, sweet and soft. Her body lifts to meet my thrusts and she throws one leg over my hip for leverage. It feels like I'm being claimed, though I know that's foolish. Trinity is attracted to me, but she couldn't possibly want more. I'm not the kind of man a woman of quality like this would want for the long term. But for tonight, maybe I can dream . . .

"Lucas," She brushes her thumb over my lip. "Stay with me."

"I'm right here," I say, answering the meaning I'd like to imagine was in that question. "With you." I stroke harder, longer, all while keeping my eyes on hers. With anyone else I'd look away, for fear of revealing the broken pieces of me, for fear of begging to be fixed.

"That's my guy," she says, squeezing her muscles with each thrust. With each moan that escapes my throat. With each beat of my heart.

And when we finally fall apart, it feels like we've found something that's only possible in this moment. Something unrepeatable.

CHAPTER 21

Trinity

We lie there, the glow of our orgasms keeping us warm. He shifts slightly so he's not lying on top of me, though I love the weight of him keeping me anchored in the now.

"Those women who thought I was the sommelier—you get that a lot?"

Not what I expected for a postcoital sweet nothing, but okay.

"It's not the first time."

"Because you're a woman or because you're Black?"

I love that he sees all the angles. "Both, I suppose. Boobs and skin color have a habit of reframing people's constructs because they've already decided how a particular situation should present itself. Preconceptions are very powerful. Anything different is a violation of the norm."

I snuggle into him, loving how his strong body feels sheltering mine. It's strange to be curled up on an office sofa naked as a babe, but it's been a strange ride since I met Lucas.

All the negativity I felt toward him has disappeared—orgasms the cure, for sure—though he's still technically the enemy, at least on paper. And now he might be in trouble because of me.

"So what about your ethical dilemma?"

I feel his smile curving against my temple. "Resolved."

"How?" I draw back to look at him, hope taking root in my chest. "You dropped Brian?"

"Got his okay."

My heart plummets. "You mean . . . you talked to him about me? About us?"

"It was the only way forward. While you were rocking it at the tasting, I emailed him and asked him to put a waiver in writing. Basically I told him either I have to drop him or he has to say yes. He signed an agreement that any future relationship with you would not be a problem."

I sit up straight, suddenly feeling vulnerable, as I usually do whenever Brain enters the conversation. I cross an arm over my breasts. "You cannot be serious."

"I can. And I am. I take my duty to my clients very seriously. Either I drop him or he waives any objection. I told you that this is what would have to happen if we wanted to do this."

"Yes, but . . ." The words dry up in my throat.

"Yes, but what?" He's looking at me intently and I'm very aware of needing to get this right.

"I didn't want you to get his permission. I—I hate that."

"I don't like it, either. But sometimes we have to do things we don't like to get to do the things we do like."

"But not that!"

His blue eyes flash. "The obstacle in our path hadn't changed, yet you still did this. Either you knew I'd have to resolve this ethically, you were hoping I'd lie to my client, or you were thinking that sleeping with me would force me to drop him, thus jeopardizing his petition. Now I know you don't like him, but I can't imagine you'd intentionally put his position in danger." His face shifts to darkness, which is so strange on him. "Would you?"

Maybe. I'm not a nice person where Brian is concerned. "You know I'm not on his side."

"Yeah, I'm starting to get that." He pauses, rubbing his chin. After a couple of taut moments, he speaks. "Did you sleep with me thinking this would be a good way to upend your bother-in-law's legal case? Bed me, now I have no choice but to terminate my representation? And if I didn't, were you going to . . . fuck, Trinity, would you have reported me?"

That's not what I thought at all, but I'm so stunned by his accusation that I'm slow to respond. That pause makes him jump.

Right to the wrong conclusion.

"Jesus Christ, Trinity, that's fucked up." He stands, naked and glorious, hands on hips. He's still half erect, which makes me want to either suck him or laugh uproariously, neither of which are appropriate responses to this situation. "What the hell? This isn't a game! I told you what would have to happen. Either I lose his business, tank my career, or get his blessing. Which would you rather?" He shakes his head . . . and his dick shakes in sympathy. I'm inappropriately mesmerized. "Besides, he was fine with it."

Oh. In the haze of my annoyance and getting lost in Lucas's dick-sand I didn't think too hard about that. "Why would he be okay with it?"

"Why do you think, Trinity?"

I can guess. Brian thinks Lucas will spy on me, take back some insider knowledge—and shit, now I'm wondering the same.

"Sleeping with the enemy?"

"I'm not the enemy, Trin."

"I mean me. Is that what you're doing? Using me to get the inside track?"

"I'm not going to dignify that with an answer."

This is going from bird crap to Great Dane turds on toast. "Maybe this isn't a good time to talk. I'm just feeling sensitive about Brian having some say over this. Over my life."

"Right, I hear you. But no one has power over you unless you give it to them."

People always say that, but saying it doesn't make it so.

CHAPTER 22

Lucas

Lizzie's room is quiet except for the sound of various apparatus. A regular beep. The whoosh of the ventilator. Sometimes I imagine I can hear her blinks.

The window to her room is open, a light breeze wafting through as early morning sunlight struggles to brighten our surroundings. It's England, so we can never take the sun for granted. The British are grateful for small mercies.

"I've met a girl, Lizzie. A wonderful, prickly girl."

Tell me about her.

I wander over to the jigsaw puzzle and add a piece. Someone has completed the left side, revealing the children talking to the Professor. I always envied those Pevensie kids —sure they had to evacuate to the countryside during the war, which must have sucked, but look how it turned out. Wandering a great house, finding adventures inside furniture, fulfilling their destiny in far-flung worlds. Who needs parents when you have each other?

Our father died nine years ago, a heart attack at the age of forty-three. I was traveling in Thailand at the time, so I missed the funeral. A nice affair, I heard later. Once he'd moved away to Scotland, he didn't make all that much effort to be a dad to us. Some might say that circumstances snatched the opportunity away from him. Events overtook us.

I could blame outside forces, but I know who's at fault here.

I add a puzzle piece that looks like the ear of Tumnus the Faun and turn back to my sister. Taking a seat, I curl my palm around hers. Her skin is cool to the touch, a few degrees away from death.

"Trinity's her name. She looks like a warrior princess—fierce hair, fierce eyes, fierce smile. And when she drops that sun on me, I'm a goner."

So what did you do?

I chuckle. Lizzie knows me so well.

"I tried to move things along. You know how I am."

Impatient. Impossible.

"That's what she's said. It's sort of complicated between us. Boring legal stuff, but it amounts to me not running something by her and her getting mad. Still, you'd like her. All this fire she brings, but it seems like it's—well mostly on behalf of other people. Her sister, her nephew. She's big on supporting other people, putting everyone else first. All this ferocity, and she won't draw on it for herself."

I shake my head, questioning the accuracy of my conclusion. I'm willing to fight for my sister, my clients, for Trinity. If I want something, I take it.

Sure, if I want to bury my guilt, I pay a few quid for a complete stranger to read to my sister.

Lizzie's breathing stops for a moment. Occasionally this

happens and it terrifies me. What if this is the time she forgets how to inhale?

I squeeze her hand. "Fight, Lizzie. I'm here. I love you."

She exhales. So do I.

The nurses say her immune system is weak, that an infection could carry her away. They say it matter-of-factly, their tone clear: Maybe it would be for the best.

I know what's best for my sister.

If she can't fight, I will fight for her.

CHAPTER 23

Trinity

It's been two days, and I haven't talked to Lucas since I left his office in my ripped leather pants looking like I'd been well and truly fucked—in all meanings of the phrase. Yes, I freaked out over Brian, but Lucas really should have checked in with me first before he got Brian's permission.

Gah! The idea that this guy has any say over my sex life makes me ill. To have Brian looming over me wielding this power is unbearable. And for Lucas to make that decision for me? No way.

Then there's Emily. What would she think of me knocking boots with the enemy? She'd feel betrayed by the one person she needs most right now. *Like you did all those years ago, Trin.* I thought I'd stowed that hurt deep, but recent events are making me rehash it all over again.

Guilt is my new bestie, so in order to make myself feel less culpable, I've agreed to babysit Arianna and by default, Chase. Emily has her Animal Flow class, where she taps into her primal self in the name of fitness. She's the kind of girl who really needs endorphin boosting, so if that has to come in the form of crawling around a germ-ridden gym mat pretending to be a tiger, I'm all for it. However, it leaves me with the devil child.

I jest. Sort of.

Ari's not *completely* evil, but she does appear to have early sociopathic tendencies that I think might best be handled by a child psychologist. Only a couple of weeks ago I tripped over a pink Barbie Glam Cruise convertible mysteriously placed on the top rung of the stair. As I soothed my sore butt, the sound of Ari's laughter rang in my ears.

Then I found the same toy in the same place the next day.

So she's not tearing wings off flies. Yet. But it's in the eyes. I see flashes of *The Omen* at work.

We're spending the afternoon in one of my favorite places in the city, the Alfred Caldwell Lily Pool. This little-known spot on the edge of Lincoln Park behind the conservatory is the best-kept secret in Chicago. A duck pond sheltered by trees, it's an oasis away from the craziness of city life. You enter by a hidden gate on Fullerton and wend your way along a stone walk encircling a lily pool. Birdsong and the gentle sounds of a waterfall fill your ears, and it's easy to forget that a busy city bustles outside the gates.

Good thing I have a moody teen to remind me.

"This is boring," Chase says.

"How would you know? You haven't taken your eyes off your phone."

He takes his eyes off it now, only to roll them.

"This is what your sister wants. Right, Ari? You want to see the ducks?"

"Ducks!"

Exactly.

I take a breath, seeking peace after my argument with Lucas.

I should have explained my objections to Brian more clearly. And I would have if I'd realized that this was evolving into something much more serious than I'd planned. Not that I planned a thing. This entire fiasco was completely *unplanned*—it's reckless, sexy, and just a little bit absurd.

Take Lucas Wright, a man who wears ugly golfer pants and dumb T-shirts and jaunty hats. I mean, who wears hats in this day and age? He's loud and raucous and not my type at all. Too young, too hot, too everything.

Why should I share anything important with a man like this? He won't be around for the long haul. I can't imagine a future with Lucas—except when I think of him not being in it, I feel ill.

I take a plastic bag of bread out of my purse and hand it off to Ari. "Want to feed them?"

"It's not legal," Chase says. "There was a sign when we came in."

"Sure thing, Mr. Law and Order."

"I want to feed the ducks," Ari says with steely resolve.

"Feed away, kid." Better she's nurturing them than decimating them. I watch her carefully, ensuring she stays close and doesn't fall in. Off in the distance, a gentle but persistent quacking fills my ears.

A raft of ducks descends on the single piece of bread Ari throws in. She looks with grim satisfaction at the havoc she's created. The raucous quacking continues.

"Duck's hurt!" Ari exclaims.

"He's just annoying," I say, but I then look closer. The duck appears to be spinning in circles, *Exorcist*-style, flapping its wings, and being a general nuisance. Another duck— maybe annoyed by Duck No. 1—is also bringing the noise, screeching in duck at his buddy.

It occurs to me that maybe Duck No. 2 and Ari are onto something. *Duck's hurt.*

Any further investigation is superseded by a series of unexpected events, starting with the appearance of a red, white, and blue blur, which lands in the duck pond.

"Hey, it's Coach," Chase says, as if this is completely normal.

It *is* Lucas, and he's doing something to the duck.

Okay, he's *saving* the duck. I think. After a titanic struggle, he lifts the duck out of the water to reveal—holy shit!—a turtle's jaws attached to one of the duck's spindly legs.

"Turtle!" Ari screams.

Duck-turtle combo beast in hand, Lucas wades through the water toward us. That turtle is determined; he's not letting go. "Grab a stick, mate!"

"What?" I screech helplessly, but Chase is on it and back with a stick he pulled from the wooded area along the path.

Lucas places the duck down in the water, takes the stick from Chase, and jabs under the surface—at the turtle, I assume. A few people, drawn by the commotion, line the pond watching this battle between man and beast unfold.

"Poke it!" Chase yells, and soon we're all bellowing variations on "Poke it!" "Do it!" and "Kill it!" (Ari. What did I tell you?)

Finally the duck stops thrashing and swims off to the center of the pond, free of the evil turtle, and followed by his companion. Applause breaks out. We all grin stupidly, happy in the communal bubble of having witnessed something special, and just a little amazed at how it all went down.

Lucas stands waist-deep in the pond, hands on hips, peering up at me with a big, goofy smile.

Aw hell, I'm falling for this guy.

"Get out of there!" I yell, mostly because I'm annoyed at how pleased I am to see him and how—*shit shit shit*—I might have more than pants-feelings for him. "That turtle is prob-ably looking for fresh meat."

He strides to the edge of the pond and hoists himself onto the path with his yoga strength. I pull on his arm as if I'm helping, but really just to feel up his biceps, which look amazing. He's wearing white (now pond-gray) jeans, red Converse, and a blue tee with the slogan: "I may not be right, but I can sure sound like it."

"Why are you here?"

"Why do you think?"

I turn to Chase. "Did you tell him where we were?"

"He's been helping me with my math homework."

Really? That's so sweet. Besides, I can't blame Chase. I suspect Lucas will always find a way.

"I'm sorry," Lucas says.

"No. Don't." I can't bear to hear him atoning for my over-reaction.

He addresses Chase. "Mate, can I trust you to keep an eye on your sister for a second?"

"Yeah, sure."

Standing and shaking off the pond water, Lucas holds out his hand. "I'll take the phone while you're on watch duty."

Chase frowns but hands it over immediately, then takes some of the bread from the bag. Lucas assesses the child care situation and, once satisfied it's to his liking, he takes my hand and leads me down the path until we're out of earshot. He high-fives two guys on the way.

"Lucas, you're wet. You need to dry off."

"In a minute. Something to say first. I handled this all wrong. I should have run the waiver business by you first and made sure you were involved in that decision. It was disrespectful. I wanted you, you see. More than I've ever wanted anything, and when I saw you at that tasting kicking ass and taking names and just being all around fucking awesome, I didn't want to wait a second longer."

My heart is pounding ten times harder than the moment ago when I thought Lucas's wedding tackle was about to be ravaged by a turtle. "You saw me doing my job and realized you had to have me?"

"Pretty much."

"Witnessing me operating in my chosen field drove you to such heights of insatiable lust that it made you lose your mind?"

"That about sums it—"

I kiss him before he can finish, an all-in, filled-with-gratitude kiss. I shouldn't be this grateful, should I? I should just accept his hard-on for my competence as my due, but no one has ever seen me like Lucas does. I feel respected and desired, which is a heady combo.

"This isn't all on you," I whisper against his lips. "I overreacted when you were just trying to eliminate an obstacle." I pause, wondering if I should tell him exactly why Brian's blessing makes my skin crawl. *Too soon,* a little voice says. "I had no idea that this would turn into something."

He brings my hand up to his heart, covered by his wet T-shirt, which is very, very distracting. "Something?"

"I can't label it, so *something* will have to do."

"How about I label it?"

I shake my head vehemently. "Don't. As soon as you do, it places expectations on us."

"You mean it places expectations on you?"

I clam up, unsure how to elaborate or even if I should. I don't want to get hurt. I don't think Lucas would do that consciously, but why would he choose me for the long haul? It wouldn't be the first time I've been tossed aside.

My gaze dips over him, taking in all the sexy, noting how his wet clothes mold to every perfect angle, plane, and bulge.

Particularly the one that's magnetizing my greedy, grasping eyeballs.

"We really need to get you out of those wet clothes—"

"And into a wetter woman," he finishes, this time with a deep kiss that fills my soul.

CHAPTER 24

Trinity

*B*ack at Emily's, I'm very conscious that the attorney representing my sister's ex is in the house, possibly judging, oh, everything. I try to see it through his eyes. Does this look like a home lacking in love? (No.) Is there too much wine in the fridge? (Probably.)

Lucas went home to his place to change and came back with Ann Sather cinnamon rolls, a move surely designed to get into my panties. It's working. Or at least, it will when I'm not surrounded by cock-blocking children. The man is also wearing another Lucas Wright special: pants that are comic book panels of Doctor Who's various regenerations and a tee that shows off his musculature to perfection.

Acutely conscious of my non-perfection in this guy's presence, I put down the cinnamon roll.

"My friend Pete is a big Who fan."

"Yeah, I guessed when I saw him at the pub quiz." He leans against the counter in the kitchen, where I'm preparing a PB and J (actually cashew butter and gooseberry preserves) for

Ari's pre-dinner snack. Apparently the original isn't done in Lincoln Park. Chase is watching *Avengers: Civil War* in the living room, while his sister plays a game on her iPad, one of three she owns.

My phone buzzes with a text from Emily.

Any chance you could stay a little longer? Pretty please?

My gaze flips to Lucas, who's watching me intently. "I need to make a quick call. Could you . . . ?"

"I'll keep an eye on them."

With a grateful smile, I go into Brian's study, which smells of leather and asshole, and call my sister. "What's going on?"

"It's Annalise. Her husband left her and she needs a shoulder."

I don't even know who Annalise is. Emily has a coterie of ever-rotating friends with names like Magda and Kendall and Quinoa.

"That . . . that sounds awful." Guilt pinches me that Lucas is here and I wonder if I should share that. But I'm not ready to get into that over the phone. Besides, Ari will probably rat me out later. Instead I ask in the sort-of-concerned-yet-abstract tone of someone who doesn't know the person involved, "Is she okay?"

"She will be. We're women and we have to be strong for one another. We can't rely on men to do it for us."

I restrain an eye roll. "How long will you be?"

"Oh, who knows? A few hours. I'm round at her place now and she's ten sheets to the wind on elderflower gin. You know something else? Ari asked for that Danish trollop the other day. Said she missed her!"

My heart squeezes. Poor Emily, forced to compete with her ex-nanny for the affections of her daughter as well as her husband. Fury at Brian's selfishness grips me hard. Emily yammers on some more about Annalise's cheating husband

and the tart he brought into the marriage bed. I make a few sympathetic noises before ringing off.

She didn't even ask if I'm working tonight. I'm not, but she just assumed I had no plans.

I head back into the kitchen to find that Lucas has completed the sandwich making and delivered it to my hungry niece.

"Order in?" He holds up a few menus. "I kind of fancy some duck."

"Uh, not tacky at all! Lucas giveth and Lucas taketh away."

He laughs. "Okay, how about I make you a grilled cheese?"

My stomach rumbles. "I will have your babies if you make me a grilled cheese."

"Might hold you to that," he responds, which has me thinking about golden-eyed spawn with night-dark hair and Lucas's smile.

He calls out: "Chase, mate, grilled cheese?"

Chase responds in the affirmative without turning. Kids these days take adult service to their every need as a given.

"Everything okay?" Lucas asks.

"Yeah, that was Emily. She's delayed, helping a friend."

He only nods. Is he judging Emily for not being here and leaving me on the hook?

The grilled cheese is amazing, but then it's Lucas, and he does everything professionally and perfectly. We watch more Avengers movies—I'm always up for my tenth viewing of America's boyfriend, *Black Panther*—and the longer Lucas stays, the more I pray that Emily will just show up and find him sprawled on the sofa, embedded in my life, taking care of me. With each minute that passes and no sign of her, I weigh my secrecy about Lucas against her leaving me to watch her kids with little thought to my plans. This ledger of injustices I'm keeping almost makes me feel better about keeping Lucas to myself. If she's going to be inconsiderate, then I can tell a few white lies.

AFTER THE MOVIE, Ari insists that Lucas—or Duck Man as she's labeled him—has to read her a story. He winks at me. "What can I say? Women love me. Ducks, five-year-olds, whiskey sommeliers."

While he's gone I think more on what he didn't say earlier. Just that nod that spoke volumes. Emily has been calling on me more than usual since she lost her child care. I've been trying to be patient, but maybe it's time I weaned her off the teat of Trinity.

I'm waiting not so patiently for the foot rub Lucas promised, but he's taking his damn time. Concerned he might be injured (Ari can*not* be trusted), I head on up in time to hear excited voices and Ari's giggles. Somehow Lucas has roped Chase into acting out one of the Lemony Snicket books.

I sneak a peek through the just-ajar door. Chase is reading the narrative from the hardcover book that usually sits on Ari's shelf, while Lucas is following along on his phone, doing all the dialogue with some mighty fine voice work, including excellent American accents. Even listening outside the door, I would know which character is speaking.

Ari's loving it. After a couple of minutes, the chapter comes to an end.

"More!" Ari screams.

"What did I say about raising your voice, Arianna?" Lucas is firm but kind.

"That I shouldn't. Not even if I'm hungry."

"That's right. You can ask politely."

"May I have another story, please?"

"Nope."

"But—"

"Sorry, sweetheart. You can't get everything you want all the time. That's not how life works. Better to learn now."

I expect a tantrum. Instead I hear a small "Okay." Lucas Wright, Demon Whisperer.

The boys emerge, grinning up a storm. *My boys,* I think proudly.

"That sounded like fun," I say. "Chase, I had no idea you were this talented."

My nephew blushes. "Yeah, well, Lucas is pretty awesome at all the voices." He splits a glance between us. "I've got some homework to do."

"Need any help, mate?"

"Not unless you're an expert on the causes of the Franco-Prussian war. I have to write an essay."

"Bloody Bismarck! What a chuffer! Listen, email it to me and I'll read it over breakfast."

Chase grins. "All right."

As he heads off, I ask Lucas, "So you're leaving?"

"Yeah. As much as I'd love to spend the night debauching you, it seems weird in my client's house."

It does. I'm acutely aware that this—that Brian—is between us, even with the air clearing of earlier.

I walk him to the door. "I know you can't discuss your clients or one client in particular, but can we talk in hypotheticals?"

"Hypothesize away."

"What would you say is the single most surmountable obstacle in any divorce proceeding?"

He frowns slightly. "Hypothetical, of course, and not related to any one particular situation."

"Right."

"People need to learn to get out of their own way. I see

too many people on both sides of the equation self-sabotaging, usually by insisting that nothing has to change. That they can go on as before. They don't have to solve anything because if they ignore it, it'll solve itself. Taking control is the answer. Recognizing that you have the means to improve your lot is the key."

Emily would prefer to pretend that Brian will either come back to her or he'll support her in the style to which she's become accustomed. Putting her head in the sand has always been her MO. I want to help her change that mindset, but I can't be seen to be taking sides against her.

I'm shocked to be even thinking this. Sides? There's only Emily's. I've never not been on hers—even if she hasn't always repaid me in kind. But her leaving me on the hook tonight is a nagging barb, one I suspect will fester if I let it.

CHAPTER 25

Trinity

Max Henderson lives in a fancy penthouse in Lincoln Park and his rooftop—to which he has exclusive access—is the location for one of those *meet-all-my-friends, we-might-be-a-couple* cookouts.

"Wow!" I say, sounding like a complete rube.

"Yeah, wow is about right." Lucas grins and puts an arm around my waist. "You look stunning."

"Thanks." In this red halter dress, I feel pretty stunning. The night is magical, the rooftops of Chicago bathed in the orange-pinks of the setting sun. Of course, Lucas manages to outshine me *and* the sun in a pair of rolled-up pale blue chinos, a teal blazer over a white tee, and a fedora. It's *Miami Vice* meets Bruno Mars and it totally works.

"You must be Trinity." A bubbly blonde approaches with Max in tow. "I'm Charlie. It's lovely to meet you."

"Nice to meet you, too. You look a little familiar—the Gilt Bar? I used to work there. Now I'm in the basement, which doesn't sound like a step up, but is." I'm babbling, nervous at meeting Lucas's friends officially.

"Right, I've been there a couple of times." Charlie and Max exchange grins. "Good place to pick up a guy."

I snort. "I wouldn't say that. The guys who frequent that place are mostly douche bags."

"Yeah, but excellent tippers," Max offers.

"Excellent tippers are in the eye of the tippee," I tease.

Charlie lets loose with a boisterous laugh. "Lucas, honey, this one's a keeper."

"She doesn't want to be kept," Lucas says. "One of those independent types you're always hearing about."

I elbow him gently and he squeezes me tighter to his side. For the last couple of weeks, we've been living in my happy place, though every now and then, a little voice tries to prick the bubble of sex and comfort Lucas and I are creating: What would Emily think if she knew?

I've become expert in shoving that voice down deep. Surely she wouldn't begrudge me a few moments of joy.

That's the word, isn't it? *Joy.* Lucas soaks me in it, and fleeting though it might be, I want to hold on to it. To him.

Charlie takes my hand. "Let's get you a drink."

"What about me?" Lucas asks.

"Keg's over there, heathen."

I think I'm going to like Lucas's friends.

At the bar, a bartender is on hand to dispense. Everyone's drinking Pimm's like we're at a royal wedding, so I go with the flow and take one myself.

"Oh, hello," I hear in a smooth, moneyed voice. Aubrey appears, looking like Snow White's wicked twin just blown in from the Hamptons. "So you and Lucas decided to get down and dirty, to hell with the consequences?"

"Aubrey," Charlie says in a tone that sounds like a warning.

"I don't mean that you shouldn't," Aubrey says, taking a big gulp of wine. I shouldn't judge, but I wonder if it's her second or third glass. Being in the biz, I recognize that slightly unfocused look. "It's just Lucas was a little worried about the ethics thing."

"Well, he got a waiver so everything's aboveboard."

"Oh, sounds serious." Charlie lowers her voice. "I'm guessing he wouldn't go to all that trouble if it was just a fling."

My heart takes flight, but the engine stalls midair. "Oh no. We're just having fun."

"With the lawyer representing your sister's soon-to-be ex?" Aubrey again, cutting through my mealy mouthed defense with the sharpness of a saber. *Gorgeous white teeth gnashing. Designer stilettos stomping.* "That's not a fling. That's a conscious coupling."

This sends us all gawking at Lucas, who's laughing about something with Max, Grant, and a pretty redhead. Lucas spots us staring and tips his hat in my direction, with a hammy wink the bonus.

"Now he knows we're talking about him." I call over to him. "We're lamenting your fashion sense. Nothing else."

"As long as I'm being discussed, that's all that matters!"

I giggle stupidly, conscious that I've never been a giggler, but with Lucas, all bets are off. At the sight of the girls watching this exchange with interest, I abruptly stop.

"Aubrey's right, you know," Charlie muses. "If it was just sex, would you go to that much trouble? Risk pissing off loved ones or ethics boards just to get your rocks off?"

"Well . . . I don't know . . . possibly . . ." This is all very pointed and personal, considering I barely know them. Once we decided to go all in, Lucas and I have made a conscious effort not to talk about my sister or the kids. At first, it felt weird, like this void that needed filling because they're such a huge part of my life. Who am I without them? But Lucas made it easy, keeping the focus on me. It turns out I have plenty to say that doesn't require twittering on about my family. Who knew?

"Your sister's okay with it?" Aubrey again, and I hear compassion for my dilemma in her voice.

"I haven't told her yet." I figured it would be over before I had to even bring it up. Yes, that's my plan. Have my fun, part amicably, then never breathe a word of my betrayal to Emily.

I had a similar conversation with Gideon and Pete earlier this week. Gid thinks I should tell Emily because secrets have a way of bubbling to the surface like a bloated, fish-ravaged body. (The man has a melodramatic streak.) Pete thinks . . . oh hell, Pete thinks the same. And they never agree on anything. I'm *so* happy they've found this cause to unite them.

But when it comes to Lucas and "the end," I don't want to part amicably. I don't want to part at all. This is something for *me*. Why should I have to bow down to Emily on this issue? Hasn't she already taken enough from me?

Holy balls, where did *that* come from? I'm happy to help my sister out. She needs me.

The silence has gone on too long. Charlie lays a hand on my arm.

"Don't mind us. We're awfully nosy and we love assigning *huge* significance to things we shouldn't. We've only just met and you're a guest and I can't believe we were all up in your business."

"Speaking of all up in someone's business, who's that?" Aubrey uses her now-empty glass to motion toward Lucas's group.

"Kelly," Charlie says, biting her lip. "I think Grant's taken her out a couple of times."

"Must like her if he's bringing her to meet the gang."

There's an undeniable sadness in her voice and I can't help checking in with Charlie to see if she's also heard it.

I'm not wrong. Charlie's expression is filled with sympathy. "Maybe you should think about dating yourself. It's been, what, a year since your divorce?"

Oh. I slide a look to Grant and the redhead. Awkward.

Aubrey looks wistful. "Maybe I'll just fuck the bartender." This is said loudly enough for several people, including the bartender *and* Grant, to hear.

Instead of scowling as I think most guys would do in the presence of their slightly tipsy ex mouthing off in an embarrassing way, Grant merely smiles at Aubrey. A secretive curve of his lips.

Two spots of color appear high on Aubrey's cheeks and she mutters, "Prick." She turns to us: "What's the drop off this roof? Two hundred feet? Three hundred?"

Laughing, Charlie pats Aubrey on the arm. "Let's get you something to eat, and Trinity, I want to hear all about these Whiskey, Women, and Song events. I might be able to help you out there."

I'm fairly famished myself, but I'm stopped from partaking by a strong set of arms encircling me, breath hot against my ear. "Ms. Jones, this party was a terrible idea."

"It was?"

"I just want to ravish you and all these bloody people are in the way."

I push my ass back against him, slotting into the concave space of his body. Fitting perfectly.

"I don't mind. Ravish away."

His chuckle is warm and as usual, gives me life. "So, did the girls subject you to the third degree?"

I turn in his arms. "A little. They seem to think it must be very serious between us because we're risking things. Reputation, jobs, family relationships."

"And what did you say?"

"I told them cougars do whatever's necessary to get their kicks."

"Still not putting a label on it?"

I shoot for nonchalance. "It's kind of early for that."

"Is it? Maybe you doubt my sincerity. Or maybe you think I'm not a relationship sort of bloke."

Maybe I do, on both counts. I'm not used to this lavish attention, and that's what it feels like: excessive and indulgent. Since we met, Lucas has been bending over backward to woo me. Doubts slam through me. Perhaps I'm just a novelty for him—it wouldn't be the first time a guy has shown interest in me because it checks off some box for him.

I look up through my lashes to find Lucas frowning. "Where'd you go?"

"Oh, nowhere."

"Hmm." Before I realize what's happening, Lucas is standing on a wicker sofa, waving like a madman. "Can I have your attention, everyone?"

Max frowns. "Wright, get your big feet off my very expensive furniture."

"In a minute, Mr. Trust Fund. So, I just wanted to thank Max for inviting everyone over, though I suspect we should be thanking Charlie, because she's obviously the organizational brains of the operation."

Charlie raises her glass in thanks. She's a wedding planner by trade, which is a fun match for a divorce attorney, for sure.

"So, cheers, Charlie," Lucas continues. "And thanks for taking on this stuck-in-a-rut for a boyfriend. Also, don't leave him hanging for too long regarding getting hitched. I for one am tired of his whining about how he can't persuade you. Just say yes!"

"Jesus, Lucas," Max mutters while everyone hoots their appreciation.

A blushing Charlie draws an imaginary zip across her lips.

This makes Lucas laugh. "You mean you don't want to be forced into a public acceptance of a proposal like some crappy movie? Not a romantic bone, you bloody tossers!" He turns to me, his smile devilish. I brace myself for more Lucas inanity. "Now, some of you might have met my date for this cookout, Trinity Jones. She happens to be a whiskey expert, so if you're looking for a hot woman to tell you all about how your alcohol tastes like bird droppings with top notes of vanilla, she's available for parties." More laughter. "But if you're looking for a hot woman for other things, like maybe a few dirty things . . ." The word *dirty* is a low rumble of sex. "Or even things that aren't dirty, then Trinity Jones is not the woman for you. Because she's the woman for me. She's taken, and I just want that to be clear. Hands off!"

He hops down from the sofa, his eyes fixed to mine. It's breath-stealing. Then he gathers me in his arms and claims me physically, just as he did with his words a moment ago. People clap, the sound of laughter and joy a buzz in my ears as Lucas fills me up.

His nose nuzzles mine. "Too much?"

"Far too much."

"Good."

CHAPTER 26

Lucas

"A stripper pole?" I cast some serious side-eye at Trinity. "Really?"

"Not for women to strip in your living room, but for your own dance routines."

"Of course." We're walking through the Lincoln Park neighborhood, on our way back to my place, about ten minutes from where Max lives. Trinity has never visited, so she's trying to guess at what she'll find.

"Oh, I know. A cozy of weird teapots that only British people would have."

"Is *cozy* the collective noun for teapots?"

"It should be, don't you think?" She laughs, her imagination running riotous circles. "Ooh! Fifty pairs of board shorts. Each pattern more outrageous than the last."

"Getting closer."

She laughs again and squeezes my hand. It's comforting and sexy at once, that hand squeeze. The full-linkage hand meld, each of my fingers interlaced with hers.

"What are you smiling at?" she asks.

"Our hands. They look amazing together."

She lifts our joined hands between us and examines them, turning them to get a good view of all the angles. I think of Lizzie's fingers, cool and stripped of life.

"They look *good*," Trinity murmurs. "You're a superlatives kind of guy. Me, I'm happy with good."

"Better than good."

I mean us. Her mouth wobbles beautifully as she holds the smile. After my declaration to the group, I'm not sure if I've scared her off or brought her closer. Maybe a little of both.

Tonight I have a late flight to London and I'd like to tell Trinity about Lizzie before I go. I'm nervous to share, but not nearly as much as I thought I'd be. We continue on our way, enjoying the sun coming from both inside and out.

"Shit," she says as we turn down the block where I live. Her entire body tenses all the way down to where we're joined. A blond woman is walking toward us in workout gear, a slouchy bag over her shoulder, and while I've never met her I know who she is.

Emily Carson.

Recognition makes Emily's eyes fly wide. They expand to saucer width on seeing Trinity's hand in mine.

Ripping her hand away, Trinity speaks first. "Ems, I can explain."

"Oh really?" She gives me a cursory once-over, verifies I'm who she thinks I am, and turns back to her sister. "This— this—are you kidding with this, Trinity? He's trying to destroy me!"

And I thought *I* had a flair for the dramatic. "Mrs. Carson," I start, only to be glared into silence by Emily's raised hand. Seriously. She gave me the hand.

"Well, you're obviously busy," she says to Trinity, and flounces off, her high ponytail bobbing.

"Emily!" Trinity calls after her, then to me: "I have to talk to her."

"Might be better to let her cool off."

"No. I have to fix this now."

I don't like the sound of that. Fixing might not be so beneficial to me, and my next words sound on the wrong side of desperate. "If she tells you to stop seeing me, will you?"

"That—she wouldn't do that."

"You're not answering my question."

"It's not a fair question. I need to talk to her."

Maybe she's right. It's not fair, and it's not fair of me to ask her to choose a side. Yet she took a risk getting involved with me. Clearly she never planned for it to go this far. I was only meant to be that one-shot deal to resolve all that sexual tension. I understand that.

Still I can't resist pulling her close. I want her to know things. To know me. Not Lucas with his stripper pole and teapots and board shorts collection (metaphors, you know what I mean!). But Lucas with his heart on the cusp of breaking twice a month as he makes a lonely trek to London and back. Lucas who wants something he probably doesn't deserve but is going to fight for it anyway because he's an ornery bastard underneath all that cheer.

"Come back to me," I say, not caring that I sound pathetic.

I watch the swallow of her hesitation as it makes her elegant neck bulge. "I'll call you later."

CHAPTER 27

Trinity

"Hey!" Ten minutes after leaving Lucas, I walk into Emily's house and stop cold on seeing her expression. Sucked down a lemon would be a fairly accurate description.

"I can't believe you'd do that to me."

"I'd planned to tell you, but it happened kind of quickly and other stuff got in the way . . ."

She turns away from me and stalks into the living room. A bottle of wine is already open—just the one glass—and she sits down, not inviting me to get comfortable.

I take a seat beside her anyway.

"He's the enemy, Trinity," she whines, sounding very like me a month ago. "He wants us to sell the house. Take my children's home away from me."

"Look, that what's I thought. The enemy thing, but I do know that he's just doing his job. Like your lawyer's doing her job."

I know Lucas. He's a great guy. Funny and sweet and

sensitive, and yeah, great in the sack. Am I really choosing my neglected lady parts over family? But surely I deserve some happiness as well. I can't always be the last girl chosen for sports ball.

She grabs her glass and takes a slug. "Is this even legal? Aren't there rules about consorting with the enemy?"

"There are but Brian said it was okay."

She explodes. "Brian knows? Well, of course, *he's* okay with it. He has you in his pocket now, playing for his team. Telling them stuff about me. He has all the advantages, the inside track." She looks around as if there's evidence on every surface that I could use against her.

I squeeze her hand; she pulls away. "You know what I think of Brian. He's a no-good cheating jerk and you could not pay me to play for his team. This thing with Lucas kind of blindsided me, but you don't have to worry. We don't talk about your case because of lawyer-client confidentiality so there's no inside track to be had."

She assesses me sharply, that lip bite I know so well telling me that her mind is working all the angles. "Maybe he could tell you things. Strategy things."

"So if Brian does it, it's taking advantage, but if you do, it's not?"

"I need all the advantages I can get!"

You've had nothing but advantages your entire life, sis. I suppress this uncharitable thought. Ems can't help being weak. But maybe it's a trap I've created for us. I like being in charge. I like being needed, and Emily needs me. Have I been enabling her all this time just to give myself a purpose?

I move closer to her and throw an arm around her shoulder, willing her to relax into me. "You are my number one, not some hot guy with amazing cheekbones, and sparkling blue eyes, and a dick I want to bronze."

"Oh my God, really? I saw a photo of him online but I

didn't expect him to be so good-looking in person. And the dick as well?"

I nod solemnly. "Praise the dick."

She laughs and leans her head on my shoulder. I love her for trying. "He's got . . . interesting fashion sense. Does he wear that hat when he fucks you?"

"Ems!" I'm all affront, but then I add a wink. "Of course not, but I'm going to ask him the next time." That sets us off giggling like teens, just like old times.

"God, I miss sex," my sister says.

"With Brian?" I bite my lip. "Sorry, it's just you said it wasn't all that in recent years."

"I know, but it's like pizza. Bad pizza is better than no pizza." She shrugs helplessly. "Mostly I miss the cuddling, that closeness you feel with another person. It's been so long that today I almost gagged on my toothbrush and got turned on!"

"Oh, God, I'm so sorry."

"No, you're not. I assume the Lucas-made orgasms are out of this world?"

"So-so."

"Bitch."

I grin, relishing the rare feeling of smugness and wanting to hold on to it for a while.

Ems sighs. "Well, enjoy it while it lasts. Brian used to make me shave his back. That's what marriage is all about."

"Ew! You're well out of it, sis."

We stay quiet for a while, both of us lost in our thoughts. After a moment, she speaks. "Remember when we went to Six Flags as kids and you had to drag me on every single roller coaster because I was a big ole scaredy-cat?"

"Yeah, I was a mean sister."

"No, that's not what I'm talking about. I needed someone

to push me, to tell me the rush I'd get was worth those brief moments of fear. You did that. You've always done that."

That was me. That *is* me. Protector and pusher. My own memories of that time have a different blush to them, though —going to Six Flags with Emily and her dad where more than once it was made clear that I was different. Other. Ticket takers, servers, the workers running the coasters would ask, *Are you on your own, honey? Where's your mom and dad?* And Evan would assure them I was with him and Emily, his words intended to soothe but feeling like sandpaper over a raw wound. *She's with me. This is my stepdaughter.*

I push those memories away. "Then we went with Chase and his friends when he was what—eleven? And neither of us would go up on them."

"With age comes the knowledge those machines could drop out of the sky at any second."

"But I used to love them," I say. The anticipation, the climb, the drop. Nothing scared me, but over the last few years, I've retreated to another place. Played it safe.

Until Lucas.

Emily wrinkles her nose. "Does he know about—?"

"No," I cut her off before she can say it and taint our truce.

She pulls back, her eyes alive with concern. "Don't you think that's something you should share?"

"I will. I just—shit, I didn't expect anything to come of it. He's supposed to be the good-time guy, the jump-starter, the one who gets the juices flowing. Not a . . . possibility."

"Funny how things can just spiral out of control like that." For once, Emily looks and sounds like the older one. Miraculously wiser after a crappy year. Why the hell do we have to go through hell to gain all the fucking insight?

We're okay for now, but this feels like a tremor in our

relationship, a precursor to the big one—and I'm not sure how I'm going to react when those tectonic plates shift.

SUNDAY NIGHT, and the Library is hopping. We have three parties in for whiskey tastings, one of which is a bit rowdy, but nothing I can't handle. What I'm having trouble handling is the deadweight of my heavy heart, telling me I screwed up with Lucas.

I left messages for him after I made up with Emily yesterday, but I haven't heard back. That he might be in pain because I chose to run after my sister has my stomach in knots.

"Heads up," Gideon says. "Three o'clock."

I look to the right.

"Your other three o'clock."

Stupid guy directions. To my left I see that the man of my fantasies has just walked into the bar. He captures my gaze with an intensity that flays me alive as he approaches, stopping short a few feet.

I look at him more closely. It's like staring at a sun that's been drained of life.

"Lucas." I grasp his hand and pull him forward. "What's wrong?"

His fingers curl around mine. His expression brightens by a few watts, and knowing my touch does this for him lifts me up.

"I know it's late, but I figured my friendly bartender would be willing to pour beer down my throat regardless of the hour. Or if you won't do it because you're a liquor snob, maybe I can convince Treebeard to help out."

We left things weird, stuck in that space of mistrust when

we should have been basking in the glow of *finally*. I want to tell him we're good, that Emily's on board.

"Would you like to go somewhere? There's an office in back."

"No." He looks uncomfortable, which is strange because Lucas is usually so at home in his own skin. "I want to just stare at you and not feel obliged to talk. I want to feast my eyes on beauty and life and everything good. Do you think you could do that for me?"

Who could refuse such a request?

"Of course." I lead him to a stool near the end of the bar, one that will give him a good view of the space if he wants to . . . uh, watch me. I call over to Gideon. "Give the man whatever he wants."

"I have a break in about thirty minutes," I say to Lucas. "We don't have to talk or anything, but if you feel like it, I'll be here."

He curves an arm around my waist and pulls me close. His eyes scorch me with their intensity. "You're a good woman, Trinity Jones. Far too good for the likes of me. But I don't care. I'm keeping you."

I cup his jaw and hold his gaze. He's not drunk. He's completely sober, yet his words are the words of a madman. Usually Lucas projects a "high on life" attitude, but this . . . this is something else.

"Maybe I don't want to be kept."

"No." He releases me with a light tap on my ass. "You're no one's possession. I don't mean that—I'm just rambling, love. Ignore me. Off now and tell the world about the demon drink."

Gideon places a pint down before him. "You okay, Lucas?"

"Yeah, mate. Peachy. As long as I've got a beer and my girl, all is good."

Gideon and I exchange looks. Subdued Lucas is weird Lucas. Philosophical Lucas is even more odd, but hey, no one can be 100 percent on all the time.

My chest warms at seeing facets of this man I never knew existed.

"Give me a shout if you need anything," I say, meaning both Lucas and Gideon.

Lucas salutes me, but it's like he has to think about it first. His default setting of bonhomie is on the fritz.

I return to work. Every time I head back to the bar, I do a visual check-in with Lucas. Sometimes he smiles, more often he doesn't. He just drinks me in.

And it's intoxicating.

My rowdy party is investment bankers, and one of them keeps trying to light a cigar even though I tell him he can't. The third time I try to enforce this rule, he grabs my wrist.

"Have a drink with us, angel."

His gaze runs point over my legs, revealed in a short skirt I wouldn't normally wear. But being with Lucas has given me confidence and made me feel sexier of late. I pull away gently, though my skin is crawling.

"On the clock, gentlemen. No can do."

"What about after?" Bloodshot eyes peer up at me through lank, sweat-drenched hair. "You can help me with my fuck-it list."

I don't like the sound of that, so I refuse to ask a follow-up question. Instead I laugh it off like I'm the dumb server who doesn't get what the important men are saying.

"No fraternizing with the clients," I say with a wink. "Keeps things simple."

"His fuck-it list!" one of his mouthy friends yells, as if everyone needs reminding. Whatever it means, it makes them all bust a gut laughing. We've finished the tasting, so now I'm just bringing rounds of scotch to them. This is defi-nitely the last one.

"What are you missing, John?" one guy throws out to the fuck-it-list guy. "An Asian chick and . . ." He trails off and the rest of them chuckle with a pointed look in my direction. One of their party looks a little uncomfortable, but remains quiet. A real stand-up guy.

I understand the fuck-it list now. I'm the "it" in this scenario, but really who I am doesn't matter. It's my supposed exoticness that's of value, a check box on some inventory.

Fuck-it-list guy stands up and places a hand on my arm to steer me away from the group. "Sorry about them, they're dicks when they drink."

And I think you're probably a dick even when you don't drink.

"No problem!" Disarm and de-escalate. A woman's weapons. "I'll bring your check." *Even though you haven't asked for it.*

"You're throwing us out? Hey, that's no way to be. They're just kidding. They didn't mean anything by it." Right, the defense of every asshole bro racist ever.

"Uh-huh." I'm not going to get into it. One step back. "Like I said, no problem. Plus we're closing up in about ten minutes." This is true, thank God.

He steps with me. We're in the middle of a crowded bar. I should feel safe.

I don't.

His fingers brush my waist. It's the last thing he does before he's shoved away with force.

I pray it's Gideon, but my mind knows it's not. My mind knows that Lucas was watching every microsecond of my interaction with this piece of shit and now he's here to play at white knight.

"Hey, what's your problem?" Fuck-it-list guy yells.

"You are. Touch her again and I will end you," Lucas grates, his accent like a Guy Ritchie street thug. "I've had a pretty shit day and I'm just looking for an excuse to pound someone. You want to give it to me?"

"Lucas, it's okay."

"Is it?" He stares at me, and I can see that whatever's eating away at him has had a five-course meal. He's being torn apart.

I only have to think it and Gideon appears, his expression telling me he has this. I take Lucas's hand. Initially he resists, preferring to get a few more death stares in, but after a moment he relents. We travel down a corridor, around a corner, and into our small office. I push him into a chair and close the door.

"Want to tell me what's going on?"

"That arsemonger laid a hand on you."

"Well, that arsemonger was a customer and I had it under control." What is an arsemonger anyway? Is it like a fishmonger? A seller of arses?

"Everything good with Emily?"

I swallow at the abrupt change of topic. "Yeah, we made up. I left you messages. I wanted to tell you."

His eyes bore into me. "I wasn't trying to make you choose. I wouldn't expect to come out on the good side of that."

I should say, *yes, I would choose you in a heartbeat. There's no question.* Instead I respond with, "She'd never ask for that. It's not even an option."

He remains quiet, the space filling with unspoken accusation. If she had asked, if my being with Lucas truly hurt her, where would we be?

I made it clear from the beginning that Emily and her kids are my primary concern. They need me. But I didn't expect this to happen with Lucas, where the notion of choosing him—choosing *us*—over Emily might ever be an option. Might even be a choice that needs to be made.

Luckily it doesn't, but the implication remains: I've failed a test.

"Luc—"

A knock sounds on the door and Gideon's voice echoes. "Trin, we're closing up."

"Okay! Gimme a sec." To Lucas, I say, "Could you wait here ten minutes while I finish out there? Please. I want to talk."

His nod is curt. We're not over this hump yet, but I'm determined that before the night is through, Lucas and I will be on the same page.

CHAPTER 28

Lucas

*W*hat the fuck am I doing here?

I dropped my overnight bag off at my office after coming straight from the airport, then hightailed it over to the Library because the one person I wanted to see most after Lizzie is the other woman who has my guts tied up in knots.

I'd thought I could fake my good humor, call on cheery old Lucas to get me through. Pretend that her choice of her sister—which I understand, God how I do—didn't break me a little. Rewire our relationship back to the fun fling we both signed on for.

Instead I sat morosely at the bar, a pint in my hand, jealously watching her every move and plotting the assassination of every prick in the bar in ways that would give an FBI profiler pause. And I wanted her to see it. To feel my possessive streak.

My phone buzzes. *Come out to see me.*

Her command? My wish.

The bar is empty, all the revelers and wankers gone, and looks like I've stepped through a portal and gone back in time. True to its name, the Library's shelves are filled with gilt-edged books, their spines alight in the amber glow of candles. It's positively . . . romantic.

Isn't that *my* job?

Trinity is sitting in a booth, a bottle of what looks like whiskey in front of her and two glasses. Her legs are my Kryptonite in that short skirt, long, shapely pins gleaming in the flickering light.

"Love, I'll do you sober," I joke. "No need for that."

"Come sit with me," she says, so simply, so earnestly my knees practically buckle.

I slide into the booth, keeping my eyes on her. She pours a measure into both glasses. "I know you don't like whiskey, but it's here if you need it."

To loosen me up, I suppose. I put it to my lips, trying to remember all those things I'm supposed to appreciate. I hate not understanding something. It offends me deeply.

"Tell me what I should be tasting." *Tell me how to feel.*

She takes a sip, closes her eyes. "This is a Lagavulin sixteen-year-old from the island of Islay. Peat, smoke, bacon" —she tastes it again—"salty sea spray. A little citrus on the way down. A story in every sip."

I let a drop slip past my lips and try to imagine another place. Craggy rocks, a surging surf, flying pigs dive-bombing unsuspecting beachgoers.

"About what happened when we ran into Emily," she says. "I didn't handle it right. I—I panicked."

"She's your family. Family comes first." If anyone should know this, it's me.

"Right." But I hear it, the thread of doubt about her place. The pressure she puts on herself to be her sister's rock. "I think it stems from not expecting this to escalate so quickly."

"This?"

"Us."

I snatch a breath at her utterance of that word. *Us.* "Did you just put a label on this?"

"I don't know. Maybe?" She shakes her head. "I don't want to overthink it or jinx it, but at the same time, I also want to just say fuck it, let's do this, you know?"

I do. Alarm bells go off in my head and my heart quicksteps in my chest. Having the ball placed firmly in my court after I thought I was playing practice drills wrenches my brain. If she's prepared to open her heart to this, just like I asked, then I need to meet her halfway. Yet now that I have the chance to spill, turns out I'm not ready.

She senses my hesitancy. "Maybe a good old-fashioned drinking game. Truth or dare."

A quid pro quo. Her truth for mine.

"As I'm an open book," I lie, lie, lie, "then the truth would be boring. I'll take the dare."

"Down that shot."

"I see your game. Can't wrangle the truth one way, you'll get me drunk and wheedle it out of me."

"Not such an open book after all," she says. "Tell me what happened before you came here tonight. Why you had such a bad day."

"Just tired from my flight."

"From London?"

Nice going, big mouth. "That's right."

"How's Lizzie?"

My breath stalls, my lungs seize up. I knock back the whiskey without even tasting it. Bad customer.

She raises an eyebrow, acknowledging what I did. I took the dare rather than speaking the truth, and that's a more damning admission than any word I could have spoken.

"Back to you," she murmurs, ostensibly letting me off the

hook, but I'm well and truly dangling. No one has ever demanded my words before. I don't know how to verbalize *this*.

Me, Lucas Wright. So gifted with the gab, so talented at making other people feel good—well, that idiot knows jack shit about emoting.

"Why didn't you go on that trip to Scotland to see the distilleries?"

She blinks, contemplates her drink. It should be an easy enough question to fake her way through. Life issues, money trouble, fear of flying.

"I'll take the dare." So we both have things we want to hide, just as we both have things we want the other to *know* we're hiding. Aren't we a pair?

"Shirt. Off."

"That didn't take long." Her fingers slide to the buttons on her black shirt and slowly unplug each one from its hole. My breathing picks up with each inch of smooth skin revealed. When she slips the shirt from her shoulders, I swallow hard.

She's wearing a cream-colored bra, pearlescent in the candlelight, a dream against her skin.

"Jesus, you are one fine woman, Trinity Jones. Looking at you is sun and starlight and what keeps my heart beating when all it wants to do is stop."

"Lucas," she breathes before I pounce like an animal. I need to touch her, will die if I don't.

Might die if I do.

She heaves a breath, the rise of her breasts brushing against my chest. Her hand cups my cock and drags over it roughly.

I fucking love it.

"Yeah, love. Harder. Stroke me, Trin. Rub me raw."

In seconds, my zipper is down and she's unpacking me with one hand while I lick the palm of her other, a lascivious, dirty stroke of my tongue. I place her slick hand on my hard-as-my-heart dick. She grips me like a champ, feeling my need for her not to go gentle.

Punish me.

"That's it. Just like that, love. Leave a footprint."

She's breathing heavily. I'm panting like I've run a marathon. Like I've run my life.

"Inside. Please, inside."

It's all happening so quickly, but that's what I need, a fast and furious fuck. I cup her ass under her skirt and pull her astraddle me. There's no time to divest her of her panties. No time for anything but this woman and her heat and wetness surrounding me until I'm home, plunging deep, fucking up into her like I could reach her heart. Make it mine.

The only sounds are ragged breaths and lusty moans from both of us. Until she points out an obvious problem.

"Lucas, we need a condom."

"Fuck." That's why she felt so good. So right.

I grip both of her hips, readying to pull her apart from me.

She stays home. "Truth or dare."

I swallow. I pant. If one of us moves another inch, I'm going to embarrass myself.

"Do you trust me, Lucas?"

It's a dare, but it's also a plea for the truth, and I can only nod, amazed at this leap she's taking. Because only a woman who believes I'm worth it would ask me that.

"Say it, baby."

"I trust you. More than anyone." The words emerge shaky. I mean them to their core.

I've no idea how we got here. That's not right, though. It was baby steps, a slow burn, a jump over the chasm, an over-haul of my outlook.

I shouldn't be here, I want to tell her. *Two roads diverged in an English wood . . . and I-I—*

She makes it *us,* bucking her hips, urging me upward. The roads that parted all those years ago veering back to each other. Above me, she's a shining beacon, the light I strive to reach.

"That's it, baby. Right there," she says into a kiss that rips me open. Moving inside her is the greatest gift I could receive, but then Trinity's a giver all the way. She wants to take care of me—not just my dick but my heart. Both are hurting and she is the cure.

I'm expanding, thickening inside her, and with it my blood vessels are flushing open. Everything is magnified.

Everything is Trinity.

I glance a thumb across her clit, then press harder, merciless. She screams and it triggers my release. I drive up and into her, wringing every squeeze of her pussy to fuel my orgasm. Taking and taking and taking until I can take no more.

Ten seconds elapse. Thirty. A full minute to catch my breath and find the words.

I'm in love with you.

I don't say that. I can't say that.

"Sorry."

"For what?"

"For being greedy."

"Lucas, you're the most generous man I know."

I can't agree. I'm selfish and petty, a bearer of grudges, a keeper of a toxic past.

She kisses me softly. "What did you mean? About the footprint?"

"Nothing, just something silly." I laugh, seeking *him* out. Happy Lucas. Chicago Lucas. "Trying to be deep."

She's staring at me now, and I should be softening inside

her but I'm still rock hard. I could go again, the adrenaline is still pumping through me.

Then it starts.

Not words, not sweet murmurs, but kisses. Across my cheeks and nose, over my eyelids and eyebrows. She pays special attention to the scar I got when I fell out of the tree that night, as if she suspects this might be the way to open me up.

It's not.

But she might be. The key to my lock, the zig to my zag.

With each butterfly caress, I feel my heart thumping, my soul opening, my mind letting go. I'm not only turned on. I'm turned out. Flayed from the inside, exposed to the harsh elements of soft bar light and a postcoital cuddle.

Trinity's kisses fill me up, make me bloom. This is what moments with her are like, each one an unfurling of tightly bound layers.

Then she reveals her most destructive weapon. Three words, arrows every one.

"Let it out."

She's here, ready to be my sponge. All I have to do is uncork the bottle and pour out my troubles. Just tell my friendly bartender.

My hands shake but I tighten them around her waist to get a grip on my emotion. My eyes are closed, savoring those words. I'm not used to talking about her—about Lizzie. I'm not used to being given this freedom.

I take a breath and do as Trinity says: I let it out.

CHAPTER 29

Trinity

For a moment, I think he won't do it. This man, a whirling dervish of energy and chatter, might not be able to express whatever has him in its grip. But then I see the spark in his eyes, that nanosecond when something unstops the blockage to his heart.

"She's in a nursing home just outside London. My sister. Lizzie. She had an accident when we were thirteen and she's been laid up ever since. Awake but . . . well, not."

My heart squeezes tight. This happened to his sister? Worse, his twin? "That's awful."

I can't imagine his pain, but now I understand so much more about this man. Those deep pockets of sadness he carries around with him. I want to fill them with love and light.

Seeming to sense my pity, he pulls out of me and smooths my skirt over my ass. It's the moment he needs to compose himself. "She loved—*loves*—The Chronicles of Narnia. We'd steal the books from the library and carry them with us on our travels."

"Travels with your mom?"

"Right. Then I escaped. Someone saw my potential and pulled me out of all that."

"All what?"

"The madness that comes with living with my mum. To the outside observer, she's all fun and games, but it's not the same when you live it. Through it."

I suspect this has shaped him more than anything else. "What did you live through, Lucas?"

His mouth twitches. "I'm okay now. Better than okay. Rich, successful, in demand by gorgeous women. Soccer coach extraordinaire, savior of ducks."

I smile, but there's tungsten in it. He's not fobbing me off, not this time.

"You know, parents can be the biggest disappointments in the world," I offer to get the ball rolling.

"You, too?"

"My mother left us to fend for ourselves, but really it was all on me. And I took that on."

He grins. "You're as strong as steel forged in fem-hell's crucible."

"I am woman, hear me roar."

"Shout it out, love."

I laugh, loving the lighter moment but knowing the dark must still be navigated. "What I'm trying to say is that we put them on pedestals, our parents, when they're flawed human beings who make mistakes."

His humor fades. "I can't forgive her. She drove me nuts with the weed and the Age of Aquarius and all that shit, but that's not it. That's not the fundamental underlying problem here. She's reckless, and her recklessness caused real damage. I don't think people realize that. We live in this age where everyone is me, me, me and thinks their individual choices override those of everyone else. Well, that's bollocks. When you're a parent, you are no longer the most important person in the room or in the world. When you're a parent, your kids come first. At least they should."

I can relate. He knows I can, which is why he's telling me this.

I curl up, fitting into the space between his jaw and shoulder. "Tell me what happened, Lucas."

He takes a few shallow breaths. "I wasn't there. I should have been there, but I'd already found my way out. At boarding school. Full ride. Out of the swamp."

I run my fingers through his hair, encouraging, soothing.

"My mum—Starshine was her New Age name—was always on the lookout for some cheap place to stay. Or some cheap guy to make her stay. But she'd latch on to men with ideals." He puts air quotes around that word, bitterness boxing it. "Men who were trying to stop highways smashing through forests or high-rises being built on pristine beaches. She said she believed, but I think she wanted to believe the guy. Any guy who would love her. But her search for that dragged us into hell."

I already know I won't like the ending, but that's not going to stop me from listening to the hard stuff.

"What happened?"

"We were living with a bunch of hippies in Kent, in the south of England. Mum had hooked up with this guy called Cal, a real guru type, like Charles Manson but less murderous. Bloke was leading the way on this protest to keep The Man from building a golf course in Clowes Wood. They wanted to knock down the trees, but Cal had his groupies out every morning stopping the work. And overnight, he'd order people to sleep in the trees so they couldn't get the jump on us in the early morning."

I nod, letting him know I'm here for every word no matter how painful.

"They'd had enough, these fat cats who needed the golf course built stat. Jesus, another fucking golf course, right?" He's started to twitch and shake his head, all that negative energy needing an outlet. All those memories fighting to break free.

I kiss his beautiful cheekbones. "It's okay. Just say it."

"I'd come in the day before from boarding school. Got a scholarship, didn't I? Fancy school with a bunch of nobs, and there's me, sleeping in a bloody forest during the school holidays. I had to—get this—run my trousers through the mud because they were too clean for the people I'd be hanging with all summer. One night I'm in my comfortable bed at boarding school, the next I'm sleeping in a fucking tree and I wake up to find the forest's on fire!"

He heaves a breath, needing to ready himself for the next part. The worst part.

"Long story short, I was able to scramble out and down, falling the last half of the way. Cut my head—" He points at that scar through his eyebrow. "But it's nothing. Barely felt it. I'm screaming at Lizzie to follow me and I thought she was behind me but she's scared. Of the fire, of the height, of everything. So she—shit, she—" He pulls away. "She jumped, Trin. And I tried to catch her, she hit a branch on the way down and sustained a catastrophic brain injury, and now . . . now she's in a long-term nursing home. Has been ever since."

He stares at me, willing me to say some trite platitude, I suppose.

"And you see her regularly?"

"Yeah. Twice a month. Make sure she's doing all right, that the nurses are treating her well."

I bet he pays for her care as well, though maybe it's different in the UK.

"Your mom must have been devastated."

His beautiful mouth sneers. "Are you kidding? All she was worried about was how it would affect her benefits and support from my dad. Sure, there were tears, but—fuck this." He turns his head from me, like he can't bear to look me straight in the eye any longer. "And then I thought I'd end up with my dad, but he'd already moved on with a new family. Couldn't blame him, really. I was able to legally emancipate myself, spent the holidays at school or with mates. First time I realized I could use the law for good. For what's right."

If anyone has the inner resources to survive such hardship, it's Lucas. But the toll? All this time, how alone he must have felt, and then the ultimate blow when his father didn't step into the void. My heart breaks for that solitary boy, living with the guilt of surviving his twin, unable to lay those ghosts to rest.

"Do you see your mom?"

"Not if I can bloody help it."

"Have you told her how you feel? How she hurt you?"

He rubs his mouth. "That's not how she operates. She doesn't think she did anything wrong. And trying to convince her otherwise is a waste of breath."

"Then waste it, Lucas, if only for your sanity. Where is she now?"

"Last I heard she was living in some commune in Wales. She calls every now and then to beg for money. And I send it to her to keep her away." His eyes are lasers. "What it boils down to is that there are givers and takers, Trin. Your sister and my mum are the kind of people who expect the world to pick up after them. And you and I and people like my dad are always going to get shafted."

I can't argue with him, not when he's feeling so raw. Instead, I kiss him softly and let him know with my hands and my heart that I'm here for him.

CHAPTER 30

Lucas

My girl looks unimpressed. "Lunch? At a . . . gym?"

"Not just any gym, love." I point to the Potbelly sandwiches, chilling on the windowsill next to a couple of cans of ginger ale. This morning I called Trinity and asked her to stop by the office so I could take her to lunch. "You want to eat, we need to work up an appetite first."

Her grin makes my heart beat loud and shine like the sun. After last night's confessions, I feel lighter than I have in years. Nothing about my situation has changed, yet I sense possibility where before there was none.

She places her hands on my chest and leans up on tiptoe to kiss me. "Why didn't you say so? I'm happy to work up an appetite."

"Not that way, gorgeous. We're going to punch a few things."

"What?" She looks around at what's affectionately known by our firm as the Punch Palace, a private gym we've set up on the same floor as our offices. In our experience dealing with clients, we've realized that they often need to work through emotions they've been bottling up for a while. We'll have masks of their exes made, slap them on our punch bag Bob the Torso, and let them pummel away.

Hitting things is remarkably effective.

I extract something from a cupboard and hold it up. Her eyes widen in surprise.

"But that's . . . you!"

"Yeah, I know. Usually we'd get these made only for exes of clients, but my dear partner Max got one made of me for his own reasons. I don't know. Guy has issues."

I apply it over the head of Bob the Torso. I had thought about getting one of Brian, but I'd rather not have that tool poisoning the room.

She gestures at the punch bag dummy. "Are you expecting me to hit you?"

I wrap my arms around her and pull her close. "What happened to you on the street outside your home made *me* angry, so I can only imagine what you must be going through. I don't know how you're dealing with it, love. You can cry about it and I'm always going to be here for a good weeping jag. You can talk about it to me or a therapist, and I'm here for that, too. But maybe, just maybe, thumping my beautiful face without actually thumping my beautiful face will make you feel better."

"But I'm not mad at you! Or anyone, for that matter." Her laugh is nervous. I get it. No one wants to look foolish or reveal too much when feeling so exposed.

"Indulge me."

I grab a pair of gloves and give her one to put on. She hesitates, then shrugs as if I'm crazy while she inserts her hand into the leather cushion. I help with the other glove, lace her up, then point at the dummy.

"Hit me, baby."

She gives Dummy Lucas a halfhearted push.

"You can do better than that."

"It's weird."

"You're weird. Just do it, Jones."

She tries again, with more of her weight behind it this time. Dummy Lucas jerks back, affronted.

"Harder."

Her next blow is the most forceful yet, and then I see it: satisfaction curling her lips. She shakes out her arms, gives a few bunny hops, and lines up another strike. *Boom!* If this was Real Lucas and not Dummy Lucas, I would not be a happy camper.

"Christ, I felt that one in the family jewels."

"I'm kind of digging this."

Tackling the workout in earnest, it doesn't take long for her to find a groove. *Pow! Wham! Slap!* We're sixties-era Batman over here. After about five minutes, I grab my next piece of equipment: a pair of blocking pads. I strap them onto my palms and raise them up.

"Think you're ready for Big Lucas now, love?"

"Wait, it's one thing to hit the dummy, but what if I hurt you?"

"You won't. I won't let you."

CHAPTER 31

Trinity

I've no idea what Lucas's game is. All I know is that after five minutes thumping his stupid face on the stupid dummy with the stupid gloves I feel better than I have in months.

Maybe I have some anger issues.

Since my attempted mugging—which I insist on labeling as such even though it could have been so much worse—I've been feeling lost. Helpless. Not Trinity.

I didn't even tell the people I cared about what happened to me. I need to hold on to that feeling of control. I take care of people—people don't take care of me.

Except Lucas. He sees what I need. He provides.

And now I'm punching these blocking pads while he stands before me, as solid as an oak, and gloriously shirtless, too. I suspect he could absorb my anger forever. Lucas, the perfect sponge for a woman's scorn.

"Feel free to kick," he says, and I do. Liberated, I raise my right foot and meet the blocking pad with the arch.

"Have you ever taken self-defense classes?"

"No. I—is that what this is?"

"Having a few moves in your arsenal can only empower you."

I slap the pads with my gloved hand. He blocks me.

"Remember, Trinity, you are in control here. You are strong. You are elemental."

I kick. I punch. I rage. I sweat. A lot of sweat.

Then I exhale, each breath leaving me with satisfaction. I'm annoyed I didn't think of this sooner, but sometimes it's impossible to see the forest for the trees. I assumed time would get me there. However, I'm guessing Lucas isn't big on time. Lucas is big on action.

Feeling pretty good about myself, I launch one last kick at Lucas's blocking pads—or what should have been Lucas's blocking pads. I land a target all right and it only *rhymes* with *pads*. Replace that *p* with an *n* and you'll have a better idea of the damage I just inflicted. My personal Mr. Miyagi doubles over, clutching his groin.

"Oh, God, I'm *sooo* sorry." I rush to help him, though he'd probably say I've already done enough. "What can I do? Ice? Kisses? Ice? Blow job?"

His eyes are closed. He has lovely, long eyelashes.

"Uh, please don't touch me, Jones. I need to get through this like a man."

I cover my face so I won't laugh out loud. "I'm sorry," I say in a whisper, as if voice volume might add insult to injury.

His eyes snap open. "Admit it. That felt good for you."

"No!" I'm horrified that he'd think that, but doubly horrified that part of me agrees. I wanted to hurt someone and my foot . . . slipped?

Lying back on the floor (and still protecting his balls with those ridiculous blocking pads), he laughs, knowing exactly what's in my head. I lie beside him.

"Maybe there was a touch of the subconscious in that kick," I admit.

"Subconscious kick to the bollocks? Great name for a band." He turns his head, his grin big and bright. "If it helps my girl, I can take one for the team."

My girl. "The team?"

"Yep. You and me. The team."

I am stunned.

I have friends. I have family. I've never been part of a team.

Tears threaten. "Lucas—"

"Hey, it's okay," he says, rubbing his nose against mine. "I'm on your side. I know you don't always think that because of how we started out. All of that is unimportant. Judge people by what they might be, not are, nor will be."

"What's that from?"

"Robert Browning."

It's about potential. We all have it, buried inside us, waiting to be polished, or to have someone shine a light on it. I think of Lucas's sister, a child trapped in a woman's body, all her potential crushed.

"Are you a divorce lawyer or a life coach?"

"Priest, psychologist, attorney—not that much separating them. But that's my job. When it comes to my personal life, just know that I'm Trinity Jones's biggest fan. And I mean that in the creepiest way possible."

I kiss him hard, pouring all my emotion into it. Is there any greater feeling than the one of being understood by another human being, wholly and completely?

As I slip my tongue between Lucas's lips and absorb his moan, I conclude: There is not.

"Hold on," he says. "Let me free up my hands."

"No!"

"No?"

"Leave those pads on." I push him so he's flat on his back and I straddle his hips, giving a lascivious grind over his groin. "I'm going to take care of business. Unless your balls are too bruised for action?"

"Too bruised for action. Another great name for a band." He raises his padded paws. "I want to touch you."

"I think you might prefer what I have in mind."

"But what about you?"

I fan my fingers out over his bare chest, feeling the flex of his muscles reacting to my touch. "You don't have to be on all the time, Lucas. Your job is not to entertain me."

He waves his pads. "Are you not entertained?"

Always, but I don't want to let him off the hook. I want to do something for this man. Lowering my lips to his neck, I start at the pulse beating at the base of his throat. A suckle, a sip, a lick of my tongue to savor.

"Trin," he gasps as if I've given him so much already. As if I'm giving him everything. His padded hands levitate a few inches off the floor before he remembers that he's trapped. I chuckle at the conclusion he's forced to draw.

"You are a witch," he murmurs, not unkindly.

"A good witch with spells"—another kiss—"and potions" —a light bite of his pec—"and sexy magic." I suck his nipple into my mouth, then lick underneath, moving down, down, down. Slowly I work my way south, dipping my tongue into every ridge, mapping his body, learning his nooks and crannies. My journey takes me down that light dusting of hair, the goodie trail arrowing over those steel-cut abs.

"What do we have here?" I slide a palm across an intriguing bulge. With excruciatingly slowness, I lower the elastic waistband of his shorts past the springy tufts of hair. Out he pops, saluting me with such joy that I can't help my chuckle.

"Don't laugh at my dick."

This only makes me laugh more.

"Trinity, love." He places one of his blocking pads over his very erect cock, and I'm laughing my head off now at the image of Lucas trying to either cover up or create friction.

"Help me out," he groans.

I take him in hand, indulging in a rough pump of his dark, delicious cock. Entranced, I watch how it flushes with blood with each stroke of my hand, how the muscles of his abdomen tighten with each erotic pull. Heat flares between my legs, damp and slick.

"Tell me what you need, baby."

The struggle to admit he needs anything, even this most basic of comforts, is writ large on his face. Lucas is such a lovely, generous man. I need him to understand it's okay for him to deserve this.

I slow down. His breathing escalates.

"Lucas. Whatever you need."

"Tell me how I taste."

Ah, employing my expertise. I know it turns him on when I showcase my stuff. I lick the broad head, tasting salt and musky maleness. "Full-bodied." I run my cheek along the side of his erection. "Meaty." Applying butterfly kisses, I go deeper down his length. "Hints of . . . nuttiness." The velvet nap of my tongue glides over the dusty-dark balls, carefully, given the blow I landed a few minutes ago.

Returning to my initial task, I slip my hand up and down, up and down.

"Harder, love." His eyelids have fallen to half-mast, his lust-stoked pupils barely visible through slits. "Faster."

I give him what he needs, while that spot between my thighs, the one where I crave fullness, blooms with every drop of pre-come dripping from Lucas's cock. The moisture smooths the glide, letting me give him more of that fast and hard stroke destined to bring him higher.

"Take off your shirt," he gasps. "Need to see."

"What do you need?"

His moan is animalistic. "Your tits. Your gorgeous fucking tits."

I don't want to let go my grip to pull off my tee, so I use my free hand to raise my shirt to above my breasts, still encased in a plain black bra. I pop one of the girls out. It's a touch sleazy, and perfectly suits the vibe.

"You wet, Trin? Tell me." He moans loudly. "Fuck, please tell me you are."

I can't get the words out. I'm so turned on right now, watching him fall apart under my touch. He's close, so close, so—

He sits upright, and before I can respond, he's on his knees before me, the blocking pads thrown aside. With both hands, he yanks down my yoga pants and plunges his fingers roughly between my thighs.

I lose my grip on his cock, but I find it again, and now it's a race to reach the peak for each other first. His rough-worn thumb works my clit, while two fingers fork inside me, curling my body toward him. We kiss. Messy, completely devouring each other. I can't focus on my (hand) job because Lucas is yet again putting me first.

That tricky bastard.

I scream as the orgasm shudders through me, radiating from throbbing center to every extremity. So strong I'm left weak, my head falling to his shoulder as Lucas wrings twittery aftershocks from my body.

He pushes me on my back on a gym mat and leans over me, his cock in hand. Two quick strokes is all it takes for him to come, a ropy spurt across my chest. Exhausted and sated, he collapses beside me with his arm across my torso.

We don't speak. We don't move. He's not inside me, but I've never felt closer to another person.

"Not sure I'm going to survive you," he finally says.

"Because I kicked you in the balls?"

He turns his head slightly to bathe me in his true-blue gaze. "Yeah, right in the balls." But it sounds like he means something else. And I know exactly what he's feeling.

Another moment passes while we lie there, then Lucas asks, "Do you have a passport?"

"I do." For the tour of Scottish distilleries I never got around to taking.

"Think you might want to come to the UK with me in a couple of weeks?"

I lean up on my elbow, but before I can respond, he speaks again. "You could stay in London while I'm visiting Lizzie and when I get back we could take in a show—"

"I'd like to meet her."

His breath leaves him in a whoosh. "Yeah?"

"Definitely." Then I kiss him before he can change his mind.

CHAPTER 32

Trinity

"Emily, you know Glinda, right?"

I'm not clear on the details, but Chase's soccer team has made it to a final of some kind, which means Emily has to actually attend or risk looking like a terrible mother. I assumed she'd know the other moms, but it turns out she's never actually come to any of the games.

I'm starting to conclude that Emily needs parenting classes, or at minimum, a good kick in her Pilates-formed tush. When she does step up, it's only in Ari's direction. I told her that Brian would probably be here and it would look better from a custody standpoint if she made an effort.

As I wasn't entirely sure that Emily would show, I asked Gideon and Pete to make an appearance. Their interracial gay-hipster-geek coupledom has Lucas's Birds in ecstatic fits. There's a lot of touching of Gideon's beard and questions about the gorgeous children they have yet to breed. Max, Charlie, and Grant are also here to support Lucas—too sweet —so we're quite a merry bunch on the sidelines.

I unfold my collapsible chair like a Jason Momoa GIF and settle in. Glinda passes around the wine and we all get ready to cheer for the boys (I'm including Lucas's lovely ass cheeks in this collective).

I point out a suitably mortified Chase to Ari. "Wave to your brother, honey."

"I'm bored!"

"Yeah, well, you're going to have to be bored for a bit," I tell her. "This is Chase's day."

"Emily, I'm bored. I want ice cream." That's right, this five-year-old calls her mother by her first name. When she makes a move for her mother's plastic wineglass, Emily deftly deflects and produces some candy item guaranteed to rot Ari's teeth before the age of seven. We do what we must for a moment's peace.

The game starts with Lucas in fine coaching form, screaming encouragement that's its own weird language. "In you go, Macker, take it wide!"

A tall, gangly kid (Macker, I assume) does as he's told and sets the ball up for Chase—who scores! We all stand and cheer, except for Emily, who doesn't realize what happened. "Was that a goal?"

"Too bloody right it was," I say in my terrible British accent, which makes Glinda laugh.

"You're so getting some tonight, Lucas!" She turns to me. "Too presumptuous?"

"Not at all. And oh yes, he is."

I catch Lucas's eye and blow him a kiss. He falls over— literally—while catching it. Such a goof.

I know we have a lot going against us, but we have so much more going for us. He wants to take care of me. He wants to bring fun and joy into my life. And he treats me like a queen, like I deserve nothing but the best. I hadn't realized how much I needed that until Lucas showed me.

I hope I fill gaps for him.

The game continues with a few inspired streaks of play from both sides. By the time the first half is over, the teams are locked in a 1–1 draw. Which is when Brian shows up with Freja.

Freja is Danish, blond, as skinny as my pinkie finger, and towers over everyone in admittedly gorgeous pink heels. Did I mention that she used to be the au pair? For all I know she still fulfills this duty for Brian—he's always been the kind of guy who needs his ass wiped. I question the wisdom of Brian's decision to bring his side piece, as it can only embarrass Chase.

In case you haven't realized it yet, my brother-in-law is a grade A tool.

Emily looks up on seeing him arrive and thrusts a plastic glass of Franzia in his direction. A couple of drops land on Brian's shirt. "Are you kidding?" Ems blurts out.

Ari spots Freja and yells, "Mommy!"

Oh dear.

"Ems, it's okay," I soothe, patting my sister's arm. "Let's go talk to Chase," but my nephew is already walking over.

"Great game, Whiskey Chaser!" I sound too cheerful because I don't want him to be hurt. He nods at his dad, then says hi to Freja. The boy grows up right before my eyes.

Pity his mom can't operate on similar maturity levels. Emily hisses at her soon-to-be ex husband, "You're late, a-hole."

Brian and Freja share a look that says *We're late because we were having sex.*

"Your son's playing an important game, Brian, and—"

"It's not that important, Mom."

Emily ignores Chase. "And you couldn't be bothered. What the hell are you going to do if you have sole custody, *Brian*? If you can't even get out of your whore's bed—"

"Whoa!" Just before I can intervene, Lucas is on hand. I've never been so glad to see his handsome face. "Let's take a time out here. Brian and Freja, maybe you guys would like to join me at the bench. You can cheer from there. Chase, mate, go hydrate and get ready for the second half. You're playing a blinder so far and I need you to be at your best. And Glinda, a little less generous with the pours, okay?"

Glinda adds more to her glass in defiance. "You've always looked better from the back, Lucas. Off you go and show us those lovely hot cross buns!"

Everyone laughs, save Brian, and the situation is instantly defused.

I mouth *thank you* at Lucas, bask in the warmth of his smile, then do a pirouette with my fingers indicating he needs to do as Glinda told him.

"Come on," Lucas says to Chase, who turns with him. Lucas walks away with his hand on my nephew's shoulder, displaying more class than the rest of us put together.

"Verra, verra nice," Glinda says.

I laugh again, feeling happy and lusty, but catch Brian glaring at me, trying to dim my sun. I give him a salute. "All right there, Brian?"

"Fine," he says gruffly, then steers Freja—and her heels—across the field to the other side.

CHAPTER 33

Lucas

We win the game 3–2.

Bloody shocking, actually. I'd already booked the Oven Grinder's back room because I was determined we'd celebrate, win or lose. The presence of both of Chase's parents complicates things, but it's imperative that they learn to be in the same space together in a civil manner. Pizza and beer can only help.

Today I'm not a lawyer. I'm just a guy falling down the rabbit hole of Trinity. These people are important to her, so I'm going to have to make an effort to be there for her. I'm only now starting to figure out that the easiest way to do this would be to remove myself as Brian's lawyer. I probably should have done it the minute Trinity Jones walked into my office, but I thought I could handle it. Where Trinity's concerned, I can't handle shit.

Over pizza, Trinity is being an amazing aunt, playing buffer between Chase's parents and keeping the peace with Chase and Ari. The love she has for her family is such a clear, bright thing. I hope one day to be part of her circle, to be worthy of her love.

"Good game," I hear at my shoulder. Brian stands there, a beer in his hand, offering it to me.

I take it, already wondering about the catch. With guys like Brian, no exchange is ever straightforward. "Yeah, it was. Didn't expect the little buggers to win but they managed to surprise us all."

He grunts. Sniffs. All we're missing is a good ball scratch.

"How are things with Trinity?"

"Good," I say.

"Yeah?"

"Taking it slow."

"Really? I assumed you'd be banging like bunnies once I gave you the go-ahead."

I grip the bottle of beer hard. This fucker needs to be very careful about what comes out of his mouth next. He stays silent, which I imagine must be killing him. I'm getting bored, so I decide to move it along.

"Brian, what's on your mind?"

"Just curious if you've found out anything."

"About?"

"Emily. From Trinity. Anything I can use." He takes a cigar out of his pocket and sniffs it. "I mean, Trinity's got a mouth on her, so I expect she can't shut up about how much she hates me. Women who shoot off like that usually reveal things they shouldn't."

"What, like where Emily has stashed the millions she's been siphoning off the grocery budget?"

"Ha ha," he says without humor. "I expected this would help our case."

"Me with Trinity? No, mate, that's not how it's going to work. That's completely separate from you and me."

He looks like he wants to throw a tantrum. Am I going to

have to baby him through this?

"Now I know you two don't get along, so I don't need to hear you disrespecting her. In fact—"

"Chase looks up to you."

The abrupt change of topic tinged with accusation throws me, so much so that I soften slightly. Divorce is hard on everyone, especially on the people who are most in the wrong. "Well, it's easier to be a coach than a dad."

"I've been trying. Man, you know I have. He's never shown much interest in anything, but he did well out there."

I wince. "Even if he hadn't done well, he's still your son, Brian. You need to figure out a way to connect to him."

"I know that! But you see how *she* is. Making me look bad. And drinking in front of the kids in a public park. That's not legal, is it?"

Probably not, but I've no intention of playing the Boxed Wine Police. Emily and Brian need to be better than this. Neither of them is a saint. "The moms like to make a day of it. It's not really actionable behavior for a custody agreement, if that's what you're thinking."

"What is? You're doing shit for my case."

This is perfect. We can part ways, I can recommend another lawyer, and I don't have to feel guilty about it. But of course, the prick gets the jump on me. "Gotta take a leak. Hold my beer."

With Brian out of my hair, a low chuckle snags my attention. Grant stands at my shoulder, his eyes gleaming in amusement.

"What's so fucking funny?"

"You. This." He waves around the restaurant. "How is this not the definition of a conflict?"

"Got the waiver, didn't I?" And I'm about to wave *bye-bye* to Brian.

"Yeah, you're dick deep in this girl's life. This what you

want?"

"Yes, it is."

Grant thinks about it for a while. That's his MO: tortured deliberation before pronouncing judgment. Just when I think he might have fallen asleep with his eyes open, he speaks.

"I get the impression you have unfinished business from before. Business that prevents you from fully committing to your life here."

That's . . . astute. My partners know I make regular trips back to the UK even if they don't know the reason. I think of Lizzie, rotting away in that bed, her muscles atrophying, her mind a whirligig. She keeps me tied to the Lucas of before. I don't want to lose her, but I wouldn't mind losing him. Sad Lucas. Mad Lucas.

But now that I've confided in Trinity, the burden might rest easier while she helps me shoulder it. Perhaps I could persuade her to move to the UK with me, drink whiskey at the point of origin, help assuage my guilt at spending so much time on the run from my previous life.

"It's hard to let go," I say.

"True."

Sensing an opening, I figure now's my chance. "What happened with Aubrey?"

For a moment I think he won't answer. "She let go before I did. She had to, to keep her sanity."

More riddles. I swear, if it's the last thing I do, I will lock these two in a room and make them fight, fuck, and forgive.

"And what about you?"

"Still glued to the fucking life preserver."

I laugh, because Grant rarely swears and his gallows humor sounds strange on his lips. "How's Callie-Kelly?"

"She's not Aubrey."

Well doesn't that just say it all?

Grant's frowning up a storm, so I place a hand on his arm,

ready to offer the same shoulder I offered to Aubrey. "Listen, if ever you need an ear—"

Grant cuts me off with a jerk of his chin over my shoulder. "I think that conflict of interest waiver is about to be sorely tested, Wright."

Leaning against the wooden pillar near the bar, we have the corridor leading to the restrooms in our sight line. Now I know Trinity can handle herself, but I do not like how Brian has her cornered in that small space.

"Here, hold my beer." I shove my bottle into Grant's hand. "And my client's beer."

"Don't hit him," Grant says lazily, in a way that sounds like I need to definitely keep that option open.

As I approach, I bear witness to this sleazy gem slip from Brian's mouth: "I still feel the spark between us, baby, don't you?"

To which Trinity replies: "I feel something, Brian, but it's more like nausea."

"All right there, love?"

She slides past Brian and grasps my hand. Her eyes flicker with nerves, like she's worried I might have misinterpreted what just happened.

I make it clear I did not. "What the hell are you playing at, Brian?"

"This is between me and Trinity—"

"Oh, there is no me and Trinity," she says. "You thundering wanker!"

I smile at my woman. "Nice."

"Been learning your lingo."

I step in and poke a finger in Brian's chest. "You make it very hard to root for you, Brian. How about you spend some time with your kids instead of hitting on your wife's sister? Who clearly hates your guts, by the way."

"Ever wonder why that is?"

True, I've been curious about Trinity's antipathy toward Brian for quite a while now. His question is sly and sends a shiver of dread down my spine. I need to know.

"Enlighten me."

Brian flicks a look at Trinity, then back to me. "We used to date. She took me home to meet her sister and, well, the rest is history."

My heart pounds, blood rocketing through my veins at the thought of this piece of shit even touching my Trinity. Because that's how I see her. That's how I've always seen her.

But today I'm seeing someone else. Someone with a secret.

Her face is an unpicked lock, raw and twisted with pain.

"Nothing all that serious," Brian continues, oblivious to Trinity's discomfort or more likely acutely aware of it. "College stuff, and then Emily came along and I knew." He looks wistful, maybe even a little regretful that it's come to this.

Shouldn't have slept with the nanny, you old cliché you.

"Ever since, Trinity's held a grudge. Never lets Emily forget what I did. Reminds her that I'm fickle, right, Trin?"

Trinity looks like she's been slapped. She hasn't said a word in her defense, not that she needs to defend herself, but her usual spirit and defiance has left her.

"Dad?"

Chase stands in the corridor, his expression a storm. I can't be sure how much he heard, but whatever it is, it's enough. The kid shakes his head, like he expected nothing less.

"Chase," Trinity calls out, her first verbal response to what just occurred, but he's already gone back into the restaurant's dining room.

"Brian, I think you need to get your house in order," I say, fighting to control my emotions. *Why didn't she tell me?* "Also, we both know this can't go on."

Of course I'm not quick enough. Brian snaps, "Too right it can't. You're fired."

He pushes past me in a bluster. At the entrance to the restaurant, Grant holds out Brian's beer, but the idiot just knocks it out of his hand. The crash of glass to the floor and the resultant beer trickle is the appropriate coda to what just occurred here.

I turn back to Trinity, the words that usually come easy to me locked in my throat. While I wait for an explanation, I line up the facts:

1. She resisted me because I was—*am*—the enemy, and when she gave in she freaked out at the news Brian had given his blessing.
2. This would have been the ideal opportunity to tell me why Brian's waiver bothered her so much. She chose not to reveal this vital information.
3. She also chose not to tell her sister about us. Admittedly it was early days, so I gave her a pass.
4. After everything I confided in her—after I asked her to come to bloody London with me and meet my sister—she still didn't fess up.

One thing you should know about lawyers is that they hate being the last person to know. That goes double for guys who've fallen in love.

Her first words on the topic are: "I promise I was going to tell you."

"Like you were going to tell your sister about us?"

She flinches. I hate it, but my hurt is a raw and raging beast. "For fuck's sake, Trinity, I looked like a right wanker when he dropped it on me. And he took great pleasure in it."

"So this is all about you and your butt-hurt feelings?"

No, she doesn't get to do that. "He blindsided me. And now I understand why you have such a problem with him."

"Because he hurt my sister. Is still hurting my sister."

"Is that all?"

The words hang between us, their meaning sharp and ugly. Deep down, I know why she didn't tell me about Brian—because it hurt her and you don't tell strangers your hurts. I'm still a stranger to her, clearly not worthy of this reveal.

"You think I have feelings for Brian?"

"Oh, I know you have feelings for Brian. I'm just trying to figure out the exact nature of them."

"This isn't a good time. I can't—not now. I need to see if Chase is okay." She tries to step around me.

"Really? We're not going to talk about this?"

"You don't want to talk. You just want to accuse. You just want to look down on me from your high horse and tell me what I must think of Brian. I'm either in love with him or I hate his guts or maybe I want him now that Emily's divorcing him or perhaps I want to see him get his just desserts for dumping me for my sister."

"Well, don't you?"

"Yes!"

He broke her heart and now I'm doing it again. Not ready to die on this hill, I reach for her.

"You don't get to comfort me, Lucas. Not after you hurled your accusations."

She pushes past me, and right past Max and Grant, who are standing at the end of the corridor. Bloody perfect.

"Enjoy that, did you?"

Max winces at my snapped query while Grant raises an expressive eyebrow. "Reckon we don't need to tell you that you made a pig's ear of that, Wright," my southern friend drawls.

No, they do not.

CHAPTER 34

Trinity

I knock back a glass of Laphroaig while Pete and Gideon stare at me in horror.

"What?"

Gid takes the bottle away from me. "You didn't even taste it, heathen."

"Don't care. Tonight I'm all about getting trashed."

"Not on the good liquor you're not. I've got some JD lying around somewhere."

I cover my face with my hands. "How bad do you think that was?"

Pete pushes his glasses up his nose and waits a beat. "On a scale of one to ten, I'd put it at a"—he shrugs—"twelve?"

My groan echoes through their cute-as-a-button apartment in Uptown. They have throw pillows with the word *Love* silk-screened on them in rainbow colors. They're absolutely adorable. "I was going to tell him, but it all happened so long ago and I thought it didn't matter."

Gideon shakes his head in pity. "You did *not* think that, you big-ass fucking liar."

I close my eyes, trying to center myself. He's right. I didn't tell Lucas because I can barely stand to think about that awful time. It still embarrasses me. Being passed over. Being tossed aside. Also, I've always known the story doesn't reflect well on Emily. Lucas didn't need any more ammunition. *I* understand what happened all those years ago, but from the outside, it doesn't look good for her.

Gideon turns to Pete. "You knew her back then and you never even told me."

"Wasn't my story to tell."

Oh, God, if I must.

When Emily was little she had pneumonia. I'm not saying that this is the reason why my sister is a touch, shall we say, helpless. But she's certainly assumed the mantle of damsel throughout her life. I know this. She knows this. But our dynamic has always been big sis looks out for little sis. It fits us, probably because we all have roles to play. These roles make us feel important, and Lord knows, we all want to feel important.

When I was nineteen and a sophomore at University of Illinois I met a guy. He was majoring in communications, which is a bullshit degree, and he had a good line in it, too. But man, he was cute, and more important, interested in me, the girl who spent her life looking out for everyone else. There I was in my sophomore year, taking premed courses and finally starting to blossom into the me I was meant to be. I'd met a guy who laughed at my dumb jokes and told me I had a great ass. Our love was young and unsure, but it was so exciting.

Then I brought him home.

My mom and stepdad had died six months before, so I was Emily's official guardian. Emily was in high school and she needed me to get her through the final year. I actually got into Stanford, but the University of Illinois is a great school, so it wasn't some terrible sacrifice. I would be getting a great education, paying in-state tuition, and taking care of business. Look at me, rocking it!

This night I'll never forget, Emily had a math test the next day and I'd said I'd stop at home, even though I had a paper due in my econ class and I really needed to be knuckling down at the library. My boyfriend offered to give me a ride. Part of me balked. It wasn't like we lived in a shithole neighborhood or had rat droppings everywhere (though the house tended to remain untidy until I had time to clean it on the weekends). But I think it was the first time I sensed that maybe my helicopter-sister attitude might be viewed as weird.

My boyfriend pushed the issue. *I just want to meet this sister you're always talking about.*

Okay, why not? It could be a quick visit, and getting a ride meant I could return to the library to pull an all-nighter and finish my paper.

I remember like yesterday how he was tickling me as I put the key in the door. "Stop. It." I was squirming and laughing and feeling all aflutter.

Two minutes later, it all crashed.

It wasn't the first time I'd been passed over for my sister, but it was the first time it had happened with a boyfriend. Possibly because it was the first time I'd had a boyfriend. Someone who was all mine.

"Brian, this is my sister, Emily," I said, my skin still tingling from where he'd been touching me. Within thirty seconds, the tingle was gone, replaced with a creeping chill that started in my gut and spread tentacles of dread in a chokehold of my heart. Witnessing the thunder bolt between two persons is generally lovely, but not so much when one of them is *your* person.

He offered his hand and Emily giggled, because she was seventeen and a handshake was a grown-up thing to do. My boyfriend was twenty, a junior, studying communications, and here he was communicating his pleasure at meeting my sister.

She didn't pass the math test.

I didn't get my paper in on time.

Brian had the decency to break up with me first. I think. I have to believe that my sister wouldn't do that to me. She asked permission to date him, keeping good form, hos before bros, like I'd ever said no to a single thing she requested of me. *We're just so in love,* she said, her big eyes wide and innocent. They married as soon as they found out she was pregnant—within three months of the thunderbolt—and Brian's family was wealthy enough to see them through and ensure Brian got the degree, the girl, and everything he wanted.

Lucky escape, I hear you say. Definitely. Any affection or attraction I had for Brian died with that tingle. *You can't steal what doesn't want to be stolen,* I insisted to myself. Emily felt bad for a while—I know she did. And I felt bad that she felt bad and went out of my way to make her feel better. I had to act like the adult because that's my role. So maybe I was within my rights to scream at her, or rip her hair out, or give her the cold shoulder. At a minimum. But I got over myself and moved on. I was the supportive sister, her maid of honor, a free babysitter for their date nights. Chase and his chubby cheeks have always been my weakness.

I'm trying not to take pleasure in the collapse of their marriage. People are being hurt, the kids are confused, and Brian is really a turdweasel, but . . . but I don't think he's a great guy. I think my sister deserves better and Chase deserves a more attentive father and role model. And if it means I won't have to see Brian's ass-chin face anymore, that's a freakin' bonus.

I didn't share my past with Lucas because when you're insisting you're in a fling with a younger, hotter, out-of-your-league guy, you adopt a certain mindset, namely: Don't share the deep stuff, especially the hurts that shaped you.

But after seeing the look on Lucas's face when Brian dropped the bombshell, I know I screwed up. I wished I'd been brave Trinity, the woman who used to love roller coasters, who would jump into anything. I wish I could have trusted my instincts.

How do I tell him that I had no idea he was the one until I was so deep that I was drowning in him?

CHAPTER 35

Lucas

"So, he's a tool?"

I eye Aubrey over my ale and wait a beat before responding. We're at the Legal Eagle, a regular haunt near the courts, though the usually easy vibe is being ruined by the baseball game on the TV.

"Show me a client going through divorce who isn't, princess. There is an incontrovertible link between toolhood and marriage dissolution, especially in the male of the species."

She snorts. "You've changed your tune. I thought it was all boo-hoo, my penis makes me sad but shouldn't disqualify me from fatherhood."

"I'm still the guy you want in your corner if you're a dad with a tricky custody issue, but Brian Carson has stepped on my last nerve. However, I know you'll do your best to represent him fully and to the utmost of your abilities."

"Stow it, Wright. I've already said I'll take it on."

I've spent the last thirty minutes filling Aubrey in on Brian's case. As much as I despise the toxic toad—and especially after what I've just learned about him and Trinity—I feel an obligation to ensure he gets the best money can buy. Aubrey is a pistol, so I know he's in competent hands.

She flips through the paperwork I've given her. "So basically, she needs to sell up, get a job, and accept ownership over her situation."

"Bingo."

"And . . ." She knows I'm hedging.

"And she leaves the kids with Trinity, probably more than a woman in a custody battle should. It's not straight-up neglect, but . . ." I know I shouldn't compare my situation, but we all arrive with baggage that influences us. Emily's not trying that hard when it comes to her kids, Chase in particular.

"You think we should get a guardian *ad litem?*"

"Might be time." A guardian ad litem is a court-appointed lawyer who works on behalf of the kids in a custody dispute. I've been hoping Brian and Emily could work this out like adults, but neither of them can get out of their way long enough to come to an agreement that's in the best interests of the kids.

"A little leverage never hurt." Aubrey looks thoughtful. "So unloading Carson opens things up for you and Trinity now."

It would if we were on speaking terms. I'm still fuming, not because it was Brian, but because she chose not to share. I unburdened and Trinity was there for me, listening, soothing. But she clearly doesn't see me the same way. She doesn't see me as the person who will make her better. Who will catch her when she falls.

I wasn't there for Lizzie—I literally didn't catch her. (And that's the correct context for *literally.* Look it up, vocab nerds.) If I can't be that for Trinity, then what use am I?

A louder than usual buzz at the bar area steals our focus. People are pointing at the TV screen, and I squint to figure out what the fuss is all about.

"Bloody 'ell, do you see that?"

Aubrey's mouth hitches and she shakes her head. "Good for him."

Ladies and gentlemen, we are witnessing romance in full bloom. The camera has zoomed in on the scoreboard at the Cubs game at Wrigley Field—and it's a doozy. The words *Max* and *Charlie,* connected with a big fucking heart symbol, are tearing up the eyes of every coldhearted cynic at the Legal Eagle.

"Gotta text him. Can't believe he's making me watch fucking baseball." I shoot off a text affirming that I knew this —a bloody proposal!—would happen all along. I so love being proved right.

"I miss him," Aubrey murmurs.

"Who, Grant?"

She rolls her eyes at the apparent absurdity. "Max. He and I used to be good friends."

"But Grant got him in the divorce."

"Right. What is it they say? Divorce is like the death of a small civilization. All these ripple effects that start small and . . ." She mimics an explosion with her hands.

I think on Lizzie and how her accident has affected me, except it's almost the other way around. An explosive event that's rippled inward, contracting my organs and shriveling my heart. The Lucas I show on the outside is not the Lucas that festers on the inside.

I am a fraud. Is that why Trinity can't trust me?

"Hey, what's wrong? You look like someone walked over your grave."

Sure. Dead man drinking.

I peer up at the TV screen. The romance has moved on, a fleeting moment to brighten up that most dull of American sports. Is that what I'm doing with Trinity? Trying to desperately craft bubble-bright moments to take me away from myself?

A small hand covers mine. "Lucas, are you okay?"

"Just fine," I mutter, and squeeze her hand back, more to make her feel better than myself. God forbid I let anyone see the pain.

Except Trinity. She's seen it, and I thought she understood.

But not enough to share hers.

My phone vibrates and I check it, expecting a response from Max. I texted the prick five minutes ago, after all.

It's not Max. Dammit, but I wish it was.

POLICE STATIONS ARE NOT my favorite places. Between the belligerent drunks and grouchy wankers, it's an environment guaranteed to put the fear of God into the most hardened of criminals. And that's just the coppers. *Zing!*

I've no doubt my current client is terrified. When I was pinched for stealing, it was the scariest time of my life. Finally, after what seems like an eternity, the door to the interview area opens and a ruddy-faced officer brings him out.

I place my hands on Chase's shoulders and squeeze. "What. The. Fuck."

Those shoulders shrug under my touch. "I screwed up."

"Uh, yeah you did." I level the police officer with my no-shit, unhand-my-client gaze. "What happens next?"

"He's lucky. No charges will be filed, but we'll be watching him. Lucky kid, having a lawyer on retainer."

"I have a good mind to tell them to go ahead and file those charges. Christ, if you needed money for a video game, I would have given it to you, you bloody idiot!"

Another shrug. We both know it wasn't about the money.

"Where's your partner in crime?" Carlos was also nabbed by security at Best Buy.

The officer answers. "His parents picked him up ten minutes ago. And we tried calling this one's mother. Left a message for his aunt, too."

No surprise, there. Emily Carson dropped out of the running for Mother of the Year a long time ago.

"Look, about what happened after the game—"

"When we all found out Trinity used to hook up with my dad?" He pushes out the words through gritted teeth.

"Yeah, that. Listen, it all happened a long time ago. Don't be too hard on them, okay?"

"She should have told us."

Agreed, but I'm trying to see it from her point of view. Not everyone is comfortable opening a vein. Trinity's spent so long putting aside her problems for everyone else that the idea of leaning on anyone is nowhere near instinctual.

"So she didn't tell us. People make choices, do what they think is best at the time. She's always the one listening to everyone else, and it probably never occurred to her that she has sensitive men in her life like you and me who'll make her a cup of tea and buy her those disgusting Cadbury Crème Eggs and let her unload all her problems."

"I suppose," Chase says, his tone one of teenage suspicion. "Those eggs are freakin' gross, aren't they?"

"Totally manky, mate."

"Chase!" A familiar voice rings out.

Chase's eyes fly wide. "You called him?"

"Yep. There's no escaping this."

Chase pulls away from me, hurt in his eyes at my betrayal. But he doesn't get far because his father gathers him in his arms.

"Are you okay?" Brian asks gruffly.

"Course I am. It was just a misunderstanding."

This sets Brian off into a haze of righteous indignation. "Who the hell did this to my son?"

"Brian," I say tiredly. "You're not going to win this battle. Just count your lucky stars that the store is not going to press charges."

A moment passes where I wonder if the man will do the right thing: be the parent his kid needs. Tick. Tock.

"Do I need to sign something?" His tone is, for once, conciliatory.

The officer, who is watching this play with interest, weighs in. "Free to go, but keep an eye on him."

Brian gives a curt nod to the man in blue, then to me, "Thanks, I owe you one."

"Full service, mate, even when I'm no longer your lawyer."

Lowering his voice, he thrusts out his hand. "About what happened over the weekend. I'd had one too many, made a bad call. Are we good?"

No, we're not. You hurt my girl, then and now. You hurt your kids and your behavior is likely the reason Chase is acting out.

But I'm feeling magnanimous. If I can work things out with Trinity, there's a good chance that I'll be clinking beer bottles with Brian at family cookouts and birthday parties. Time to let bygones get gone.

I take his outstretched hand. "Good luck, Brian. And listen to Aubrey, she'll put you right."

Before Brian can answer, another voice, one filled with anguish, calls out. It should be Chase's mom, but it's not.

Trinity stalks in like a mama bear ready to do battle for her young, and damn, it's hot. Her eyes widen on seeing me; her lips purse on seeing Brian.

"What the hell is *he* doing here?"

225

CHAPTER 36

Trinity

The Chicago Police Department called forty-five minutes ago, but it was too loud at the bar to hear my phone, which was charging instead of stuffed down my cleavage. My sweet, chubby-cheeked nephew is in the pokey! I assume it's a frame job, probably with Ari at the foundation. Emily wasn't picking up so I expected to find her here. Instead I find Foreskin.

Not really caring for the answer to my own question, I hug Chase hard. "What happened? Are you okay? Oh my God, were you in lockup with winos and criminals?" I sniff, seeking out the scent of urine, flop sweat, and brown bag vino.

Chase winces. Since he witnessed the drama of finding out I'd once dated his father, he's been cool toward me. It breaks my heart. "I'm okay," he mutters. "Lucas is here. And he called Dad."

Lucas called Brian. Of course. "Well, I'll take you home."

"He's coming home with me," Brian says. "If his mother

—" He stops and takes a look at his son. What I never thought would transpire in a million years happens right before my eyes.

The man shuts the fuck up.

Brian doesn't want to bad-mouth Emily in front of Chase. I suppose I should be grateful for this brief character growth spurt, but I'm not.

"You can see him this weekend per the agreement."

"Trinity . . ." Lucas says, the first thing he's said since I arrived.

God, he looks good. Better than good. And serious. And a little bit tired.

I'm reminded of something Pops would say: *A person isn't who they are during the last conversation you had with them— they're who they've been throughout your whole relationship.* I know Lucas was sucker punched by the news I'd once been with Brian. I have to give us a chance to make that right.

"I can't just let you go with him," I say to Chase, giving him the opening to express his wishes.

"I'm his father," Brian says.

So much I could say to that. "Yes, but—"

Lucas cuts in. "They'll be fine, Trinity."

I don't want to get into a shouting match here, at the police station of all places. Chase isn't objecting, either. "I—I suppose it's okay. But call your mom?" Who should be here. Her absence is a dark, rain-heavy cloud. I hug him again and give him a sloppy kiss, then watch them leave, feeling like I've failed and let Emily down.

A few seconds later, Lucas has steered me out of the station and onto the street.

"Lucas—"

"What happened at the weekend, Trinity—can we talk about that?"

"Yes, of course."

"I overreacted," he says. "Who you were with before is none of my business, and I can only say that it took me by surprise. That's my excuse. I was jealous. Madly so. And I felt blindsided when my client dropped it on me. I already felt he wielded too much power over me because of this conflict situation, and he seemed to relish telling me. My reaction was petty and I'm sorry."

I'm stunned by his apology, at how unvarnished it is. Lucas has to be one of the most sincere and honest people I know. I try to surround myself with such people, but it can be hard finding it in a partner. And that's what Lucas is starting to feel like. My partner.

"This isn't all on you. I should have told you, but—"

"You didn't. You had your reasons."

He thinks he knows my reasons. Jealousy, resentment, love unrequited. My feelings for Brian might have once been a complex tapestry woven with all those emotions, but no more.

I've never been a big sharer, not even with friends. People come to me with their troubles, not the other way around. Now I'm languishing in undiscovered country, fumbling around without a map. I need to fire up my rusty compass and give Lucas what he needs.

I need to open up.

"Yes, I have feelings for Brian, but not in the way you think. I didn't share with you what happened because I— well, I never talk about it. In fact, I've never shared it with anyone. Pete knew because we went to college together, but I brushed it off, said it was no biggie, when really what happened felt so personal and hurt me for a long time." The admission presses the space around my heart. I haul in a breath, and it's surprisingly jagged. "Can I honestly say I don't harbor some resentment toward him? No, I—I can't. For a long time, I felt invisible, undesired, unloved, but I put my hurt aside because holding on to it interfered with my relationship with my sister. She needs me, and I need her, so I had to get over it."

"Your feelings, your problem?"

"Yes. We all have to take responsibility for how we feel. Learn to . . . manage it."

He clearly doesn't agree. "Emily has no responsibility here?"

"You can't steal what doesn't want to be stolen." I say it as if that should settle the matter. It's been my mantra for fifteen years. "So now you understand how I feel about Brian. Perhaps my resentment is seeping into this divorce process, but when push comes to shove, I know what's best for my family. I wish you'd called me tonight, not Brian. Who I thought you were no longer representing."

Lucas stares at me, his blue eyes on fire, then says slowly, "He's Chase's dad."

"Oh, *now* he wants to step up."

"Chase has a mother. A father. Who are both capable of caring for him if they put some damn effort into it. You are not the parent here, Trinity. Though you've been playing one to both Emily and her kids."

The words sting. "I'm sure Emily just lost track of time."

"I don't doubt it. Booze will do that." Those cobalt-blue eyes I usually want to get lost in are glass-hard. "Emily's been trying to shut Brian out for a while, and I'm not so sure she's doing it for the good of the kids. She's using her children as a means to get more for herself. Money, the house, a way of not taking responsibility. You can't keep covering for her, Trinity."

"I—I'm not. She's my sister. And you're not even Brian's lawyer, yet you're still working for him. You didn't have to do that. You don't owe him anything." *Your duty should be to me,* I want to scream at him.

"No, I don't, but I know what it's like. What Chase is going through."

"You can't use your personal experience to decide this."

"What else am I going to use? What else can any of us use? You told me once that my choice of profession sounded like a crusade, that I had to have a good reason. I do. I know Brian's a dick, but it's not enough to deny him his rights. And did it ever occur to you that maybe you should take a page from my book, Trinity? Acknowledge your pain, recognize that what Emily did to you—continues to do to you—shouldn't be glossed over to keep the bloody peace?"

I've negotiated my version of the truth so peace will reign, but that's too gray for Lucas. He'd prefer to apportion blame where it's due. He has a cause to promote, a score to settle.

"You need to quit making excuses for Emily."

"Excuses? I'm not—"

"Tell me in all honesty that Emily's a good mother."

"She—she adores her kids." It sounds weak and ineffectual in my mouth.

"Right. I've no doubt she does. But you've been enabling her for so long, Trinity, that you can't see her for what she is. A bloodsucker. All she does is take, love. She's bleeding you dry."

I'm stunned, not at the words but at the *yes, yes, yes* my traitorous heart is chanting in agreement. He's right, but I refuse to reckon with it because as soon as I do—as soon as I accept it as fact—I lose some important part of myself. Big sister Trinity. Caregiver Trinity. The role I took on gladly as a girl. Who am I outside of these parts I've been playing for so long?

I can help Emily. I can shape her into a better mom.

"She's my sister. She is *not* bleeding me dry. Not everyone is an emotional prodigy who emerges from the womb fully formed. Some of us need a little help along the way. I'm happy to be that for my sister. Is this about me? Are you trying to punish me because I was with Brian once and I didn't fess up?"

"Don't be daft. I just don't happen to agree with how your sister is getting away with everything. She's so damn helpless and she's using you to shield her bad behavior."

I'm starting to understand that Lucas feels more than anyone I know. Every case is personal for him. Every relationship. And it can all be traced back to a single source.

"Your mom screwed you over. I get it. I've lived it myself. But you can't use that as a yardstick by which you measure every single experience. You can't punish every person because they fail to live up to your standards."

"Like you're punishing Brian because of what happened years ago? Maybe Chase's arrest is the wake-up call your sister needs, Trinity. Maybe it's the one *you* need."

Anger flares. "Stop making this about me."

"You're not Chase's mother. Maybe you look at him and think in another lifetime you should've been, but you're not. Brian picked her. And dammit, I'm glad he did because you're here with me."

He doesn't sound all that glad about it. He sounds miserable.

"I told you what would happen if you screwed over my sister."

"Dammit, Trinity!"

I jump at his outburst. A couple of cops heading inside hover near the entrance, ready to intervene. "I won't apologize for trying to do my best by those kids."

I'm shaking at the force of his words. "We can't agree on this. We *won't* agree on this." Not when I know I'm the best chance they have.

He moves in and cups my shoulders. His heat brands me, yet my heart is icing over.

"I know this is hard, Trinity. You've carved out a certain place, a role that's comfortable for you in your family. But that doesn't mean it's healthy. You're going to have to choose."

This again. "What? You over my sister?"

There's a wryness to his expression, sadness in his kind eyes. "No, love, I'd never expect that. What I mean is you. I need you to choose *you*."

"Don't—don't be absurd. That's not what this is about."

"Isn't it?"

"My sister needs me. I've always been the stronger one."

"I know, but the best thing you can do is let her stumble. Fall. Screw up. You can't be there to pick up the pieces every time. For fuck's sake, you didn't even tell her you were attacked."

I jerk away from him, his touch burning instead of soothing. "She's got enough going on." As do I, but I can handle it. Or at least, I was handling it until Lucas blasted into my life pushing and probing and making me question everything. Who I am and where I fit in. I'm sick of myself, and if I'm being honest, I'm sick of Emily—but I'm not ready to give up on her.

"And what about you, Trinity? When's it going to be your turn? When are you going to take on the lead role instead of hanging back in the chorus?"

"My turn? It doesn't have to be an either/or proposition, Lucas. I can be a good sister and still find time for me, for a relationship. But maybe that time I find will never be enough. Nothing is half measures with you. It's all or nothing, and I don't think I have what you need."

Those words appear to strike him like cannonballs, and

when he speaks, it's low, seemingly torn from somewhere deep inside.

"I won't apologize for wanting more, Trinity. For wanting to be wrapped in us until I can barely breathe. What's the point in half measures? If something—someone—is worth it, why not give it everything you have in you to give? All the want and need and energy and love? I've lived half my life feeling guilty for just surviving. For being the one who made it. I want more. I want beauty and life and beer and football. I want that with you."

I don't know how to respond. I think he just told me loved me right in the middle of telling me I'm a screw-up.

And I love him, love him, love him. But it's not enough, not when we're at such cross-purposes. Not when he thinks I'm so wrong that nothing could ever feel right between us.

"Lucas—I can't. We can't."

And then I turn and walk away.

CHAPTER 37

Lucas

I'm miserable and everyone knows it. My mood is not helped by Sadie sticking her head around the door of my office two days after my clash with Trinity and asking, "You ready?"

"For what?"

"Lucas, darling, don't say you've forgotten our lunch date!" I close my eyes, remembering now that I have a standing monthly lunch date with Susanne Henderson and Sadie, and today's the day. That's Susie's voice outside my door making me feel like a chump.

"He did forget," Sadie says. "But then his mind has been elsewhere for a while."

"I'm coming, I'm coming!"

I grab my jacket and head out to meet the ladies. Susanne is Max's mother, a British blonde in her midfifties, and an absolute stunner. Like Sadie, she thinks I need looking after. Usually, I don't mind playing this up because I enjoy the attention, but I'm not sure I can handle their anal probing today.

"Susie!" I hug her and do the Euro double kiss. "Left that old git you call a husband yet?"

"He's keeping me in lavish style, darling. I'm afraid you'll have to up your game to compete."

Sadie sighs. "You never ask if I've left *my* husband."

"Because your former marine, current fire captain husband, would probably kick my ass if I laid a hand on you, sweets."

The ladies giggle. It's a game we play.

"Mom, what are you doing here?" Max walks out of the lift, having just come in from court. He kisses his mother, then splits a look among all the parties. "Is this an intervention for Lucas? Please say it is. I have *so* much to say."

"I'm taking them to lunch, Maxie," I tell him, enjoying his surprise. These days, it's the little things.

"You mean to say, Mom, that you've come all the way from the North Shore to be wined and dined by this limey idiot?"

"Hey! Less of the idiot. And can I help it if I'm too charming?" I put both my arms akimbo. "Ladies, shall we?"

We exit with the heat of Max's glare burning holes in my back. Ten minutes later we're seated at a nice Riverwalk eating establishment with G and Ts for our first round. Sadie and Susanne exchange a look.

"Okay, out with it."

Susanne opens her mouth, then waves at a point behind me. I look up to see Aubrey coming toward us. She takes a seat at our table.

"Don't say you started in on him without me."

"Wait. Is this an *actual* fucking intervention?"

"Language, Lucas," Sadie says. "We've added Aubrey to the think tank. It's always good to have a millennial on board."

"I'm a bloody millennial!" I protest.

Aubrey regards me with pity. "Yes, but you're the problem."

"I am not the—"

"Sadie tells me you've been snippy, Lucas," Susanne cuts in. "You are never snippy. Also, that you're engaging in public arguments in historic pizza parlors with a lovely woman who's out of your league."

Thanks, Max and Grant.

"You haven't even heard about the one outside the cop shop."

"Surprised you got this far," Sadie offers gleefully. "In fact, we were pretty sure she wasn't going to go for it."

"We?"

"Max and me. We lost a bet. Grant had your number."

Damn bunch of no-good gossips. "Why wouldn't she go for it? I'm considered a catch, you know."

She sips her G and T, flutters her eyelashes. "Yes, but you're so much work, hon."

I know that!

"And yet she likes you," Susanne says with a pat on my hand and a gentleness in her voice.

You might say I'm ripe for mothering. No one knows about my mum or Lizzie, but these women—minus Aubrey, who I'm convinced is here to acquire ammunition for some nefarious plot—have gleaned enough to feel some ownership over me and my problems. I should be annoyed that they think I need looking after, but the truth is, I do need it.

"Trinity and I have a different way of viewing the world. Ultimately, I think people are selfish tossers who should be allowed to make mistakes and fail. Trinity wants to coddle people and wrap them up in cotton wool."

"So she likes to care for people," Aubrey says. "What's wrong with that?"

I find this rich coming from the woman with edges sharp enough to slice an opposing counsel from throat to balls. My glare in her direction makes this clear.

"What's wrong with it is when you spend so much time looking out for other people that you forget to live your own life." I practically shout the words and earn a few weird looks from other diners.

Susanne tilts her head. "And you've never looked out for anyone?"

"No." The lie tastes like stale ciggie butts on my tongue. "Better to think of number one."

Sadie scoffs. "You don't believe that for a second."

Maybe I do, maybe I don't. I certainly have been thinking of my sister less and less, as if there isn't room in my heart for both her and the woman I've fallen in love with. I told Trinity to start thinking of herself, to grasp the brass ring—her own happiness—when we all know I'm talking about me. I want to be the prize.

I am such a fucking diva.

"So, she's a do-gooder," Aubrey says from behind her menu. "Can't you just support her do-goodery?"

"Not when it's enabling other people's bad behavior. Enabling hurts people, Aubrey."

"I suppose," she says quietly.

Sadie's mouth hitches at one corner. "Should I get the mac and cheese? Seems so heavy for summer."

"You always get the mac and cheese," I mutter.

"Hard to teach an old dog new tricks."

I roll my eyes. "Subtlety, thy name is Sadie."

Susanne puts her menu down; an eyebrow tilt summons the waiter. "Darling, you'd know I'd adopt you if Max wouldn't throw a fit about all the attention it would divert from him."

"Bloody Max. Ruining everything."

"But I—*we*—can still impart wisdom honed to sharp, jagged points by years of messy motherhood. Now we all come with baggage, some of us more than others." She flicks a glance at Aubrey, who suddenly looks incredibly sad. "You never talk about your mother, but I know she failed you somehow and that's made you quite, well, intolerant of parents who aren't pulling their weight in the child-rearing arena. Ultimately, you want it all to be hunky-dory and you don't like to see anyone take advantage, especially of someone you love."

I shift in my seat. "Maybe."

Our waiter chooses this moment to take our orders so I can stew on what Susanne just said. Once he's gone, Sadie picks up the baton in true tag team *Sex and the City* brunch style.

"You have to let her figure this out, but at the same time, maybe you could be a little less—"

"Pushy?" Aubrey says, ripping a piece of bread off the loaf just dropped at our table.

"I was going to say needy," Sadie says, "but pushy will do."

"So I'm a needy, pushy, intolerant, baggage-laden bugger with too-high-standards who can't abide when my woman won't put me first."

"Sounds about right," Aubrey chimes in.

"But you're very intuitive," Susanne soothes. "If we'd said any of this to Max or James, it would have taken them all day to get it."

Bully for me.

All three of them smile at me, bathing me with the attention I crave. I should be in heaven, wallowing in all the drama and self-pity I've manufactured.

Instead I'm in hell.

CHAPTER 38

Trinity

*E*mily is pacing the living room, her hands balled into fists of fury.

"Well, his new lawyer is a bitch. Aubrey something. Total cow!"

I cross my arms over my chest. "So where were you when your son used his one phone call, Emily?"

She snaps to attention. "My phone was out of juice and Magda was over with little Ainsley. I've grounded Chase for the rest of the summer. That Carlos is such a bad influence."

I'm not so sure. I'm beginning to think Emily is just not handling her separation with a whole lot of maturity and Chase is getting the short end of the stick.

"You have more than one kid, Ems."

Her eyes widen. "I knew this would happen. I knew he'd turn you against me."

"Don't be so dramatic." My heart keens in pain, remembering my last conversation with Lucas. *"I want beauty and life*

239

and beer and football. I want that with you." And I couldn't give it to him. "We're not together anymore."

Emily drags me to the sofa. "He dumped you?"

"So sure I'm the dumpee?"

"No—that's not what I meant. You're beautiful and confident and totally kick ass. You can get any guy you want."

This is so ridiculous I laugh hysterically.

Emily interprets it differently. "That bastard, look what he's done to you. I knew he was using you to spy on me."

I don't know that at all, and what's more important, I don't believe it. Lucas and I might have our differences, but I always trusted that he had my best interests at heart. Protecting me. Helping me unlock the person I want to be. I felt enveloped with him, and that's what he wanted back. Something more all consuming than maybe I have it in me to give.

"Lucas wasn't—isn't like that."

Emily pats my hand. "Sis, I know you'd like to think he wanted you for, well, you. No one likes to think they've been used, but let's face it. He sold me out—sold *us* out—to Brian by calling him to the police station. Like a double agent when he supposedly didn't work for him anymore."

"No." I pull away from her. "Lucas called Brian because he operates under a very specific value system. I don't agree with his reasons here, but neither do I believe he targeted me to get intel on you. We never talked about you. He was too committed to maintaining an ethical separation." I can't explain to her about his sister, about all the pain his mother's negligence caused him, and how all his decisions are filtered through that awful experience. It goes bone deep with him, and it's not my story to tell.

Emily's expression is filled with pity, and her silence makes it bloom into something malevolent.

"Do you think I can't get a guy that amazing? Is that it?"

Her pause hurts me more than I'll ever admit. "Of course not! I mean, yes, he's a catch and he's a total hottie and younger, but there's no reason why you can't win a guy like that. Just not *this* one. He's all wrong for you."

Really? *This* feels wrong. This state of not-with-Lucas feels unnatural.

I try to get us back to the real problem. Not Lucas and me, but what he said was the most important issue here. "This is about the kids, Ems, what's best for them. If you want Brian to support two households, then downsizing shouldn't be outside the realm of possibility. Getting a job should be on the table. And not spending all your time boozing should definitely be on the checklist."

She barks out a laugh. "He's brainwashed you."

I sigh, annoyed with her obtuseness. Just plain annoyed.

Yet I still can't let go of my part. It's ingrained in me, the loving sister who knows best.

"I'm on your side, Emily, but . . ."

"But, what?"

I inhale sharply. "Why does it always have to be about you?"

"It's—it's not!" Her eyes well. "He chose someone else. You don't know what it's like to be passed over for the younger, newer model."

"Don't I?" My anger uncoils and sharpens my tongue. "All these years I've watched you with Brian. With the man who was mine before he was yours. Who I know you slept with while he was still technically my boyfriend—"

She opens her mouth. I hold up my hand.

"Don't, Ems. I fucking can't with you right now. I don't want Brian. This isn't about that, but this playing the martyr has to stop. Time to grow a pair and take control of your life."

And maybe time to take my own advice.

∽

THE TURNOUT IS MUCH BETTER than I could have possibly expected.

My first Whiskey, Women, and Song event is a hit. Charlie with her wedding planner connections was able to snag me a private room at a bar in Lincoln Park for free. Aubrey corralled her lady lawyer posse, while Glinda ensured every soccer mom agreed to forego the Franzia rosé and give whiskey a shot. Two of Lucas's Birds have already thrown up.

It's a great success.

The Alanis Morissette–style singer who's playing for tips —and making out like a bandit—has just rested her acoustic guitar for a break during her set. I'm walking around, practically orgasming at the sight of women networking and gossiping and coughing their way through the whiskey tasting. Bringing people together warms my ice-compacted heart.

I know Lucas has a penis—a lovely penis, in fact—and that this effectively disqualifies him from tonight's event, but I still expected him to stop by. Even when we're on the outs, I've never doubted his support. Unlike Emily, who has elected to take our argument and make it all about her.

She didn't show.

I might not have invited her.

"So this one has a kind of"—Penny, Charlie's bestie, sloshes her Glenfiddich around like mouthwash and swallows—"mossy flavor." She consults the tasting chart. "Is that right?"

I laugh. "Only if you think it tastes that way. There's no right or wrong, but for a lot of people, it tastes of a memory. A certain nostalgia."

I think of my granddad in his leather chair, the scent of old books, the lingering smoke of a cigar. I think of the time before when it wasn't all on my shoulders. When I didn't feel so alone.

I think of Lucas.

"Back in a second," I mutter, emotion building in my chest. Over at the bar, I fuss with glasses and a bottle of Ardbeg.

"You okay?" I hear behind me.

Aubrey stands there, her dark head cocked, her expression one of mild disinterest.

"Yes, fine! Better not consort with me, the enemy and all that."

"I think we can be professional here. And as hot as you are, I'd need a couple more of these drams in me to make a move." She scrunches up her mouth, building to say something. "So, I want to apologize for how I behaved at Max's party. I was sort of obnoxious."

"Oh, God, no!"

"I was. Don't argue with me. You'll never win." She grins. "I didn't cross paths with my ex much until my firm moved into his building this summer and then at this party over at Max's. We've been doing this great job of keeping our distance and I knew he was coming, so I liquored up. I'm a bit embarrassed." She puts her drink down on the bar and stares at it accusingly. "I was getting all personal with you and shooting my mouth off, and then he shows up with someone. I thought it would take longer, I suppose." Her eyes go suspiciously shiny.

I have no choice but to take her in my arms. She's small and fragile, and as she relaxes into me, I marvel at how the human condition can be both so lovely and so painful.

Aubrey sniffs against my neck. "What's this for?"

"You looked like you needed it."

She pulls away in a slow glide. "Hey, you give good hugs."

"I know."

"Modest, too." She looks at me directly, her eyes soft with emotion, but mostly with kindness. "So in all my years as a divorce lawyer, I've learned this much when dealing with couples, kids, friends, and family: It's impossible not to take a side. And if you're on the wrong end of that, it can hurt like a mother. When I split from Grant, I lost more than a husband. I lost part of my identity, and sometimes I wish I could just have a do-over with some of the fights. Take back some of the sharp words. Explain things better without all the emotion getting in the way."

"Two divorce lawyers in a relationship—that has to be weird."

Her smile is knowing. "You need to be on your best game, that's for sure. What I'm trying to say is that maybe with Lucas you can try to see where he's coming from."

I know this is personal for him. What happened with his sister is a weight on his broad shoulders, the guilt of surviving still heavy after all these years. Yet he still found time to be here for me. When I was ill, when I needed to dig deep to find the me I used to be, when I finally realized that sharing was painful but cathartic.

If ever anyone needed to be called on her shit, it's me.

Aubrey nods at a point over my shoulder. "I'll leave you to it."

"Hey, sis." I turn to find Emily, her big blue eyes blinking in trepidation. Oh, my heart. She came out to support me, found a way even though I didn't invite her. Maybe she's more resourceful than I gave her credit for.

"Ems!"

"Looks like a good night." She arcs her gaze over the space, her mouth in a wobble.

"I'm so glad you made it."

"Trin, I'm sorry," she says, her voice shaking. "About Brian. About Chase. About taking you for granted and being an all-'round bitch."

"No, no, that's not true. We both settled into a groove that worked for so long, and maybe we just needed a reset." I hold her arms to get a good look at her. Her eyes are red, raw from emotion. "I've tried to be there for you, but—"

"I haven't been there for you?"

"No! I haven't let you be. I wanted to be the one everyone relies on, the strong shoulders, so I could—I don't know—feel superior, I suppose. I've underestimated your strength, Ems. You can survive Brian and you don't need my help, but I'm here if you do."

"Jesus, Trin. How could I do any of this without you? I'm already a mess, just think what I'd be like if I didn't have you in my life." We fall into each other's arms, our beef not forgotten, but I hope halfway to being forgiven.

For the next hour, I squire Emily around, introducing her to people, and watch as she networks and builds new friendships. Who knows? Maybe she'll find a job out of a conversation she has tonight. And if she doesn't, we'll figure it out—as a team.

A little later, my phone buzzes. It's him! I take a deep breath and answer cheerfully, feeling confident that it's a good night for reconciliation.

"Hey!"

"Hullo, Trin. Not disturbing you, am I?"

"Not, not at all. How are you?"

"Oh, hot as ever. You know."

He sounds off, his voice a slight slur wrapped in faux cheer. God, I've missed him. "Lucas, are you . . . drunk?"

"I might have had a few. Drank some of that shite you ply to your punters."

Shock bolts through me. "You're drinking whiskey?"

"I am. Keeps you in my head. I knew you had your event tonight, so I raised a glass or two in your honor. Going good?"

"Yeah, great. A nice showing."

"Well, I know I'm not a woman, but I would have snuck in if I was there, love."

Then why didn't you? Why are you not here?

"I just wanted to wish you well and say I'm sorry and hear your voice before—before I go to sleep."

His voice breaks on the second *before* and I realize that something is terribly wrong. And sleeping? Why would he be sleeping at 9 P.M.?

"Baby, where are you?"

"Nowhere. Everywhere. Citizen of the world, that's me. I —" He inhales a shaky breath. "I shouldn't have bothered you. I'm sorry about what happened. About everything. You're right. Family is all that matters and I had no right to tell you different. To tell you how to deal with your damage. I brought my personal stuff into it and fuck—Trinity, I screwed up."

He sounds so broken. I search for the right words, for the glue that can stick him back together.

"You didn't screw up. You just feel so much. In fact, you said a lot of things that made me think about how I've been handling everything. We've all got baggage. You know I do. It's okay to unpack it every now and then. I'll happily help you sort through it."

He snorts. "You don't need my baggage, love."

"Oh, but I do. I'm the best baggage handler there is. Emily's, my own. Lay it on me, baby. Let me take the weight for you as you've never failed to do for me."

"God, I love you," he says, just like that.

My heart explodes into a million tiny fragments. I'm

searching for them, trying to piece them back together, but he's still speaking.

"I should go. Just needed to feel your footprint."

"Luc—"

He's already hung up.

CHAPTER 39

Lucas

*J*jolt awake to bells ringing, calling people to church on a Sunday morning. The peals are supposed to sound joyous, I suppose, yet all I can hear is mocking.

Lizzie exhales a long, juddering rattle of a breath, and I hold one of my own, waiting.

The beeps continue. Proof of life.

Three days ago, a sniffle turned into a cold that turned into a lung infection. She made it out before, but I don't think she has the strength this time, possibly because *I'm* not strong enough. For fifteen years, we've held on together. Last night she slipped into a coma.

I squeeze her hand.

"Hey, Lizzie, remember that time we sneaked into the movies to see *The Lion, the Witch, and the Wardrobe?*"

She giggles, as soft and joyous as a church bell.

"Yeah, you had a lady boner for Liam Neeson, even though he was voicing a lion, and you were like a silent Beatlemaniac every time he spoke in his deep, lion voice." I raise my hands to my face and mimic a screaming teen.

Shut yer piehole, Lucas!

I laugh, joining in with her—but she's only laughing in my head. The incongruity of it washes over me. All this time I've been playing both sides of the chess match, speaking my part and hers, living two half-lives as if I can somehow meld them into a single decent one.

My own laugh turns into something maniacal. Christ, I need to get a coffee, maybe even take a shower, because I suspect I smell like a fucking distillery. At least I'm starting to appreciate whiskey.

I close my eyes to fight off the demons and I imagine Trinity is here. Just hearing her voice—when was it?—over a day ago offering to take the weight for me broke something wide open in my chest. *Her* voice is the one in my head now, replacing Lizzie.

I shoot to a stand, thrown by that conclusion. That's not what I want. Is it?

I snatch the door open, needing air, needing to get away if only for a moment. Jenny is standing there, and with her is the woman I've conjured from my dreams.

"Hi," my Trinity says.

My Trinity.

"Lucas, I was just coming to tell you about your visitor," Jenny says, splitting a glance between us. It's a wonder she's not being sizzled alive with the zinging electric current.

"I need coffee." It's a strange way to greet the woman you love, especially when that woman has traveled thousands of miles to see you. I turn to Jenny. "Will you—"

"I'll text you if anything changes."

Jenny slips into the room and closes the door, leaving us alone in the corridor.

"Why are you here?"

Her smile is heartbreakingly sweet. "You asked me to come."

True. Not outright, but the act of placing that call was a plea for this woman to be at my side.

"I hope you don't mind. I asked Grant to use your firm's resources to track where you were."

I've been ignoring Grant's and Max's calls. "There's a family hospitality room around the corner. Coffee's terrible, but they sometimes have Jaffa cakes."

"Jaffa cakes?" she asks, walking alongside me.

I smile, for what feels like the first time in days. "Jones, you're going to love Jaffa cakes."

CHAPTER 40

Trinity

So Jaffa cakes are awesome, like chocolate marmalade cookies. They shouldn't work but they do. We're not all that different from a Jaffa cake, Lucas and I. Sweet and tart (guess who is which?).

Coffee and cookies in hand, we take a seat in side-by-side armchairs. I wish it was a sofa. I want to press my thigh to his, hold him close, and breathe him in.

"I didn't expect you," he says. "If I'd known a drunken ramble would get you on my side, I would have tried it much sooner."

"Tell me about Lizzie."

He swallows. "What's there to say? She loves the Spice Girls and Narnia. Has a laugh that makes you feel like you're wearing a sweater on the inside. Is clever and bright and—" His hand moves to cover his mouth, as if concerned the next sound will be a scream.

I kneel in front of him, push his knees apart to get closer.

Then I hold his head with both hands. His stubble-rough jaw scrapes deliciously against my palms.

"She's clever and bright," I echo. "Of course she is. She's the one who got all the personality from the Wright gene pool."

He snorts, swiping at a stray tear.

"She—she's not going to last long, Trin. I think I've been holding on forever, and now that my focus is elsewhere, I don't have enough to keep her going."

His focus? Does he mean me? I'd hate to bear that responsibility, but the man has to live, to move on. We both do.

"I'm here for whatever you need. And if you don't want me here, if it makes it all too much, I'll go."

He cups my face in return. "Lovely Trinity, always taking care of people."

"Not always." I shake my head, remembering my fight with Emily. "I told Emily she needed to grow up. Accept some responsibility."

"Ah," he says. "Went over like a lead balloon, I assume?"

"Yeah, but it was a huge relief to get it out. This weight I've been carrying. And I owe it to you, for making me see. I guess I've always known that I enable her, but we never really understand what's best for us. Not when we're so close to the problem. We've made up, started afresh."

"I can't believe you're here."

He kisses my nose, the dark circles beneath my eyes (I didn't sleep a wink on the plane). He kisses my cheekbones, reverent whispers across their planes. He smells of whiskey and leather, of longing and Lucas. Of home.

"Did you think I wouldn't come for you, Lucas? After everything you've done for me?"

"So you feel obligated? A Cadbury Crème Egg and here you are."

I pull on the lapels of his jacket, frustrated at his ever-present self-deprecation. "I'm not so easily bought. I'm here because you've been bearing this for a long, long time, and I'm offering my shoulder. My body. My heart and soul. All these pieces of me are strong because you made me feel worth the trouble. You gave me strength when I had none, care when I needed it. You saw the real me. Not the forgotten daughter, the abandoned girlfriend, or the put-upon sister. But me. Trinity Jones."

As the words spill from my mouth in raspy utterances, the notion that I'm making this all about me crosses my mind. But what I'm really trying to do is force him to realize how special he is. How beloved. Not just by me, but by Max and Grant, Sadie and Aubrey.

He is not alone.

I plead with my eyes for his understanding. And when he speaks, I know he's heard what I have to say.

"Trinity, my love, would you like to meet my sister?"

I can only croak the words out. "I'd be honored."

As he stands, he pulls me to my feet. Hand in hand, we walk back to Lizzie's room where inside, Jenny is mulling over a close-to-complete jigsaw puzzle.

"Nearly done," she says, and I don't know if she means the puzzle or her patient. She quietly slips out, the door closing with a soft snick.

"Hey, Lizzie, I want you to meet someone."

Damn, she's pretty. Dark haired and pale, the proverbial English rose. I wonder if she has Lucas's clear blue eyes—or if she'll ever open hers again.

"Hi, Lizzie," I say shyly. "So nice to meet you at last." I squeeze her hand, surprised at its warmth. There's life in the girl yet.

Lucas watches her closely. "We've been reading *Prince Caspian,* and we stopped at a really exciting bit. The gang's about to do battle for Narnia."

Lucas pulls a chair forward and sits me down in it. Then he plucks a thick tome off the nightstand and takes a seat close to Lizzie. I curl up and listen to him read. He does all the parts, just as he lives. Lucas Wright, man of a million roles.

When the battle is won, Aslan tells the oldest Pevensive children that they can't return to Narnia, that they've learned all this world has to tell them. They have to go back to their other lives and live out their days there.

In that moment, Lizzie takes her leave, as if she was waiting for all to be right with Narnia once more. Lucas clasps her hand as she slips away and I sit on the armrest of his chair, my hands on his shoulders, giving him my strength.

I hold him through his sobs.

I tell him he is loved.

And then I step outside so he can say his final goodbye.

CHAPTER 41

Lucas

One month later

England's green and pleasant land stretches before me, a blanket of verdant growth over rolling hills and sparkling streams. The nation's unofficial national anthem, "Jerusalem," springs to mind, threatening to drown me in nostalgia for my public school days.

The camp can be seen from the motorway, and as I approach in my rental, my heart beats to a junky rhythm. Deciding it's probably safer for the car, I park at a distance and walk the last third of a mile. Rusty motor homes dot the landscape, no doubt considered a blight on the countryside's beauty by the locals who live here all year around. Grime-faced kids, their eyes wide and wary, view me with suspicion. My dark-wash jeans and button-down don't exactly help me fit in.

But then I never did.

"I'm looking for Millie Wright," I say to a tall kid who

seems to be in charge. My accent is rougher, so as not to give away the journey I've taken from where they are now to the stellar heights of designer hats and business-class flights.

"Never 'eard of her."

"Starshine," I amend. "She about?"

"Down the end, 'round the corner."

I nod my thanks and continue on my way with the kids following at a safe distance. Safe for me, that is. They could beat, strip, and rob me in twenty seconds if given the go-ahead. Cool stares of supposedly responsible adults flank my journey, and while I don't acknowledge any of them, I don't avert my eyes, either.

I turn a corner, and my breath traps in my throat. There she is, dear old Ma, sitting on the steps to a van, a fat spliff between nicotine-stained fingers. Her hair is matted, a muted (for her) mix of pink and green. Seeing her in the flesh, I realize that a part of me expected she'd be dead. I sent her money a year ago, but I haven't heard from her since.

"'Allo, Mum."

She turns her head, her eyes betraying no surprise at seeing me. I'm expected.

"Moonbeam."

That stupid fucking name. I could protest, but I'm not here to argue. "Okay to sit?"

"If you don't mind getting your fancy trousers dirty."

Ignoring the jibe, I take a seat. She offers the spliff, half-heartedly, knowing I won't indulge. That I'm too straight edge for that.

"They said you weren't having a funeral," she mutters. "No service. Nothing."

"Made it easy for you, didn't I?"

She snorts, like I'm in the wrong here. "She was already gone. Years ago."

Perhaps. Perhaps I'm to blame for holding on—to Lizzie,

to that chip on my shoulder, to that old version of me floundering in self-pity and righteous indignation.

Some people don't "family" well, and I include myself in there. I could blame her forever or I could take Trinity's advice: free my heart and let it all go.

"I forgive you, Mum."

She turns those eyes on me, same as mine, same as Lizzie's.

"You were never meant to be out here in the open, Lucas. Not everyone can hack it. Not everyone understands the Mother."

She doesn't mean herself. She means the earth, the giver of life. Taker of it, too.

Yeah, but you didn't give us a choice, Mum. You let your id rule and your selfishness be your compass.

"I s'pose not," I merely say, not taking her bait. "Tell me how you've been."

We talk for a while, with surprising ease, skirting hard topics and painful memories. I could call her out, air every grievance, but it won't change a thing. All my bitterness died with Lizzie.

"You need anything?"

"Jake's back has him laid up. Can't work." Jake's the man she's been living with for the last few years. They subsist on poached game, society handouts, and willful ignorance.

I put my hand in my pocket and contribute to the cause.

As I stand, she peers up at me, her hand shading her eyes like she's getting a good look at me for one last time. She thinks I won't be back, though who knows? Time might give me the distance I need. Regardless, I'll continue to send her money as long as she asks for it.

"Got summat for you." Thirty seconds later, she's back from inside the trailer with a hardcover book. I recognize it immediately: *The Lion, the Witch, and the Wardrobe,* with a plastic cover on it. A library book.

Millie hands it over. "She thought you'd be coming."

She? I look more closely at the binding. The spine has the library call number but doesn't say where it's from. I open to the front page, but I already know what I'll find there.

Chicago Public Library. Harold Washington branch.

"Pretty girl," Millie says. "Knew to bring a gift unlike some people. Good quality whiskey."

Which didn't last long, I imagine.

She knew I'd be here. Knew I wouldn't give up. Knows me better than I know myself because damn, I didn't know where I'd be until I woke up this morning.

"She had a long lifeline, too," Mum says. "Couple of kids in her future, though I told her she needed to get a move on. None of us are getting any younger. Or wiser."

Never a truer word. Every day I get older, but definitely not wiser. I'm such an idiot.

Every day I'm here is a day away from Trinity.

"Did you want to keep it?" I ask, holding out the book.

She snorts. "What would I want with a library book?"

What, indeed.

CHAPTER 42

Trinity

The ache in my heart can't be filled by whiskey but I'm doing my best to try.

After Lizzie's death, Lucas took some time away from Chicago, from life, from me. *I can't be the man you need right now,* he said. I could have tried to persuade him, but we both needed to figure things out. If it's meant to be, we'll make our way back to each other.

I've taken some space for myself—a solo tour of whiskey distilleries in the motherland. Today I'm on the shores of Dornoch Firth checking out one of my favorites, the Glenmorangie. Pops would have loved it here. A crisp salt-tinged breeze stings my eyes, though that could just as easily be tears.

I miss my guy.

Our tour guide is an old coot with a Scottish burr so thick you could slice a claymore through it. I know the spiel, but I enjoy it all the same. After the tour, I take a moment to wander among the casks, marveling at the history.

"Whiskey woman, aye?"

I turn to find our tour guide—Mr. McGonagall—standing there, a puckish gleam in his eye.

"I'm a fan, yes."

"More than a fan, I wager. A woman versed in the mysteries of *uisge beatha*." Water of life, the Scottish Gaelic term for whiskey.

"Do I have that look?"

He grins, revealing a gap tooth. "He said you'd come. Told me to look for a goddess among us."

Clearly this guy has been drinking too much of his product. "I should check out ye olde shoppe," I say, backing away.

He's still grinning as he pulls a hand from behind his back and unfurls his fist, palm up.

My gasp echoes among the oak casks. "But—but?" I whip around, my heart frantic and seeking. "Where?"

"He told me you'd be here, lass." Reverently, he places the gift in my hand.

A Cadbury Crème Egg.

"But it's September."

"No matter to a man in love."

Dazed, I wander out of the cask house, wanting to run, afraid of hoping too much. The late afternoon sun fills my eyes, blinding me to the possibilities. But not for long.

The possibilities stand before me. Of life and love and a future I've only dreamed of.

"Hullo, love."

He's lost weight but it looks good on him. Highlights those cheekbones. Stubble blankets his jaw and my fingers itch to touch. My body craves but I hold back.

"Trinity, I'm so—"

I capture his words with a kiss. Seems my body has the better of my brain. It always has where this man is concerned.

Our tears mingle and sustain our connection. He pulls away an excruciating inch. "Let me speak."

"As if I could stop you." I kiss him again to do just that. His presence is a salve, but I worry as I always have done. That he's here to get closure—and that closure will leave me behind.

"How's this new adventure treating you?" he asks.

"Good. Terrible. All I hoped for. I've missed you so fucking much." I can't stop talking, spilling what's in my heart. "I know that you're here, so it's a good sign. But you might still be on your journey and I need to hold on to you, just a little longer."

"Ever the worrywart, Trinity Jones. I'm glad you managed to make it here after all this time. That you took this moment for you." There are little lines around his eyes and a streak of gray in his hair. I'm jealous of the time it took to grow, of the weeks I wasn't around to see it bloom.

"I got your message," he adds. "A *stolen* library book, love?"

"I sent them a donation." I wanted to visit the woman who shaped the man I love, but mostly I wanted to let Lucas know I'm here in his life no matter how he chooses to grieve. "How did it go with your mom?"

"Okay. Now that Lizzie is gone, my feelings for the woman who gave me life are more . . . neutral, I suppose. I don't think she was meant to be a mother. I can't hate her for something that refused to come naturally to her. I told her I forgave her, but I'm not sure I meant it or that she even understood." He gives a rueful shake of his head. "Still, I felt better. Lighter."

"And now? How do you feel now?"

"Ready to begin. Here. With you."

I kiss the corner of his mouth in gratitude and hold him tight.

His lips brush my ear. "For the last few days, I've been doing my own tour with Lizzie, taking her ashes to see the sights. We saw Stirling Castle. And the Isle of Skye. And I'm pretty sure I spied a wee monster in the loch."

"Nessie?"

"The very one."

We both laugh at that. I've missed this feeling, this warmth.

"I've one more trip to take, and I'm hoping you might come with me."

Anywhere. "Name it," I whisper.

"There's a train journey between Fort William and Mallaig on a steam engine—"

"Over the Glenfinnan Viaduct?"

"Yes. And I thought when we go over it, I could give Lizzie the send-off she deserves." He looks at me hopefully, testing his idea.

"I think she'd love that."

His eyes close, as if that's the answer to a prayer. I want to be the answer to that and every question he ever has. "I'm sorry I went away for a while. I didn't want you to see me like that, but all this time without you has made me realize something."

Hope is a fluttering bird in my chest. "Yes?"

"That these sides I try to hide—sad Lucas, mad Lucas— are part of me. I need you to see all of them, Trinity. I need your hand over my flayed flesh, your touch on my soul." He places my palm over his chest. "Your footprint is already tattooed on my heart. You've made your mark. What's mine is yours, if you still want it. If you still want *me,* warts and all."

"Lucas, you crazy fool," I murmur through hiccupping tears. "I've wanted you from the beginning. When I shouldn't have. When I should. When it was wrong and when it was right. I will want you when the sun rises and when it falls below the horizon. In good times and in bad. In the days of Cadbury Crème Egg feasts and of grilled cheese famine."

"Best vows ever."

I laugh, because they are. "I have a confession, though. I don't even like Cadbury Crème Eggs!"

He blinks. "What?"

"I did when I was a kid, but when you brought that one over when I was sick, I realized my tastes have changed. It's just not my thing anymore. I've matured."

His grin is huge. "Maturity. Sounds boring."

"God, it is, but it has its advantages."

"Such as?"

"Knowing what you're about. Who you are and who you're meant to be. What your heart is made of. Who it belongs to. I love you, Lucas."

"About bloody time!" He inclines his forehead to mine. "And I love you, Trinity."

On the shores of a Scottish loch we commit our hearts to each other, knowing that at last, we've found the person who completes us, deep and to the bone.

He will catch me when I fall.

I will soothe him when he aches.

We won't take this adventure for granted, but I know that with Lucas, there'll never be a dull moment.

Lucas

Who doesn't love a wedding, especially when it involves a divorce lawyer and a wedding planner? There's a certain smug glee to be wrung from this because of the parties involved. Max and Charlie had us on tenterhooks for a while, so we're all here—in a bloody cold church in November, mind—to celebrate these two crazy kids as they trip toward the altar. We're about ten minutes to liftoff—though that's a guestimate given how brides have prerogative with timing on their day of days—and there's an expectant buzz in the air as people settle.

"Can't believe he didn't include me in the fucking wedding party," I mumble in my pew four rows back. Aunts and uncles and third cousins twice removed, many of them wearing bloody big hats that will block the view of the plebs in the cheap seats, are taking up prime real estate that really should have gone to close friends. I plan to have words with Susanne later.

"Watch that sexy mouth in a house of prayer," Trinity

whispers, leaning in close so her scent reminds me that my head was buried between her beautiful thighs less than thirty minutes ago.

As lovely as the memory is, I refuse to be distracted, not when I still have grievances to air. "What kind of wedding planner goes this minimalist for her own shindig? Only one bridesmaid. One groomsman." Max chose his brother to be his best man, which I *suppose* is understandable. The rest? No clue. "Bad marketing, if you ask me."

"No one is asking you," Grant, seated on my other side, grumbles out of the side of his mouth.

"At least he didn't choose you," I say. "That would have really hurt my feelings."

Trinity laughs. "You're such a diva."

Before I can protest this rather accurate characterization, Aubrey slides into the seat beside Trinity.

"Hey, princess." A neon pink cast on her forearm covers her hand, its shiny newness glaringly obvious as it sits in a sling. Three perfectly manicured nails peek out of the opening.

Trinity touches her upper arm. "Are you okay? What happened?"

"Just something stupid." She squints at the collection of hats in front of her, then looks over her shoulder. "Maybe I should sit back there."

A shadow enters my field of vision. This shadow has a name: Grant "The Ex" Lincoln. "What happened?" he grits out to Aubrey as he leans across, getting right in my personal space.

"None of your business."

"How did you get here? Because it looks like you can't drive."

Aubrey's eyebrow arch is beyond dismissive. "Big city, Grant. Lots of cabs."

A muscle ticks in Grant's jaw. "What are you going to do about going home for Thanksgiving, Bean? Unless you're suddenly okay with flying."

Trinity mouths *Bean* at me, and I can only shrug. I've never once heard him call her that.

"Nothing for you to worry about," Aubrey shoots back, her cheeks rapidly coloring.

"You don't like flying?" Trinity asks.

"Um, no." And then louder: "But I'll figure it out."

Grant snorts beside me.

I wave a hand between them, my matchmaker brain churning overtime. Hey, it worked for #Chaxie. "Would you two like to sit together?"

"Certainly not!"

"Hell, no!"

They turn away from each other—and us—leaving Trinity and me mystified. God, I'm so glad to be out of that world of single misery.

Trinity narrows her eyes and moves her lips close to my ear, yielding a delicious shiver.

"What's going on in that wicked mind of yours, Lucas Wright?"

"Just thinking about earlier," I say, so low she has to practically sit in my lap to hear me. "When you made that little squeak and—"

"Lucas!"

We grin like fools. The last couple of months have seen us grow closer with every glorious passing second. She even moved into my place in Lincoln Park (though she was very disappointed I had no stripper pole). Emily and the kids are living in a smaller town house in Edgewater, and the divorce decree should be granted any day now. The sisters made up, but my girl has figured out that her own life needs nurturing as well. I'm so proud of her.

Now that we're in this for the long haul, I was a little worried she might not be able to handle unadulterated Lucas 24/7, but it's amazing how good she is at absorbing my energy. With her I can be on, I can be off, I can be a blubbering mess (I'm man enough to admit I still get blue). Mostly, I can be myself.

"You okay?" she asks.

I move my mouth over hers gently, sweetly. "With you I am."

Her golden-brown eyes heat with the sun of her smile. In them I see all the love I'm not sure I deserve, but that I'll hold on to for dear life anyway.

I pat the breast pocket of my jacket.

"Still carrying my card around, weirdo?"

"Sure am, Whiskey Woman." She doesn't need to know that there's a ring in there as well, one I plan to slip onto her finger before the day is through. In fact, if this wedding doesn't start soon, Diva Lucas might stand on a pew and pop the bloody question.

I don't carry with me quite the same anti-marriage bias Max once did, but I'm conscious that any overtures from me in that direction might be viewed with skepticism. One, I'm a divorce lawyer. Two, I've recently lost someone who was part of me for my entire life. Jumping headfirst into marriage could be interpreted as a craving to fill the void she left behind.

But if I'm being honest—and I always try to be—Trinity is no substitute for Lizzie. She's her own person and certainly not a bit player in the Life of Lucas, or in her own life for that matter. She grounds me like no one else and lifts me up the few inches I need when I'm down.

"I think I need to mess up your makeup," I say before taking her mouth and making it mine.

A small whimper I'm immensely proud of emerges from

her throat. "Lucas," she breathes against my lips. Her eyes shine with emotion. "Have I thanked you properly for wooing me?"

Stand on the pew, LuLu. Steal the bloody show.

That little voice sounds like Lizzie, who pops in to visit on occasion. But Max would kill me if I stole his thunder on his big day, and as for Charlie? The woman wouldn't go nearly so easy. I see a good old-fashioned hanging, drawing, and quartering in my future. Lizzie's mischievous giggle echoes in my head.

Aiming for the adult response, I inhale a yoga-quality breath and speak my truth. "You're here. You're mine. It's all the thanks I need."

Organ music winds up and we stand, ready to bear witness to two lives becoming one. I'll keep the proposal for later, when Trinity and I are alone, snuggled in bed, lusting, loving, and laughing.

Where we're the best version of us.

ACKNOWLEDGMENTS

Thanks to Andie J. Christopher, Robin Covington, and Pamala Knight Duffy—your input was invaluable.

ABOUT THE AUTHOR

Originally from Ireland, *USA Today* bestselling author Kate Meader cut her romance reader teeth on Maeve Binchy and Jilly Cooper novels, with some Harlequins thrown in for variety. Give her tales about brooding mill owners, oversexed equestrians, and men who can rock an apron, a fire hose, or a hockey stick, and she's there. Now based in Chicago, she writes sexy contemporary featuring strong heroes and amazing women and men who can match their guys quip for quip.

Laws of Attraction

DOWN WITH LOVE

THEN CAME YOU

Rookie Rebels

GOOD GUY

INSTACRUSH

MAN DOWN

FOREPLAYER

DEAR ROOMIE

REBEL YULE

JOCK WANTED

SUPERSTAR

Chicago Rebels

IN SKATES TROUBLE

IRRESISTIBLE YOU

SO OVER YOU

UNDONE BY YOU

HOOKED ON YOU

WRAPPED UP IN YOU

Hot in Chicago Rookies

UP IN SMOKE

DOWN IN FLAMES

HOT TO THE TOUCH

Hot in Chicago
REKINDLE THE FLAME
FLIRTING WITH FIRE
MELTING POINT
PLAYING WITH FIRE
SPARKING THE FIRE
FOREVER IN FIRE
COMING IN HOT

Tall, Dark, and Texan
EVEN THE SCORE
TAKING THE SCORE
ONE WEEK TO SCORE

Hot in the Kitchen
FEEL THE HEAT
ALL FIRED UP
HOT AND BOTHERED

For updates, giveaways, bonus scenes, and new release information,
sign up for Kate's newsletter at katemeader.com.

9 781954 107212